PRAISE FOR K.T. BLAKEMORE

Blakemore's rip-roaring action and lively characters capture the imagination. This series is off to a fine start.

— PUBLISHERS WEEKLY

Blakemore's madcap novel sparkles with scintillating wit, heartfelt warmth, and snappy repartee.

— HISTORICAL NOVEL REVIEWS

K.T. Blakemore crafts perfect characters and adds the right amount of action and a dash of suspense to create the ideal story to keep you entertained for hours. Five Stars!

— READERS FAVORITE

Highly recommended if you like Westerns, road trips, great voice, and female friendship stories. I'm very much looking forward to the sequel!

— COFFEE & INK

Magnificently written, Good Time Girls is a tough, gritty and often humorous wild ride of danger, death, narrow escapes and yes, love. K.T. Blakemore owns the time period as if she had lived through it, and the characters as if she knew them personally. Open up the book, but hang onto your hat.

— JAMES ROBERT DANIELS, BESTSELLING
AUTHOR OF *THE COMANCHE KID*

Told in humorous, and sometimes touching, McMurtry-esque prose, this book will keep you entertained and glued to your chair far into the night. If you like bold women and stories of the West, you will love this literary adventure!

THE GOOD TIME GIRLS

ALSO BY K.T. BLAKEMORE

How to Survive Cactus: A Good Time Girls Short

WRITING AS KIM TAYLOR BLAKEMORE

HISTORICAL SUSPENSE

The Deception

After Alice Fell

The Companion

HISTORICAL YOUNG ADULT

Bowery Girl

Cissy Funk

THE GOOD TIME GIRLS

K.T. BLAKEMORE

SYCAMORE
CREEK
press

The Good Time Girls

By K.T. Blakemore

Published by Sycamore Creek Press

Edited by Kerry Cathers

Cover Art by James at Goonwrite.com

ISBN-13: 979-8-9877480-1-5 (hard cover)

ISBN-13: 978-0-9905843-8-4 (paperback)

ISBN-13: 978-0-9905843-9-1 (ebook)

First Edition April 2023

For my mother
&
To audacious women everywhere

CHAPTER 1

KANSAS CITY, MO
CALHOUN'S CIGARS
1905
I MEET AN OLD FRIEND

"I'll take a box of *Peter Schuyler's*."

I knew that voice. *Her* voice. Part alto, a lot tenor, the esses elongated like the silks of a spider web, and complicated with gravel and rock.

My hand froze halfway to settling a carton of quite stale *Romeo y Juliets* on a shelf. There had been no comforting ding of the bell, no warning of a potential customer. And this was my fault directly, for the chain had broken last week, or perhaps the week prior to that. I had been much greater concerned with the boys desecrating my wooden Indian out front, and greater concerned than that with the abysmal sales of the *Romeo y Juliet* Cubano cigars to pay heed to the broken bell.

I had become careless. Which meant this woman—whose voice I so sadly knew—now stood behind me, and for all I could tell had a pistol pointed at my back.

The brown cigar box hung from my fingers. I had a flash that I should sling it at her. My luck would be to miss her head and end up with a cracked window of which I did not have the funds to repair.

An ice of sweat fizzed down my spine and pooled at the waist of my corset, collecting and sloshing around my rib cage. I kept my movements slow and indifferent, as if old friends who might kill me commonly visited my shop.

"*Peter Schuyler's*," I said, "are harsh on the throat. I've got better cheroots, should you be of a mind."

"But I only like *Peter Schuyler's*."

I had only the counter and register as a barrier between us. With a gritted jaw, I slid the cigar box to its place, shrugged out my shoulders, and bent to pick up another. I gave a quick click of my tongue. "I've got a good sale on *Romeo y Juliet's*."

"I asked you for *Peter Schuyler's*." There was a rasp of her boot heel against the floor.

I yearned to scrape my tongue across the roof of my mouth, but all of a sudden, it felt too thick, too swollen, and any words I wanted to let out scuttled back down my throat. I dropped to a crouch behind the counter, ready to grab the big shotgun from its hooks. It was too long in the tooth to be of much use except for waving around and smacking things. Another item I had grown careless of. "Are you going to shoot me?"

"Maybe when you stop quivering on the floor and stand up."

"I got a gun down here."

"I'm very disappointed. I thought you were finding my cigars."

With a quick twist, I grabbed the shotgun, shoved the stock against my shoulder and stood up. The barrel smacked against the edge of the counter; I stumbled back to give it clearance and swung it round to face her.

I squinted, for the sun was bright through the window, expecting to find her pointing a pistol right back at me.

But she wasn't armed. She wasn't even looking at me. Various news cuttings I'd framed and hung on the side wall of the shop had caught her attention. Her split skirt was a fine burgundy velveteen, cut to ride, generously fringed at the knees. She twirled a wide vaquero hat in her hands, rolling and unrolling the brim. Her hair was still a horse mane of black that struggled against the heavy ribbon she'd tried to tame it with. She had that straight forehead and thick eyebrows and the nose with a notch at the bridge.

"You might want to put down that gun." She sidestepped to peer at another picture. "It's wobbling, you have the wrong eye shut and you're about to shoot out the glass."

"Put your hat to the floor and show me both your hands."

"Well."

"I mean it."

She did as requested, and I lay the shotgun on the wooden counter, though I kept a finger hooked over the trigger.

She turned, arms out and palms up, and I caught my breath and held it as she approached. A dreadful jagged scar cut her face from right cheek to left chin. It glowed a sallow yellow against the sun-worn hue of her skin and puckered at the corner of her mouth and up along her cheekbone, as if the knife that had cut it was withdrawn then plunged in again.

She smiled, her teeth white and even; one of the many things she prided herself on. "Hello, Ruby Calhoun."

"Hello, Pip Quinn." I could not continue to stare at her, nor at the copper-penny eye that regarded me when she stared one way, and the green scheming one when she looked the other way. I busied myself with maneuvering the gun back to its hooks.

"Well, it's nice to see you."

I took a swipe under my nose and sniffed. "I'da been happier with a postcard."

"Kansas City?"

I spread my fingers on the counter and felt the sticky sweat. "Nothing wrong with Kansas City."

She shrugged. The fringe along her short jacket swung until she slapped a hand to stop it.

"Where'd you get the costume?" I asked.

"You don't remember it?"

I lifted a shoulder. "I vaguely remember the act. Vaquero Vixens or—"

"Vivacious Vaquero Gals." With a purse of her lips, she meandered

3

back to the picture frames, leaning in as if reading the headlines and such and such. She tapped the glass that contained a pen and ink of me.

In it, I wore a hat so jaunty angled it threatened to slide from my head. The newsman who came to interview me at the prison added in a few costume pieces: a white shirt and boy's trousers, a holster and kid's toy six shooter to angle in the belt, and a pair of tall-heeled brown boots. I was particularly fond of those, as the espadrilles the prison assigned me had come apart at the toe. The piece de resistance was a long heavy shotgun which the photographer had handed me. I'd said I did not use such a weapon. He'd replied it would balance the composition. Then he'd rolled down a canvas with a stage painted upon it and that was that.

"He said he'd sell it to *Cosmopolitan* what with the Pearl Hart craze," I said. "It ended up in *The Youth's Companion*. As a warning."

"Uh huh."

"There's another somewhere up there of me with the raccoon an admirer sent."

She tapped the picture again. "You're tiny as I remember. Like a bug."

"I'm tall enough."

"How'd it go, having a raccoon in your jail cell?" She lifted a photograph from the wall, wiped a gloved finger to the plaster that had loosed, and ambled over to the plate window to get a bit more light. "This isn't you. It says Ruby Calhoun but it sure isn't you." She waved the photo around for me to see.

I knew it to be of the *Wild West Show*, and I knew it to be the recreation of the stage robbery that I had attempted. My stomach grew sore from resentment. "Bill Cody hired someone else. Her name is Myra Somethingorother."

Pip narrowed her eyes at me. "To play *you*."

"That would be show business. As you know." I came around the counter and grabbed the photo. "I didn't like the terms, anyway." As I tried to hang the picture, the tack slipped flat to the wall. I dug my nails to the head to pull it right, then put the picture of the much-prettier-than-me, and blonde to boot, stage-robbing girl back in its place.

My foot caught the brim of her hat and sent it to skitter across the floor.

With a quick jerk, she grabbed it up and brushed the crown. I could tell she was angry; the scar got whiter as her skin grew redder. She kept dusting off the hat with the back of her gloved hand. "This is new."

My hands shook so wildly I gripped my gingham dress at the buttocks and pressed myself to the wall. "What do you want, Pip?"

"I want a box of *Peter Schuyler's* cheroots."

"Then you'll leave?"

"Then I'll leave."

"Where's Big Henry?"

She looked over her shoulder to the window, and her eyes searched around. "He's dead."

"Well. I'm sorry for that. You loved that horse."

"Yes, I did. I loved that horse."

"How'd you get here, if not—"

"You still got your nerve, Ruby Calhoun?"

I clamped my jaw and rubbed my tongue along the back of my teeth.

Pip pulled at the half of her lip that was good and stared at me with her more-honest brown eye. She gave a quick nod, pushed her hat towards me to hold, dug an old leather wallet from her skirt pocket, and pulled out a small square card. "Take a look at this."

A coffin, an *X* and a *1*. Crudely drawn. But it had its effect.

"What is that?" I pressed my hand to my throat. Pip's hat slipped from my grip and dropped to the floor.

"A calling card. From Cullen."

"He's been released, then." My stomach soured greatly. "When?"

"Last week. He's on his way to Hutchinson."

"Why?"

"See his mama."

I reached to take the card from her, but the curse upon it changed my mind. It meant you were good as dead. "When did you get it?"

"Ten days ago. It was on my pillow."

"Jesus."

She pushed it back into her wallet and shoved the whole away. "You got those cheroots?"

"Sure." I slipped behind the counter, dragging a milk crate into place and stepping on it. I grabbed a box and hopped down.

She dug around in a small waist purse for coins.

"You just take 'em." I slid the box across to her.

Her hand smacked down on mine. "I'm going to kill him first."

We did not look away from each other. I had no words ready for such a pronouncement. So, I raised my eyebrows and left them there. "In Hutchinson?"

"In Hutchinson."

PIP LEFT THE SHOP WITH THE CIGAR BOX TUCKED UNDER HER ARM. She had no horse, no money, and a great big target on her back. I suppose she'd come all the way to Kansas City from wherever she'd tucked herself to see if I, too, had received such a burdensome threat. I suppose she'd come to ask for help. But I had foresworn violence, and thusly she went away with her hat and the smokes and a lesser image of me.

"I'm going to kill him," she'd said.

No doubt in the tumble of her mind, she'd been secure I'd jump at the chance to join her; that I would drop my entire rancid business and quiet life and say, "Sure, Pip! Count me in for murder in the first degree!"

I gave a quick wipe of my nose and pressed my thumb to my sinuses—damn headache caused from all the dust and fresh cut wood. The edge of the city would be brick and stone before the year was out, but now it was a pile of timber and horseshit.

"Kill Cullen Wilder..." I shook my head. "He'll get you first, and that's a sad sad thing."

I trudged to the front door and flipped the latch. Turned the sign over so it said ALL CLOSED UP, walked to the back of the room and shoved the waxed calico curtain aside. I lifted the bucket next to my food stores and retched.

In a wash of fatigue, I dropped to my bed, grabbing an iron bar on the bedstead as I sat. I rested my chin upon my fist. The four-paned window above me had a crack to each corner and a view of the latrine that I shared with the haberdasher next door. Last year, there had been no latrine, so I was grateful for the facility if not the view. There had been no haberdashery, neither, nor the need for one until Olaf Hagerstrom had built it and stocked it last March. There had been no barber shop across the street nor the blind seamstress down at the turn. There was always Lady Anne's Dance Emporium three doors to the right and I surely did owe that establishment money. Otherwise, I might slip through the back alley for a sip or two of ale.

All this industry and business comforted me.

I went to bed tired from an honest day's labor and woke with the groans and griping of anyone in the working class. I did not have a need to watch my back anymore or count the tips China Mary chose to share with Pip and me and count them again to figure what she'd shorted us. I didn't have to think of Cullen Wilder. Or Pip's scar and how it came to be, and how once I spent three days under the opium to escape my guilt for its untimely occurrence.

My new life had little drama. The worry over selling those damn *Romeo y Juliet's* occupied the majority of my attention, and I took comfort in that, too.

I sighed as big as my stays allowed and glared at the rusted punched-tin ceiling. An ache came upon me, quick and sharp and familiar. It came with a wish for my snug room at the Tucson jail where I had a quince tree outside the cell and a canary that liked to sit on my shoulder. At least until Charley the raccoon came and ate the poor bird.

I thought back further to the whys and wherefores of my incarceration and that led right back to Pip Quinn. Who I had spent a good six years forgetting. I was not in any way going to follow her on some quixote-ish mission to kill a man. I wasn't about to follow Pip Quinn anywhere.

She had her wretched and now doomed life to lead. I had mine. That was that.

With a slap of my knee and my brain mass and guts more settled, I returned to the front.

And stopped on a dime. Right outside the glass, I caught the rolling walk of Willie Bledsoe as he paced directly in front of my wooden Indian.

"Hey hey hey." I raced across the room and grasped the door handle. It jiggled and caught as I worked to unlatch it. Willie had his pocket knife out and glared at the statue, as if angry at it for being ignored. I pounded the plate glass with my open palm. Then the door gave, and I reached out and grabbed Willie's collar. He stumbled back, his arms stretched out in front of him, his legs flailing, and heels digging into the walkway boards. I thought: he's six months away from outgrowing my hold on him. Which made me truss up his collar that much more until the skin rashed and swelled at his neck. He blinked those washed blue eyes and tried not to cry.

"You stay away from my wooden Indian." I shook him hard so his shoulders jiggled, then shoved him to the bench against the store wall.

His head clanged on the tin sign for *Red Dot Junior Cigars*. "I haven't done nothing."

"You're desecrating my Indian. That is a work of art."

His fat lips pursed and wobbled. "Who cares?"

"You cut off his nose last week. He had a fine nose and now it's a niggle of a nothing. I think I should cut off yours."

"I didn't do nothing to your stupid Indian."

"Maybe I'll just cut off your stupid head."

The boy's mouth yawed so wide I could see the back of his throat. He screamed. I clamped my hand to his mouth and glared around. But no one paid attention; they were concerned with avoiding the manure that never got picked up, only ground down.

"You listen to me. I see you out here one more time with that knife, I will turn it directly on you. The first time I see you, I'll cut off your head. The second time, I'll cut off your pecker. Do you understand me? For I am not lying. I am Ruby Calhoun, a most fearsome bandit you should think twice about crossing."

Willie's eyes grew round and a satisfaction warmed my chest. My words had gotten through to him.

He twisted away from me and lurched from the bench. A sweat-dark glove grabbed his arm and whipped him around. He was nose-to-nose with Pip Quinn and upon witnessing her terrible smile, he wet himself. His piss-drowned wool trousers puckered and stuck to his skin.

"You're going to have a hard time finding that pecker, Ruby."

He squeaked and peed some more.

Pip released him, giving him a good kick in his backside as he tumbled away. She resettled her hat and stepped off the walkway. "I'll be at Lady Anne's."

CHAPTER 2

KANSAS CITY
1905
I Think of the Past and Future—Fancy Nan—A Song is Warbled

After Pip left the steps of the cigar shop, I took a rag of vinegar and water to the glass-fronted case of humidors, cutters, and silver flasks. My eye caught on the rosewood box I'd put front and center in a place of honor. I crouched down to stare at it, growing heavy of heart as I traced the fine walrus ivory relief. This gift, much like Charley the raccoon and the short-lived canary, had been accorded to me by an admirer. This time it was a Rufus Parsons, who had it delivered upon my second-year anniversary in prison. Rufus never showed himself physically, so I was left with my imagination as to his looks. Which meant he was a tall man with deep blue eyes that didn't trick.

A stagecoach and tall saguaro cactus had been carved in the ivory, as had a line of passengers with hands held high and me and Joe Harper with our Colts. It was not a point of pride, but rather, like the sketch on the wall, a reminder to stay on the straight and narrow.

I swatted the top of the counter and stood.

"I hope Mexico is suiting you well, Joe Harper."

I thought I would write to him, to apologize for bringing him into the sorry mess, but I did not know where he'd holed up after his escape. He said once he'd always wanted to see the ocean, so perhaps he's bootless and rubbing his toes in the sand.

The letter, I concluded, would be torn up anyway. He had much animosity about my two-year sentence as opposed to his thirty-year. I told him at the time that a lady crying can cause miracles. He could have blubbered on the floor same as me had he been of a female persuasion. But he wasn't. He was just dumb Joe Harper who blamed everything on me. And that had not appealed to the jury stuck in a courtroom with the windows shut and the weather approaching a hundred and one degrees. I think they took out much of their discomfort on him.

I slumped my way to the back room, wrung the rag in the bucket, and hung it on a hook. The wall clock ticked. All these minutes had become days and without any effort rolled themselves into years. A sharp image seared my eyelids. I saw my older self buttoned up and self-righteous and dull as dirt.

With a shiver of horror, I saw myself dead, a pinched up respectable body found on the floor of this very shop, with the hungry blowflies my only friends. The last lines written about me destined to be:

CIGAR STORE OWNER FOUND DEAD. ONCE HAD AN INTERESTING LIFE.

Just as quick, I thought of Pip, who had an interesting life, and that life was to be cut short through all the faults of our own.

And I thought: damn you, Pip Quinn.

Because she had to remind me of that life we once both led.

I FOUND PIP QUINN ALONE AT LADY ANNE'S. SHE KEPT HERSELF IN the dim, along the back wall, observing the mostly empty room that stunk of beer breath and pickled cabbage. A piano player drooped over his keys, forehead resting on the front board of the old upright, the ashes of his cigarette drifting across the back of his hand. I had not an iota of a clue what song he played; something with flats like a good Delta blues but scuffed around like an old dirge.

Fancy Nan dragged her feather boa behind her and gave him a quick roll of her eyes before half-heartedly flipping the tassels on her tits. She did it one way then the other, which caused most of the men to sway before returning to nursing their lagers and rye.

I pushed past a hurdy-gurdy girl, giving her the same stink eye she gave me, though for different reasons. She was in my way of getting to Pip and I was in her way of plying an old man in coveralls with thinned-out whiskey and the promise of a feel.

Pip looked to be in a blue funk and her eyes held the sallow yellow of too much liquor. She knocked her heel against the flocked wallpaper, as if she could force the piano man to pick up the pace.

Fancy Nan bent forward then back in an arch and did something with her legs that might have been salacious except she could not hold the pose and her bottom smacked the floor. She didn't seem all that interested in getting up and instead waved the boa around.

Pip crossed her arms and tipped her head to the side. "What in the hell. What is this?"

"It is a Tuesday," I said.

"This counts as entertainment in Kansas City?"

"Most everyone's down the street at the flickers."

"Uh huh." Her mouth hung open as she followed the path Fancy Nan took from center stage to drooping herself across the piano top.

"It's a good moving picture. It's called *The Little Train Robbery*. It's not as good as *The Great Train Robbery* because there's kids and all in it and I don't think the story holds up all that terrifically, but then there's a short that precedes it about Palm Beach and I would truly like to see an ocean and walk a beach someday."

"I should just leave you to your own card."

"What?"

"You'll get one."

The hurdy-gurdy girl sidled up to us, her violet skirts sheening in the electric light, her gray skin and fondness for opium wrestling below the powder and paste. "You're not allowed in here anymore." She smacked my shoulder so hard I stumbled into the old man in the coveralls.

He shoved me away with a spit at my feet. "You knocked my drink."

"I don't give a rat's ass about your drink." My shoulder throbbed and I rubbed my hand to it. "I just been abused." I turned to Pip. "She didn't need to go and do that."

Miss Hurdy-Gurdy gave a small nod and snapped a finger to the bouncer to haul me out of Lady Anne's for nonpayment of many bills. Which the man unkindly did.

IT WAS A HOT STEAMED-UP NIGHT. I HOPPED FROM THE SIDEWALK into the traffic, jogging left then right to avoid the drunk fellas who could barely walk and the drunk bicyclers and the buggy drivers who could cause a catastrophic fatality in the blink of an eye. Pip followed. She had retrieved her sombrero from the hat check, and when I squinted at her, I saw that wide brim turn this way and that as she one-eyed the space between streetcars. After two tries, including one that ended with a fella grabbing her arm and pulling her to the curb, she got the timing right.

She loped up, shaking a clod of manure from her boot and stumbling around to keep her balance. "This town smells like a sewer. And cow shit. And cows."

"Stockyards do smell like shit. I'll give you that."

"It all stinks here. And it's loud. So overbearingly loud."

"You didn't have one of the Special drinks, did you?"

"Did I? Was that the pretty green one?" She pulled in a great breath, arching back to peek at the sky, then landed in a dump on her ass.

"You're going to be green tomorrow morning, too." I grabbed her from behind, looping my arms under hers and sticking my shoulder in her back to get her moving and out of the way of an oncoming street-car. I kneed the back of her leg to bend it so she could step up on the walkway.

"Maybe I won't be alive tomorrow to puke it." She set her feet wide and slapped down her hat. "Maybe I am meant to enjoy this one last drunk." She pointed a finger at me. "Maybe that is my fate." Then she pointed right next to me, closed one eye, and pointed back.

"You had two Specials, didn't you?" I started down the sidewalk, waving a goodbye. "You probably won't be alive tomorrow morning."

"I'm not so drunk."

"Good night, Pip."

"Hey." She wobbled after me, one hand sliding along the door of Beerbohm's Butchers. "Hey! You just stop."

I slowed and turned back to her.

"Why are you leaving me," she asked, "when you were the one who came to find me?"

"No. You came to find me."

"Then you came to find me." She rubbed the back of her hand under her nose. "I didn't ask you to do so."

"But you said you'd be there. You said, and I quote: 'I will be at Lady Anne's.'"

"But I didn't ask you to come. I just said I was going there."

"Needless as that may be..."

"So, why'd you come?" She sat on the brick-edged window of Darletta's Millinery and Gloves.

"Perhaps I was concerned. You've got a death card in your pocket, and it came to my mind you might be in danger."

"I'm not in danger here."

"How do you know that?"

She shrugged. "Does it really concern you if I'm in danger, Ruby?"

"Well, I—"

"What hotel do you recommend here?"

"The Baltimore, I guess. If you got the money."

"What else?"

I knew by that response the nature of her purse. "You need a bed?"

"You have an extra?"

"No."

But I did have a floor. And she knew I'd give her the hospitality. "Where's your bag?"

"By your back door. Behind the trash bin."

"Of course it is."

❧

My head buzzed as it should with a good cigar. I leaned back on my pillow, wrapped my arm behind my head, and followed the meandering of smoke. I took another puff, set my tongue against my lower teeth, and pushed smoke through my nose. The bed coils squealed as I shifted to my side and peered down at Pip who lay on the floor with her head on a rolled blanket.

"You okay in that nightdress?"

Her legs, moon pale and thin as reeds, knees knobby like a boy's, poked out from the cotton chemise. She tapped a long ash from her cheroot into the ashtray near her hip. "I'm okay."

"All right, then." I watched her take a long drag of her smoke and blow concentric rings. It was a talent I could not match, no matter how many times I tried.

"What happened to everyone?" I asked. "From The Paradise? Verna and Tommy and—"

She blew another ring. "Maggie hanged herself."

"When?"

"Right after it all...Darby walked into the desert and just kept walking. We found her. Well, never mind that."

I studied her. It pained me to realize I could not remember Pip being pretty, though she surely had been. "Where've you been keeping?"

"This way and that." She took a sharp drag and coughed. "I'd prefer to leave that alone."

I rolled back in place and took a few last puffs before snuffing out the cigar. "You mind if I turn off the light?"

"Suit yourself."

The oil lamp flickered as I twisted the knob.

"Lady Anne's got electricity."

"Lady Anne's got money." I pounded my pillow into a more comfortable lump and settled back, my fingers twined and resting on my stomach, and listened to the hiss of the cheroot Pip smoked.

Through the open window came the faintest echo of a piano, as if the Paradise was around the corner and not half a wild country away.

I cleared my throat of a frog and started to sing along with the tune.

Whether she loves me or loves me not,
Sometimes it's hard to tell;
Yet I am long to share the lot –
Of beautiful Daisy Bell.

Daisy, Daisy, give me your answer, do –
I'm half crazy, all for the lust of you.

Pip gave a chortle. "That's the real truth."

It won't be a stylish marriage.

Then she warbled out: *I can't afford a carriage.*

Together, we sang a two-part harmony that used to stop the miners and guarantee extra tips:

But you'll look sweet, upon the seat
Of my pole that is hard for you!

She put out her cheroot and there was the scrape of metal as she slid the ashtray to the wall. "You've got a sweet voice, Ruby."

"Thank you." I massaged my temples then dropped my arms to my sides to tighten the sheet just right. "You're really going to kill him?"

"We crossed him. He doesn't let things like that go."

"We didn't do anything wrong."

"He thinks we all took the money."

"But we didn't."

"You're going to get a calling card, too."

It grew quiet, the floor settling and the privy door squealing as Olaf finished his business for the night.

"Sing me another song, Ruby. Maybe a nice ballad."

"How about *Sweet Alice Fair?*"

"That sounds fine."

I hummed a bit of the tune.

I'd seen the few lines in the paper about Cullen. Enough to let me sleep at night, knowing he was locked up. I'd made a vow then to become a somewhat solid citizen. I needed none of those pressures and threats.

"Pip?"

"Yeah?"

"You'll need to go tomorrow. I can only extend my generosity through tonight."

She sighed and rolled on her back, crossing her arms behind her head.

"I have responsibilities here. I can't just up and traverse the Plains with you to kill Cullen Wilder. You must understand." I picked the front of my tooth with my thumbnail and watched her. "I'm not ungenerous. I hope you do not think that."

"One night."

"And breakfast. That'll get you in the right frame of mind to move on."

CHAPTER 3

ORINDA, ARIZONA
1898
How I Met Pip Quinn—Frank Calhoun, the Damn Bastard—
A Job Request

"Chick chick. Chick chick. Come here you little shit." I squeezed my arm through the ocotillo fence and grabbed for the hen. My fist caught nothing but air. She shimmied in a circle, kicking up little rounds of dust, fluffing and settling her feathers like a showgirl, one eye a smooth ball of disdain as she stared and gave me a cluck. I pressed my shoulder to the fence, turning my good eye to watch, and winced at the tear of fabric and prick of thorns that brought a wet well of blood.

"Damn and hell."

The hen scurried closer, then took off in a flapping jump to the side. With a waddle and a sigh she took roost in the one slit of shade in the yard.

I jimmied my arm free, stood, and kicked the fence. That made my bad eye throb in anger. On top of it, my stomach knotted and burned, but there wasn't a thing I could do to entice the chicken closer.

I spun round, hands clawed to the hips of my skirts. The chicken sat in clucking insolence in the middle of a square yard, hogging the shade from a sun-bleached shed of questionable strength. Four steaming laundry tubs took up residence against the faded green boards, and, by the surviving paint on the sign, I ascertained it belonged to a Wu Lin.

The back of the shed sat sideways to the yard. Across the rock and yellow dirt, a red brick building loomed up, its white-paned windows half-open for any respite of breeze.

I knew what lay behind me, for I had the misfortune of spending the night there: rocks and prickly pear and mounded barrel cacti for a pillow. A jack rabbit eluded me and stalked me from the safety of the hedgehogs and their spitting spiteful needles all morning. There was a strip of creek that someone thought should be called a river, but it was a trickle of dust and cow patties and slag.

I gave up my quest for the chicken and stared at the huge sky. I wiped sweat from my face, careful to go gently around said bad eye, and I thought: How the hell did I get myself here and how the hell do I get out?

Then I spit, because the chicken was still alive and monopolizing the shade and I had not one cent nor one iota of dignity left to my name. I grabbed a limb of fence and shook it, letting out a grunt of frustration.

A man slipped out to the tubs, clothed in a long black cotton robe that seemed detrimental to his health.

He lifted a long wooden pole from a hook on the wall and arced it into the tub. He stirred, sluicing both water and a graying foam that slipped over the lip and plunked to the soil.

I flicked my gaze to the black and white symbols that ran lengthwise along the corner of the shed then cut a look to the hand-lettered yellow paint once again.

"Excuse me, Mr. Wu Lin, but is that your chicken?"

I pointed.

He stirred. More water and foam flipped and folded over the edge.

"Hello, Mr. Wu Lin, but could you please answer—"

The squeal of a window casing stopped my words.

"You'd have better luck talking to a wall."

I looked towards the voice. There on the third story, a woman leaned out, her elbows and tits resting on the ledge as if this was the most common way to take in the morning sun and address a stranger. Her dark hair was piled in a mass atop her head. She took a long drag from a cigar and popped out three Os, then gave a lazy gesture towards the laundry.

"You got to earn his ear." She looked me up and down, one hand latched to the cigar, the other tucking back a curl. "That's some shiner."

I shrugged back my shoulders. "You should see the other fella."

She gave a snort. "You trying to steal that hen?"

"I was thinking about it."

"You been in town a long while?"

"Since the train yesterday."

"Where you staying?"

I lifted and dropped a shoulder and glanced back at the demonic scrub. "I haven't set my mind on anything yet."

She took another drag of her cigar and let the smoke laze around as it left her mouth. She peered down at me. "Did you leave the fella out there in the wild?"

"I left the damn bastard in Tucson."

She laughed and flicked the cigar out the window, sending the chicken squawking and shaking its head. "Come on in then. Let's drink a toast to damn bastards."

❧

THE PARADISE—A HOUSE OF ILL, BUT WELL-KNOWN REPUTE—WASN'T particularly remarkable in any way. The front parlor, empty of customers, had seen better curtains and cleaner carpets. The settees, long and low to safely accommodate crowds on Friday nights and pay days, had a sheen to their flowered surfaces and bits of horsehair poking through the fabric. Wilted daisies sat upon side table doilies.

But the glass beads of the lamps sparkled, and the piano was a fine one, all scrollwork and turned roses.

I sat at the edge of a wingback chair, coffee cup and saucer balanced upon my knee, and nodded my thanks as my hostess poured a good finger of whiskey into the cup.

She had dressed before gathering me from the scrap of yard. She'd thrown on a robe of purply silk and white herons, and left the belt loose, so any time she gave a quick turn, the robe fluttered open and displayed her bits and bobbins.

She followed the liquor with a drop of milk and sat on the piano bench. She crossed a leg and rested her chin on her palm and watched me. There was a loud thump from upstairs, and a louder *Damn it to hell and back*. We both glanced at the ceiling and followed the random thud of feet as the girls awoke and made their way from their beds to the washrooms. The pipes squealed as they turned on the taps.

"I do appreciate the coffee," I said, though the fumes of it, coupled with my empty stomach and sleep deprived night, caused the edges of the room to fizzle and blur.

She opened a black lacquered box from atop the piano and popped a cheroot to her mouth. "You want one?"

My stomach gave a flop and grovel. "I think I might pass at this moment."

"It's a *Peter Schuyler's*."

I demurred.

She lit it, crossed her legs, and swung a foot. "You going to give a toast?"

I swallowed and nodded. "To Frank: I wish you a dog's year in hell, you lying, low-life, groveling excuse-making son of a bitch." Then I took a sip of my whiskey-spiked coffee. "That's enough words for him."

She lifted the whiskey bottle. "To Frank."

Then she took a big swallow before tipping the bottle again to my cup.

By my third sip, the room took on a fuzzy and circular shimmer. When I turned my head, it felt like I was inside a big ball that someone kicked around. I did wonder if I had been given a draft of something more potent, a drug that would keep me docile while being traded into white slavery. If I was in any sharp mind, I would have looked for the door. Instead, I blew out a breath and shimmied all the way back in the cushions and watched all the colors.

"Did you sleep outside last night?" Her voice floated towards me.

"I've done it before."

"Me, too." She leaned her elbows on the piano's fallboard, blew a smoke ring, and for good measure, blew another that settled in the first.

"That's a talent," I said. "What's your name?"

"Pip."

"That's a funny name." I lifted my cup, but my hand shook immensely. "You have beautiful hair."

Next I knew, I was lying on a wide bed nearly suffocated with pillows and cushions and the sweet smell of competing lotions and perfumes. I cracked open my eye. Pip sat by my side, holding a plate of bacon and fried eggs. She was in the midst of taking a wholesome bite of a biscuit when I stirred.

"You bring that for me?"

She chewed her biscuit, then set the remaining half on the plate. "You almost hit a marble spittoon."

"I fainted?"

"Indeed, you did."

I wrangled myself upright, wiggling myself into the pillow for comfort. My shiner was swollen tight, and throbbed when I turned my head.

"Here's a napkin." She draped it over my thighs and handed me the plate and a fork. "Eat up, Ruby Calhoun."

"How do you know my name?"

"Because you're a fool. You got your whole life in a wallet in your pocket."

I slapped my hand to my thigh. The plate slid dangerously, causing an egg to slip and fold over the lip. "You took my wallet."

"You should be more careful."

"Did you drug me, too?"

"Never know. You could have been the law. You know they're sending lady Pinkertons—"

"I'm not the law."

"Never know."

"They looking for you?"

She smiled, a wide beautiful smile. "I am an abiding citizen."

"Well, you just keep my wallet. There's nothing in there worth anything to me."

"I think you might want the picture of your girl." She slipped the wallet from a fold in her robe and took out a photograph of my daughter. Well, the half with her in it, as the Damn Bastard was posed beside her, I tore that half off and threw it out the train window somewhere around Florence.

"What's her name?"

"Emma. She's three."

Pip leaned the picture against the table lamp, then sat back in her chair and sighed. "She alive?"

"Uh-huh." I tore off a chunk of bacon and chewed.

"She with the bastard?"

"She is of no concern of yours." I swallowed and coughed. "I am looking for a position of any kind. Should you know of one."

Pip smiled again and, as her cheeks lifted, so did the bright shine in her eyes. "I know a few."

I could not frankly determine which of her eyes to focus upon, as one was green and the other like a bright penny, so instead I cut into my egg and sopped the yolk with the last bit of biscuit.

"Your cook is good."

"China Mary doesn't pinch pennies on the food."

"Is she your boss?"

"She is indeed. She owns everything in here including my ass, my tits, my —"

"I won't be a sporting girl."

She tilted her head. "That takes away one job."

"I'm good at laundry. I did that in Tucson."

"Wu Lin already has that handled."

"I can cook. Some."

"There's always a need up at the mining camps. Though I think they might expect the sporting along with it."

I pointed to an advertisement pinned to the wall across, to the right of her dressing table and mirror. The flyer was curled at the edges and ragged at the pinhole, as if it had been lifted and moved many assorted times. The illustration was of a plump black-haired maid in pantaloons and yellow corset, twirling a parasol and winking directly at the viewer. The print was too small for me to make out, and I gave a quick curse under my breath for having only one working eye. Still, I could tell the pretty girl in the picture was the same girl whose room I occupied now.

"You got an act," I said.

"I do."

I squinted to work out the name of the theater: Orpheum. Spokane, WA. "How the hell did you end up in Orinda?"

"I had my own damn bastard."

I took a minute to nod and ponder that. I wiped my mouth, folded the napkin to my plate and handed it to her. "You got another parasol? I believe I could be of much benefit to your act."

"I don't need a partner."

"I sing, I dance, and I know my way around a guitar. I could be of much benefit to enriching your act."

"You haven't seen my act."

"I don't need to see it to know two girls are better than one." The sheets caught on my feet as I twisted from the bed. I roughed them off and stood. "Can you play that piano downstairs?"

"Of course, I can."

"Then you play it, and I'll show you what I've got. I have played not only the best houses in Tucson, but the Chicago World's Fair far back in my youth. And I have been told I have the voice of a gilded canary. I am not a boaster myself, just merely telling you the truth. For you can always trust Ruby Calhoun for that."

CHAPTER 4

KANSAS CITY

1905

We Learn of Big Henry—A Hat, a Coat and Olaf—Doctor
Kate Tries to Knock Me Down—My Sister the Harridan—
Card Tricks

We both slept fitfully upon our return from Lady Anne's. Sometime in the night Pip had crawled from the hard floor into my bed and proceeded to saw and snore and shove me into the wall. Just as I had accommodated to the six inches spared my comfort, it was dawn, and Pip rolled out of bed and threw up in the bucket.

She pulled the bolt on the back door and was gracious enough to set the brew outside. Then she sighed, dropped her forehead against the wall, and mumbled a string of curse words. Slow as molasses, she turned about, rubbed the scar along her cheek with a thumb, and set to swigging her mouth out from the pitcher of water I kept at the sink. Then she crawled back into bed and slapped the pillow over her head.

I sneaked out quietly in the early hours to purchase six eggs, four sausage links, two buns and a tin of coffee. I hadn't realized the extent of my bill at the Market, not until Myra set three eggs, two links, one bun and no coffee on the counter and effectively cut off future purchases.

I returned to find Pip sitting upright in the wicker chair, her head resting against the back and eyes upon the ceiling. One knee bounced up and down.

I set the satchel of goods on the table by the cookstove. "You look like a poached egg."

"Thank you ever so much." Pip's stomach gave a long groan.

"I wasn't expecting a guest for breakfast. I usually head over to Lady Anne's before I open the shop. Their cook makes a fine corned beef hash."

Pip's face grayed.

I gave a lift of my shoulder and turned back to rustle up the fry pan and oleo from one of the shelves. "I'm making us eggs. Dry or runny?"

She moaned and wiped sweat from her upper lip.

"That Lady Anne Special is all dregs from the bottles. Mixed all up. And a pickled cherry to account for the "Special" in it."

Pip pressed her lips tight, her gray skin blossoming red and leaving the scar a bright jagged white.

I soaked a towel in the pitcher and tossed it her way. "Clean on up. You can tell me the story of poor Henry while I cook."

Her shoulders shuddered and she covered her face with her hands.

I set down the pan and tapped her shoulder. "Are you crying?"

She shook her head. "I don't cry." Her voice was muffled behind her hands.

"Then tell me the story while I fry this all up."

She bawled out a sob.

I stared at the curtain between this room and the shop and waited for her to snivel it out. The extent of her crying jag disconcerted me, and though I could put some of it down to the liquor, it seemed to come from a well much deeper and darker. I recalled the full might and glory of Henry, and how Pip had braided bells and ribbons in his mane and tail and paraded down the middle of Broad Street as bare as Lady Godiva. Henry's chestnut coat had gleamed as bright as her derriere and blushing cheeks. She'd done a few tricks like balancing on one foot and flipping into a shoulder stand, and Henry, not ruffled at all by the crowd Pip drew, had trotted right to the steps of the Paradise and kneeled like a knight to let his lady dismount.

"He stepped in a hole. I had to shoot him."

"Ah, hell. When?"

"Last July. Out by Holbrook."

"Why were you out by Holbrook? There's nothing there."

She shrugged and wiped her nose with the towel I gave her. "Just passing through. Damn snakes and their damn holes. He was the last good thing I had."

"You need to eat. Soak up the poison and your woes." I returned to the stove and struck a match to the gas burner. "You could use some fattening up, Pip. You poked me every which way with those bony elbows."

I sent her back to bed after our plate of shared eggs. She had not realized the extent of poison in that specialty drink and thus her need for a settle down.

This taken care of, I found my way next door to Olaf's haberdashery. Olaf was a young man, with keen blue eyes and a hairline slipping away before his youth. He had a habit of running his hand across the top of his head then leaving it there as he spoke. Except for this odd habit, and the hypnotizing quality of his fingers wiggling and tapping his forehead, he was a fine-looking man with a chest of thick blonde hair, and a narrow waist. He did not complain when I took him to bed and did not make a fuss when I rose in the morning to open my shop. He had his own business to look after, and our variegated arrangement of sharing the outhouse, wiling away slow afternoons over a game of gin rummy, and every so often taking a good old-fashioned rumble and tumble, was amenable to us both.

This morning we skipped his bed and utilized for our tryst an order of wool suit coats that had been delivered from his wholesaler on 8th Street.

After said encounter which did lower the state of my nerves, Olaf lounged against the shelves with his trousers around his knees and a supreme grin on his face. He rubbed a circle on the crown of his head. "Now will you marry me?"

"You ask that every time you're half-dressed and half-cocked."

"I ask that because it's a good idea."

"And, as I told you before, I am averse to marriage."

I twisted my skirt around and rebuttoned it.

"I need a coat for a friend of mine. And a hat. Hers is outrageously large." I stood and sifted through the coats, holding them up to my shoulders until I found a nice fawn brown one that would be a grand addition to my wardrobe. "Can you shorten this?"

At the bottom of the pile was a good sturdy gray twill jacket that looked right for Pip. I pulled out a sleeve, resting it on my arm for a quick measure, then pulled the shoulders taut. "This'll fit her just right."

I wove through the boxes and out to the front of the store, removing the list I had jotted from my pocket. Pip would require a real hat for her journey, not one of those useless creatures with crushed velvet roses, speckled ostrich feathers and taffeta doodahs. A good medium-brimmed Stetson with a round crown would be of better use.

Olaf had a goodly choice of Dunlaps and Fedoras, none of which suited my need. I lifted a brown crusher from the rack by the window, but it was too large, so I set it back.

I circled to peruse the hats hanging above the long glass cabinet. "That one," I said. "Steam that to twenty-three and an eighth inches."

And so, I found a high crown medium-brimmed Rough and Ready tight enough to pinch Pip's forehead and stay put in a sharp wind.

"Olaf?"

He stood behind me, caressing my shoulder and making me ticklish. I maneuvered a step out of his reach. His expression grew morose. I thought he would make a good addition to the melodrama shows, for his expressions would be crystal clear from the back gallery.

"Why are you being sad?"

"You come to see me. Then you go away. It hurts my heart."

My list included more stops than the floor of Olaf's shop. I had to go to Doctor Kate's, and my sister's. This last made me more frustratedly annoyed than I should have been to the man who gave me sixty percent off all wears and wares.

"I'm sorry for your pain, Olaf." I handed him the Rough and Ready, took my own straw one from the counter and pushed the hat pin to my hair. "You'll give me a discount on her, too, won't you? Since she's a friend and all." I pulled open the door. The bell jingled merrily above me. "You take care, Olaf. She'll be over later. I left her a note to stop by."

"Ruby—"

"Her name's Pip and don't hold her face against her. Pluck up your shoulders, you look like a pile of dung just landed on your head."

❧

THE STAIRWAY TO DOCTOR KATE'S SMELLED OF CLEAN LINEN AND disinfectant. You could stop at the stairwell, take a breather in the window seat, and bask in a bit of sunshine coming through the clean glass. It smelled of lemons, too, and honest good people. It did not smell at all like the rest of us.

Doctor Kate made sure of that. She kept the brass nameplate on her door shiny bright, and the walls were blinding white and bleach scented. She was the kind of doctor who waded through the floods to aid those in the West Bottoms and took in women who had been wrongfully used. She gained the respect of the society matrons and their money, too. It was rumored that the ladies' money paid a good penny for the new floors and medical equipment, and they paid a penny more for Doctor Kate to smile and keep her mouth shut when their daughters graced the door.

One secret led to the next dollar and that led to respect and the honor to walk with the refined set on the Paseo.

I admired Doctor Kate. She had come up from questionable roots. No one knew specifically what those roots were, and, thus, many muttered rumors were told and quashed as suddenly as they bubbled. For the doctor had a ledger. And she was meticulous in her recordings of sins and foibles and syphilis and the like.

She knew, as I knew, that for a woman to rise in the world, she needed to steal, cheat, outmaneuver, grift, flaunt, and, in her prosperous case, keep good records.

I slung my purse over my elbow and knocked on her door.

"Doctor Kate. It's Ruby Calhoun." I bent to look through the keyhole, but the cover was drawn tight.

There was a muffled noise, then, and the shift of a chair.

A gust of air whooshed up the stairs and ruffled my skirts. But whoever had opened the street door had gone out or was wandering the first-floor hall in search of the law office or other such business.

The door in front of me opened with a click. Doctor Kate stared down at me over her eyeglasses and stiff-necked collar. She gave a quick glance of disappointment that she must have thought I did not see when I called upon her for a small iota of morphine for my spirit's pains.

"It's a very lovely morning," I said.

"I am not giving you any drugs."

"But Doctor—" I pressed my lips tight and shook my head. "It says right on your sign: Female Complaints and Nervous Disorders. Of which I have both."

"No." She wrapped her fingers around the knob and yanked the door shut.

I rapped with my knuckle and switched my purse to my other arm. "Doctor Kate, I have tried to remove myself from this life seven times. Please don't leave me the chance for an eighth."

She opened the door a slit so her nose stuck through and she could peer down at me. "I have sworn a Hippocratic oath to do no harm."

"Exactly why I ask you for a draught."

"You were here last week."

"Friday, actually. The week before. A very long time ago."

"No. You can ask me again. I'm not giving you any more morphine. You can ask me every day, but the answer will always be no."

I gave a shrug and a dogged sigh. "It's just my head's been a bit spinny. And I am overanxious. I'm anxious to the point I might have to tell a newsman about your ledger and that alley door."

"Hm."

"Yeah, hm. *The Star* is just a streetcar and transfer up the road."

"You think you're bright, don't you?"

"Two bottles of your Speciality will suffice."

She pulled her nose back in and closed the door. A metal cabinet squealed. I heard the satisfying click of it opening and closing. Then she was back quick to the door. "That's the last of it for you."

I took the brown package with the pretty silk ribbon she offered, exchanging it for a two-dollar bill. "I do believe you've saved my spirits today."

⊗⊱⊗

MRS. CJ MALTHUS—OR MY PINCHED-MOUTH HOLIER-THAN-THOU sister Rose—stood on her whitewashed porch and stared at me. She had pin-curled her blonde hair to an inch of its life, and the frond surrounding her forehead framed eyes bugging out worse than they did on normal occasions. I flinched a bit but held my ground.

She did not take well to my request to store my next shipment of cigars in her back shed.

"It could all catch on fire," she said. She pursed her mouth ever tighter. "There would go the whole neighborhood." She waved her hand, the delicate handkerchief flapping around. She clawed it in and wiped her nose. "A miasma of flame. Did you think on that, Ruby, or did it not cross your mind?"

"I have to admit that the conflagration of your neighborhood was not on my list to think on."

The sun poked at my neck. Rose had not invited me up from my place at the foot of the porch steps. I rubbed the skin and looked to the street, wondering how much time I had before the next streetcar came and if I had timed it right to get a glimpse of Emma and John as they walked to school.

I had not had an opportunity to spy on their well-being in the past months, and wondered how tall they'd grown, for John was ten now and Emma eight. I wanted to make sure my sister hadn't dressed John up as some Little Lord Fauntleroy and forced Emma into a corset so she could grow up as a lady and not like her good-for-nothing-mother-who-is-never-discussed.

"You think I could—"

"No." Her bosom shook with vehemence. She poked her finger

under the watch pinned to her left breast and gave it a hard look before dropping it back to its resting place. "No. You go on, Ruby."

She crossed her arms and raised her nose at me.

"They're not your kids," I said.

"Who feeds them?"

"That's not the point."

"That is the point. That is always the point." The streetcar rumbled around the corner, the sparks arcing on the electric lines, the transport tipping side to side. "That's your ride."

I balled my fists, flexed them out, then dug into my shoulder bag and grabbed a roll of bills. "I feed them, too." I slung it to the porch. It bounced off a planter and Rose scooped it up and shoved it in her pocket. "You leave that shed open or I'll dump the cigars on your lawn."

I stomped away, throwing the gate open so it banged against the perfect picket fence, then I banged it again for good measure. "You are a harridan of the first order," I called out. I ripped a hank of ivy she'd trained to drape just so from the posts.

"Go on." She clomped to the edge of her porch. "Go on like you always do, you miserable—"

The streetcar passed the house and cut off her words. I jogged to the corner to catch it. A largish man leaned from the car's back steps and reached out his hand. I grabbed ahold and took a leap to the steps, swinging into a wooden seat. I gave him a nod. He leaned against the back wall, his round body and hips nearly blocking the advertisement for Mrs. Browning's Pile Relief. His clothes were a fancy check, with brown velveteen on the lapels. He pushed back his brown bowler and scratched a dark sideburn. "Almost missed it."

"There'd be another." My skirts were bunched under me. I shifted a bit and pulled at the fabric to set them right.

He snipped the end from a cigar and pulled a fancy lighter from his vest pocket. The smoke cloyed and stuck around us. I twisted to pull open a window, but it stuck tight and left but an inch of fresh air. "*Higaldo*, huh?"

He raised an eyebrow and tilted the cigar to give it a look. "I guess it is."

"I know it is." I picked at the paint on the window frame and took in a gulp of air. Then I froze. A passel of kids walked down the street, heading to St. Mary's and St. Luke's, the girls a batch of curls and ribbons and the boys kicking the walkway and shoving each other around. A too tall lanky boy looked at the streetcar. My John, with those almond-shaped eyes like Frank's and that same emerald-green that had ensnared me in his father. His head was shaved all the way to the nicked surface, and I noticed this was the same for them all. Lice had taken root and been removed.

He did not acknowledge me. He did not know me. And, as happened on previous occasions, my heart hammered my chest and I sweat too much.

I stood and strode to the rail, looking for Emma among the girls, searching for the mop of red hair and not finding it.

Emma looked like a dried mushroom when she was born. Nose twisted all awonk. Ears curving and whorled with tiny veins so red in the thin skin of them. She'd smelled of fermented lemon as if she'd popped from black spring soil and landed in the shadows of tall saguaro. She'd smelled of regret and panic and her lips stretched in a stoic line. She had not cried at all. Not even a noise, though the midwife gave her a good strong smack. Emma had taken a big gulp of alien air then clamped her mouth tight and refused to take another.

But the world being the world, and not at all kind, had decided another breath was required of her, so the midwife smacked her again and got her breath going. Emma the shrunken mushroom would have rather crawled back inside my belly and enjoyed the peace and quiet.

Frank had bent over her, hat in hand, suit coat dark-sweated under the armpits, stubble on his chin from a night at the tables, half-drunk and said, "Will you look at that."

Then he'd put his hat on and shoved his hands to his pockets. He'd rolled two coins between his fingers, the muffled click a sure sign it was all he had left of his stake.

Emma had squirmed, her mouth pursing and relaxing, two bubbles taking a rest at the corner of her tiny mouth.

"They don't stay this ugly, Frank."

"She is ugly, though, isn't she?"

I'd bent so my body curved over hers and buried my nose in the soft spot on her head. I'd known with all certainty she would grow up a beauty, and I'd known with more certainty, I'd need to keep her away from my sort of living and men like Frank. So to Rose she went.

I ground my teeth and wrapped my fingers tight on the streetcar's brass railing. The man's elbow bumped my shoulder. The streetcar took a turn to the brick and stone of the city proper. I had not seen Emma at all. Perhaps she was early to school, with her head over some geography book. Or piano. She could have gone to her piano lesson at Mrs. Durant's. I had a quick flash of thought that I might be able to catch a view of her with her music books under her arm.

I dropped my shoulders and returned to my seat. "Can you put that out?"

He didn't. He held the monstrosity above his shoulder up away from me. He squeezed in the seat next to me, his thigh pushed against mine. His free hand rested on his knee. He twisted the ring on his pinky finger, settling it so the opal that graced it showed above the tufts of hair on his fingers. His nails were neat and buffed to a satiny sheen. I shifted to the left to put a space between us, for I should have figured him out sooner than I did. A gambler. Just like my no-good Frank, with that patient way of lounging and smoking and waiting for the right game to play. Velveteen collar instead of velvet, coat hemmed one too many times at the cuffs, the rough cheap cigar, the ring with the opal that I would lay one hundred dollars down to declare a piece of glass, and that glint of greed in his eyes.

"What's your game?" I asked.

He frowned, drawing his bristly mustache down, and gave me a confused shake of the head. "I'm not sure of your meaning."

"You know what I mean. Got a penchant for faro, the wheel, or just taking young women for a quick ride?"

His frown unlocked, and his lips curled up. The clean spaces between his teeth and the shine of his gums confirmed again his line of business, for there wasn't any other type of man kept himself so very much on show. My guess was he had a book of toothpicks right at hand, and—if I were a betting woman—would say he snapped a pick off and shoved it between his front teeth when he was losing his shirt and about to bet his last pair of socks.

"I sell Bibles, Mrs. Calhoun."

"How do you know my name?"

He didn't answer me, for the streetcar had lurched to a stop by Central Bank. He shouldered his way through the passengers who had climbed the stairs, muttered "Pardon me. Excuse me greatly." And hopped to the cement. With a great smile he lifted his hat to me before departing, the smoke from his cigar trailing behind as he waddled away.

"How do you—"

I jumped up to follow him, shoving between a rose-patterned bustle and a heavy net bag that smacked into my shin. I pulled at my skirt, which had found itself pinned under a man's wide shoe and took a tumble forward when I'd freed it. By the time I'd grabbed the rail and taken to the steps, we were on our way, and the man long lost among the derbies, fedoras, parasols, and awnings. I was left with a sharp feeling in my stomach, and a wavering sense of dread. I pulled at the strings of my shoulder bag and grappled the interior, sure he'd lifted my coin purse. I pulled it up and unsnapped it. It was empty, save for a single card:

"Son of a bitch."

I hugged the bag to my chest and stared at the other passengers.

"Son of a goddamn bitch."

CHAPTER 5

ORINDA
1898
China Mary Offers Work—Tommy Gee Gives Advice

T he girls called the roof of The Paradise "Little Eden," and I could not disagree on that count. They had one day a week to themselves, and that was Monday. Verna Rolfe liked to lounge in the morning sun, taking in the cool air and a toke of opium or two. She spread her straw-blonde hair in a wide fan on the pillow of her folding lounger, letting the lemon juice she'd worked in the strands do their work. Pip showed up smelling of hay and horse, having spent the early hours riding Big Henry around the arena at Pascoe's Livery and Feed, working out some new stunts. Then red-headed Maggie Halloran brought up the *Silver King* news and read to Darby Price, the paper spread across their cross-legged laps. She had taken a motherly shine to Darby and was working on teaching her letters. Darby herself was a little nothing of a girl who'd ended up under the tutelage of China Mary because her daddy had lost a bet. At least, that was the story. The moral of it was to never lose a bet with China Mary.

I had hesitated at China Mary's invitation to join the girls, though she offered a nice little room with a view out across Broad Street and beyond it the craggy rough wild of the Pinal Mountains. I would, unfortunately, see those in too much detail, but now it was not the mountains that frightened me. Nor was it a sense of judgment or right-eousness that led me to choose other quarters.

"I am a light sleeper," I told China Mary.

She gave a grunt from the doorway to the room. "You have a skinny ass."

"Some men like it."

She widened her eyes and stuck out her chin, looking much like one of those Gila lizards I had encountered down in Tucson that were big enough to lasso and saddle. "Then make money with it. Assets, even bony ones, are meant to be used. I make you a good offer. Low rent, free food, half-price drinks, Mondays free, and medi-cine on the house. This is a popular establishment. Many girls want in here."

"Then why're you offering the room to a skinny ass flat cakes woman like me?"

"Lots of tastes out there. The miners are from all over the world. I think the Oslovians will find you to their taste."

"The Oslovians. All the way from Norway?"

She shrugged.

"Who had this room before me?"

The ribbons and lace of her small cap floated around when she shook her head. "We don't talk about traitors. Take the room."

I turned my gaze to the street. A boy in short pants and huarache sandals trotted up the middle. A double yoke sat upon his shoulders, each side holding a bucket of water. The dust puffed from under his heels as he shimmied around a buggy, then a lumber cart, keeping his knees high and footfall soft. I saw not one drop of liquid hit the dirt.

"Tommy's here," I said.

And that was enough to garner a gold-toothed smile and a clap of the hands. The only thing—beyond money—that made China Mary's day was her personal delivery of well-water. She had a deep distrust of the public water pumps and I did sympathize with that view. Pip had warned me the first few nights I hid in the attic to avoid the water altogether, unless it had been boiled three times and run through a sieve.

The Paradise's attic served much the same purpose as any attic, storing a mishmash of broken items and mismatched parts. It also passed as a furnace, should Dante lose his Inferno and need another. Hence, by the fifth morning I had lost all my senses, stumbled directly into China Mary's generous stomach, and dropped in a dead faint at her brocade slippered feet.

She lurched over me, her dress a green sateen that wavered. I shuffled back, away from her pointing finger and in fear of a long lizard tongue.

"No more free ride. You take the room or you get out."

<hr />

I WANDERED DOWN BROAD STREET, STARING INTO THE WINDOWS OF saloons and gambling halls, looked with yearning at the diners in the Cafe Royal, and blocked a hand over my eyes when passing the confectioners. Pip had not said one word about my joining her act. Indeed, she said my voice was sweet but a little on the reedy side.

I took a side street called Push Alley that turned and ambled away from the scrub brown adobe and baked brick of the town and took a few good breaths under a mesquite tree. The house it belonged to was clapboard, maybe a room or two, but the yard was neat and raked, with prickly pear and cholla kept safely to the side of the lot.

Real people had real houses like this. My sister Rose had a house like this, with even more rooms and none of the cactus. Everything trim and proper and thought out. Rose had married a banker. I missed the wedding. She swore she sent an invitation but I know she didn't. Where the hell would she have sent it? This riverboat or that riverboat? This boarding house or that opium den?

She'd been right about Frank. My sister saw him for what he was—an itinerant snake-eyed no-good sneak thief, boaster, and godless gambling man. I saw him the same way, which was why I married him. I am still not one hundred percent clear if I did it to spite her.

I took to the riverboat life with arms wide open. It was colorful and loud, and I liked to stand behind the men at the poker tables, with their razor-sharp eyes that caught out bluffs and tics in the other players. I liked the rich food—the fish stews and tapioca puddings, vanilla flambeau—and the late nights, and watching the paddlewheel churn up the muddy waters. I liked Frank's attentions and the days we never left the bed. Just ordered food into the suite and fed each other and took each other on silk sheets.

But then I got pregnant and that made me fat so Frank left me on shore.

"You're bad luck," he said. Sometimes he left me money for a room and other times, when he lost, he left me with a black eye.

Then came John. Little ruffian who yelled out and didn't stop yelling.

Frank paid our fare to Kansas City. One way for John, roundtrip for me. "Just until the luck turns, darling girl. Just until it turns."

I kicked a rock and stomped back to the main street.

Tommy Gee, his black hair sticking out in hanks both oily and dusty, sat against the wall of McCullough's, eating the last of a tamale, licking clean the husk. His eyes followed me as I passed. "You should take the room."

"I shall not take that room."

He shrugged, rolling up the husk and stuffing it in a pocket. "Suit yourself." He lifted the yoke to his shoulders. The empty buckets swung around. "Stay out in the desert then."

"I've done it before."

We were near the same height. He came close enough I could smell the linger of his lunch.

"Was that a pork tamale?"

"It was chicken."

I ran my tongue along my teeth, then swallowed.

"Lady," he said, "I seen a drunk miner fall in the dry wash and drown two minutes later in a flash flood. And I found two fingers and a watch just out there."

I followed the wave of his hand out eastish way. It took in the road to the copper mines and everything out beyond it. "Did you keep the watch?"

"Four miners died at the New Dominion smelter, and there's holes all over from the surveyors drilling and prospectors shoveling. Then there's the javelina. Eat your eyes out while you're sleeping."

"Well, what's beyond all that?"

"Apache reservation."

I put my hands to my hips and stepped back, giving him a once over. "Why, that's a damn lie. They're all in Buffalo Bill's Wild West Show. I saw them with my own eyes."

"Where?"

"Where what?"

"Where'd you see 'em?"

"Chicago. At the Columbian Exhibition."

"When?"

"Why, eighteen hundred and ninety and three."

He gave a long whistle, as if that was somewhere in the ancient past. "Well, they're back home."

"All right, then. What about that way?" I pointed west, up at the Pinals.

"That's just sure death." He chucked a shoulder and set the buckets swinging again. "Then you got China Mary up that way and the law abiders down that way."

"Huh."

"Uh-huh. Rotary Club and all."

I twisted my heel to the dirt and contemplated each of the choices.

"You should take the room."

"But I am not, nor do I wish to be, a gilded lady."

"Like I said." He pointed around. "Death, death, more death, and Do Gooders. But your grave is your business, lady."

So, I took the room and sat along with the girls Monday mornings to watch the sun come over the ridge of the San Carlos Reservation, at which the Apaches did indeed reside, though not of their own accord, and not without a good damn fight. Monday evenings, Pip and I created our acts, her having realized I would not give in to her request to be a mere costumier and lackey and that I did indeed have a greater talent than her when it came to a song.

CHAPTER 6

KANSAS CITY AND THEN JUST KANSAS
1905
THERE IS IMMINENT DANGER—I'VE BEEN STOOD UP—ENDICOTT
LEE—A TELEGRAM

"What did he look like?" Pip glared at me. She hadn't left like she'd promised, and I nearly fainted with relief with seeing her in my room. That dissipated into an urge to shove her in the privy for bringing such wretchedness my way.

I sat at the small table, neat and clean from breakfast. The only item upon the oilcloth was the devilish card.

"Ruby. What did he look like?"

"Large. Not tall large, just largish. In the hips. And a mustache like a broom." I pulled at my collar and smoothed my hands along my chest. But all of me itched and quivered, as if my skin had turned inside out. "He had beautiful hands. Gambler's hands. I've never seen such neat nails."

"What else?"

"I don't know what else. He had an opal ring. On his pinky. And a dimple. Just one. He knew it looked good on him." My throat swelled with dread. I pushed away from the table, the chair leg shrieking across the boards. "Why'd you come here?"

She picked at the corner of the blind and peered in the alley, then stalked into the main shop to spy through those windows. She came back and grabbed up her carpetbag, slinging it to the mattress and pulling out a stocking roll. "Here." It made a dull clump when she put it on the table.

"What is that?"

"It's a gun, Ruby."

My hand shook as I reached for the cotton and unrolled it. The pistol was small, an easy one to hide in purse or coat pocket. "It's tiny."

"It'll do what it needs to. We'll get a Colt in Wichita."

"Wichita." The gun had a fancy grip, as a lady might like, but the two barrels were plain of adornment. My head thudded. "Why Wichita?"

Pip ripped open the drawers of my wardrobe, shifting through my clothing and underwear, throwing some to the bed frame and shoving the others back inside. "You got a suitcase?"

"I don't—"

"We have to go."

My mouth filled with bitter saliva. "This is your fault. I was at my children's house, Pip. My *children*. He followed you here. Then he followed me there. What if he—I need to make sure they're all right."

"We make them all right by leaving and getting him to follow us."

"How does that make it right?" My knees quavered and I grabbed at the table. "I'm going to be sick."

"We'll take the train to Wichita, then figure something from there."

"Go away. This is your doing. I'm staying here and I'm not having anything to do with this. Take the card with you. I got kids to worry about."

She kicked the bed post with the back of her boot and gripped my arm. "Wipe the snot from your nose and get yourself calmed down."

"I hate you, Pip. If anything happens—"

"You want to save those kids you gave up? Then you get on a train to Wichita with me and we make sure we're loud enough and stupid enough that jackass gambler follows us right over the bluffs and out of Kansas City."

"No."

Her fingers dug in between the muscles. "What are you going to do when Cullen or one of his men comes through your front door and shoots you in the head?"

I gasped a breath and wheezed.

"Him or you, Ruby. He might be your first customer of the day. You won't know. But he will be your last."

"I don't want to die."

"Then we go. We find him first." She let go of my arm and let out a long breath. "You got enough money for a cab to the depot?"

I pointed to the tea tin. "Just a few dollars."

"When's the next train?"

"It leaves at ten forty a.m. If you want Wichita." I chewed on my nail and stared at her. She pulled the chair over to the wardrobe and reached for my suitcase, swinging it down so it landed with a thump on the bed. "That's the Missouri Pacific. Number Three. It'll be in from Independence. It's a local if you don't mind the stops. The Santa Fe comes later. That's at eleven a.m. but it doesn't go to Wichita."

Her mouth hung open as she stared at me. "It doesn't."

"It goes to Topeka. Express. It arrives at one twenty-five p.m. Then Newton at five forty, then Hutchinson at seven oh-five."

"Ruby—"

"Timetables calm me."

"That's the train, then. We can be done with this by supper."

I put my hand to my chest and dragged a breath through my teeth, trying to catch some air. Like I was underwater and drowning and one good breath would make everything all right. "I don't want to die."

"Then pack that case, put the pistol in your purse and we'll go."

"I got you a coat."

She let out a breath. "What?"

"And a hat. I got myself a coat, too." I pointed at the wall. "They're at Olaf's. I left you a note."

"What the hell are you talking about?"

"Look at your jacket. Your elbows are about to pop out. And your hat is...well, it's like having a target on your head from twenty miles away. I'll go over and—it's good twill. Then we can go and—"

She took a step forward, her hands in fists, then stopped herself short of punching me. "We have to go *now*."

"What do we do after the train? We don't have a plan, Pip."

"I'll give you a plan. You go next door and get the useless coats and that very special hat. I will pack your case and we will get two tickets on that eleven a.m. train."

She picked up her belt and tightened it on her waist. An embossed holster had been added; perhaps it had been there the night before, though I had not spied it. The gun she removed from the satchel stunned me, for it was a long-barreled pearl-and-silver-handled splendor. A Colt of the finest make and highest price.

"Did you hear me, Ruby?"

"I heard you."

"And don't blather on about where we're going. Think of a good lie."

"Like my aunt died. Or you're getting married. Or I won the trip in the last *Kansas City Star* contest."

"Never mind. Don't say anything."

"Should I take the gun next door with me?"

Her jaw clenched up tight. "Just...get the damn things."

◈◈◈

I HELD ONTO OLAF'S COATTAILS AS HE PUSHED AND MANEUVERED through the station to the platform. He held my case above his head, and I was grateful for that. We had lost Pip at the entrance and no amount of tiptoeing and jumping would have helped me find her. I worried she had been dragged into the Wichita crowd and onto the wrong train.

Olaf glanced back with a smile, twisting just enough to take my hand and squeeze it. "You don't mind Third Class? It was the last of the seats."

The coal dust made me sneeze and I slowed to take up my handkerchief from the deep pocket of the brand-new coat. It was too heavy for the bruising day, but the suitcase already bulged full and I feared removing the coat in public would cause the little gun to slip out of the side pocket and land on the ground. Security might then become involved and Olaf's questions would grow more pointed. I was not certain he fully believed my story of an ailing mother.

Earlier, as we rode the 12th Avenue El, his little looks and raised eyebrows and tsk-tsks had been followed by frowns. "But I thought your mother...I read that *Youth's Companion* article."

I had waved my hand in dismissal and stared out at the tenements and shacks that littered the bluff. "She got better."

"And moved." His left eyebrow jiggled, not sure if it wanted up or down.

"That rag got the story all wrong. You know how papers are."

Pip, who wore her new hat jaunty and low on her forehead—proving I knew what looked best on her—had leaned forward and said, "Her mother is dying of the clap. It's embarrassing to talk about."

He shut up.

On the platform, I ducked to avoid the swoop of a bird as it winged from one high corner of the train shed to another. Maybe, when the new depot got built, the bird could settle down and return to a normal life.

"You did a good job on this coat, Olaf. I promise to pay you when I return."

He squeezed the ticket to my hand. "It's a gift."

"Do you see Pip?"

He blinked and looked around.

I wished she hadn't traded the sombrero for the more casual hat I'd picked for her. It would be something easy to find, even from my level. All I saw were coats and feathered hats and conductor's striped uniforms, the porters taking trunks and luggage this way and that, and beyond that melee, the great train wheels.

My gut churned up. I glared at the station clock, which ticked its way closer to 10:40 a.m.

"All aboard!"

Olaf scooted me to the right line, his hand resting on my back. "I'll hand the suitcase through the window."

I looked at him, at those doe eyes that annoyed me to hell and back. I pressed my hanky to my lips. "I can't go without her."

We moved forward. Olaf shook his head at a porter who reached for the suitcase. "I'm sure she got on the wrong car. That's all. You can find her at the next stop. You have the tickets after all. Just catch up with her in Paola."

"Paola?" I flipped the ticket to see its information. "This is the wrong train. Olaf, this is quite the wrong..." I flipped the paper to purvey the opposite side and a hurried line of handwriting. *Change of plan.*

I did not think there was a plan to begin with. But Pip wasn't here to discuss that problem.

The conductor dragged me up the steep narrow steps. I grabbed the brass pole and leaned out to see if Pip was anywhere in sight. She was not in the pile of folks embarking Second Class, nor was she getting waited on hand and foot at the sleeper cars. "Jesus Christ in a bottle. First Class has got an awning."

Olaf gave apologies to all around for my rude language.

Then I was packed between a lady in fiddly-diddly muslin and doused in lemon verbena, and an old man in droopy pants who needed a shave. I looked for my seat, then peeled out of the line and slipped onto the bench. Olaf was outside, the top of his head showing. He reached up, waved, and knocked on the window and waved again. I shimmied the glass open, taking one more look around in dismay before pulling the case from him. It stuck between the bench and the backrest of the seat in front. I yanked it free, wincing at the rip in the chipboard.

I placed it down in the empty space that should have been filled with damn Pip Quinn and sat.

Olaf's fingers curled around the window frame. "You be careful."

"Yes, Olaf."

"There's four silver dollars in your purse."

"Thank you for telling the entire passenger list."

"And don't worry about the shop, I've got—"

The whistle drowned out whatever else he had to say. The train lurched and began its forward chug. People waved hankies from open windows and well-wishers jogged along. Olaf kept his hand curled on the frame until he couldn't keep up.

I stood and leaned out. "Olaf!"

"Yes, dear."

"Take care of my wooden Indian!"

He smiled and ran his hand over the top of his head, his blonde hair gleaming in the sun. Smoke billowed past, obstructing the view, then poured itself through the windows on one side of the car before exiting through the other.

"Close the damn windows!" The woman in verbena and daisies stomped onto the bench across, waving her fan and coughing. Her hair flew every which way proving to me once again that the Gibson Girl style was unattainable for the masses.

The wooden box was sealed up and we were left to steam.

❧

THE TRAIN CHUGGED ALONG THE STOCKYARD RAILS, HIGH UP SO I could see the misery in each crowded cow pen. It was a hive of movement, the cows with their necks stretched and eyes rolling, silent lows from their open mouths. A cowboy rode along one row of pens, poking a stick at a haunch then whistling for his dog to slither along. A group of men from Armour Packing, in three-piece suits and matching black hats, pointed as they assayed the lots. Above it all, a black throng of flies shifted like a layer of soot over the cattle.

Out beyond, the ropy mud brown Missouri River fingered its way into the Kaw. We were over the river, the train taking up speed, passing the manufacturers and abattoirs on the Kansas side until they were a blur. Then there was but the wide flat Kansas plains.

My breath grew jagged and edgy, looking at such empty space. Just the gingham sky and the sunbaked fields, all the winter wheat harvested and nothing but a few broken stalks to break up the view. I'd been this way once before, dragged myself on a boxcar with one good arm and the other broke because Frank thought I'd gone out on him when I had not. I'd been singing. He'd lost a bundle on cards, and I'd made it back singing.

My eye caught on a lone figure with one hand raised in a lazy wave, a hello or fare-thee-well to all us strangers passing by. A series of fence posts flared by, the barbed wired flicked and shiny and new. A roll of dust traveled a farm road. All of it empty. The only thing waiting at the end was the barrel of Cullen Wilder's gun.

I shivered, a sharp cold suspicion that Pip wasn't on the train at all. That this was a setup. I'd left her for dead once; maybe this was her final retribution. She could be laughing her ass off on the platform in Kansas City, thinking how she'd pulled the wool over Ruby Calhoun's eyes, and was sending me to my just desserts.

Well damn her to hell. I'd get off at the next station and turn right around and get on with my life. I shifted my hip and reached in my pocket for my pencil and the schedule, unfolding it and flattening it to my lap.

Paola 12:28 p.m.

That's what I would do. Get right off this train at Paola at 12:28 unless there was an accident on the tracks, like an errant pronghorn or seasonally late tornado. I ran the pencil along the return column and was pleased to see and circle the return No. 8, which departed at 4:02 p.m. and would thus get me back in Kansas City for dinner. Between the timetable and the decision, I felt much better.

I glanced at the ceiling, following the shallow arch of it from the front door and its exit to Second Class. The back door led to the baggage and grain and boxcars. Between each the knuckle couplers clanged and the chains swung and rang out, loud even through the thick wood.

A finger poked my back between my shoulder blades. "What're you doing up there?"

It was a freckly kid with an overbite. He cocked his elbows along the bench's back, dropped his chin to his arm and peered down at the schedule.

"I'm looking at the timetable."

"Where you going?"

I folded the paper and shifted it back to my pocket. My thumb caught on the pistol. I jerked my hand free. I patted the weapon through the fabric before twisting to look at the kid. "Where are *you* going?"

"Lomax." He stuck out his tongue and rolled it, then pulled it back into his mouth with a slurp sound.

"Good for you."

"You been there?"

"Nope."

"Me, neither." There went the tongue again, this time accompanied by rapid blinks and rolled back eyes.

"Are you having an attack of some kind?"

His shoulder lifted right up to his ears and dropped back down. Then there was a loud thwack and his head snapped forward. He grabbed at the back of it and grimaced.

"Leave the lady alone."

I twisted more to see the origin of the slap and locked eyes with a haggard-looking girl. Her dress was a washed-out brown poplin, not even a collar to speak of. She pulled at a strand of her hair, which was as thin as her skirts and about the same solid brown.

"You could have given him a concussion," I said.

She pulled that hank of hair to her lips, bit down and slid it through before letting it drop and linger on her chest.

"Is he your kin?"

The boy scooted forward, his knees wide, and one aimed directly at the girl's thigh.

"Don't you touch my leg," she said.

His lip pulled up in a smug smile and he made sure to shove his knee against her leg and push.

She rolled her eyes and returned to chewing her hair.

"That's Ernice." He flicked the top of my suitcase. "What you got in here?"

"Doodads and crawdads."

"Can I see?"

Ernice made a smacking noise with her lips, like she was chewing her tresses of hair. "You can't look at a woman's underthings, Endicott."

"What in the hell. Your name is Endicott?"

"Sure."

"Endicott." I rubbed my eyebrow. "That's the sissiest name I've ever heard. Except Finian."

"What should it be?" He was somehow now draped over the seat, his face turning red from being upside-down.

"You look like a George to me. That's a good solid name. I think you should call yourself George."

"That's my dad's name." His face grew redder.

"Is that who you're going to see? In Lomax?"

"He's dead. My sister and me are going to stay with my Aunt June and Uncle Verle. They got a farm. With pigs."

The sister grabbed Endicott's suspenders and yanked him up. "Sit back down and leave the lady alone." Then she ignored us and stared out the window.

In the seat behind the kids, an old man snorted in his sleep, his head cocked back and mouth open wide.

The boy scrambled around and over the seat to stare at the man. He slid a quick look at his sister, who pretended we did not exist, then hopped the seats and squeezed in next to me, a cigar held between his thumb and forefinger.

"Did you just swipe that from that poor man's pocket?"

"I did."

"Well, look at that." I accepted the cigar and admired the label. "A *La Magnite*. You surprise me, Endicott. I did not peg you an Artful Dodger."

He reached for it.

I gripped it tight. "Nope."

"But I took it."

"And I'm going to smoke it." In the stress and strain of escaping Kansas City, I had not thought to bring along cigars.

"Women don't smoke cigars."

"I do."

"Then you're not a woman. Maybe you're a sissy boy in a dress."

"Maybe you're right. Maybe my name's Endicott."

"No, it ain't."

"Get your hand out of my purse."

He snaked his greedy fingers back, then wiggled them so I could see they were empty.

"You met your Aunt June and Uncle Verle before?"

"Nope."

"Where're you coming from?"

"Kimmswick. You been there?"

"Nope."

"We got a butter festival."

"No ma, either?"

He pulled in his chin. "Nope."

Hot air blasted in as the front door clanked open. A porter, sharp in his flat cap, pressed blue suit and white gloves stepped into the car. He turned with military sharpness to close the door, muffling the clangs and thunks of the train's various parts. His eyes swung left to right, then he walked right to me.

"Mrs. Calhoun." His voice was near a murmur, as if we were in a private conversation, something rarified and not meant for the ears of the huddled Third Class masses surrounding us.

"I am she."

He presented me with a small envelope. "Telegram."

Endicott's head wagged. "She in trouble?"

"Shh." I handed Endicott the cigar and grasped the missive between my thumb and index finger. "How'd this get on the train?"

The porter bent close. "We have our own telegraph line."

Here it was. The kiss-off from Pip. Something like: SORRY TO LEAD YOU ON—stop—HAVE A GOOD DEATH.

I took in a breath and tore off the flap, my hands shaking as I unfolded the paper.

MR MUSTACHE ON OUR TRAIL. TRICKED HIM ON THE SANTA FE TO TOPEKA. HAHA. SEE YOU IN PAOLA.—PIP

I sighed and refolded the telegram, slipping it into the envelope.

"Do you want to send a response, Mrs. Calhoun? It's been pre-paid."

"I don't..." I gulped and swallowed. "This was sent to the train?"

"No, ma'am. It was sent from the train."

"She's *on* the train?"

"Do you have a return response?"

"Did she send this from the parlor car? In First Class?" I narrowed my eyes and glared down the corridor to the door. "Is anyone allowed between these cars? Because I could just take a stroll—"

"Only the porters and the conductors are allowed between cars while we're moving."

The boy bounced forward. "A lady got crushed in the knuckle last month. In Peoria. Did you read that? Her skirt got caught and, wowee, there must have been some mess."

The porter's mouth twitched. But he didn't give Endicott heed. Just kept his hands clasped behind his back waiting for me to give an answer.

"Mrs. Calhoun?"

"Let me think." I pressed my temples and rocked forward. I needed a smoke. I needed a good swig of Dr. Kate's medicinal tonic. I needed to know where Pip got the money for a Pullman ticket. And I needed to know how soon the man would figure it all out and switch lines. Maybe he'd turn back to Kansas City and grab up one of my kids. We should have let him track us all the way to Hutchinson. All he'd do now is get mad. Then what? "Okay. Here's the response: What's after Paola?"

"One word, please."

"Pardon?"

"She paid for one word."

"One?"

"Yes, ma'am."

"Fine."

"Yes?"

"I gave it to you." I crossed my arms. "Just take out all the spaces."

He cleared his throat and stared at the frosted globe lights. Then, he nodded and returned to the upper classes. And Pip.

"You in trouble?"

"You asked that already. Sit back down." I swatted at Endicott. "No wonder your sister looks like she's eighty-two."

"I heard that."

"Yeah, well, if the shoe fits..."

The door slammed open and thudded closed, and the man who should have been on the No. 1 California Express in the direction of Topeka instead stood wide-legged in the aisle, smoking his stink of a cheap cigar.

He blew out a puff and smiled so the dimple came out. "Mrs. Calhoun." The cigar, bit now between his teeth, stopped any more words. He smiled around it, pointing at the poor man who smelled like a delicatessen, then ambled over and moved my suitcase from the seat to the overhead storage. He sat with a humph and continued to smoke.

I grabbed the man's cigar, dropped it to the floor and stomped my boot on it until it was good and out. I held my palm out to Endicott. "Give me the *La Magnite*."

He gave it to me, squeezed his shoulders between us and stared at my new unwanted seatmate. "Who're you?"

"Sit back down, Endy. I mean it."

Maybe he saw something in my eyes that meant I was serious or about to throw up my breakfast in fear. But he obeyed, leaning back and watching the clouds skitter by.

My skin, already heated from leaving my jacket on, now poured sweat. I took my handkerchief from my belt and wiped the back of my neck, watching from the corner of my eye as the man unbuttoned a small leather case, picked up a cutter and snipped the cigar's tip.

"I haven't had the pleasure of one of these."

I scrubbed at my forehead and my upper lip. "Me neither."

With a flourish that showed off the pinky ring, he slid the cutter to the case, took up a match and scraped it along the bottom of his shoe. Holding the flame to the cigar, he lit and puffed, his cheeks sinking and expanding. "I heard you sing once. At the Paradise." He twisted his ring around and settled his bulk in, making himself at home. "Boudreaux. My name is Barnabé Boudreaux."

"I don't remember you."

I pushed the muzzle of the gun into his doughy waist.

His eyebrow rose and he gave a small shake of his head. "Oh."

"That's right, *oh*."

He peeked down at the handkerchief-draped weapon. "That little thing? Won't even leave a bruise."

"How about if I lift it to your temple?"

"That might sting."

I pushed it harder and gave a twist. "You just keep your eyes forwards and your mouth shut."

"All right already. There are children here. You wouldn't—"

"Oh yes, I would."

The gun quivered. I realized Boudreaux was laughing. He guffawed hard, and his eyes screwed tight. He wiped them and doubled forward in another round of apparent glee. Then he lifted his hands up and pulled his lips into a tremble.

"Are you mocking me?"

He eyed me up and down, before swinging his arm in an arc and clamping my wrist, squeezing until I could no longer hold the gun. It slid down my thigh, the grip facing skywards, the cylinder nestled between our legs.

"Damn."

In a smooth move, as if he was dealing cards at a felt table, he dropped my wrist, scooped up the gun and slipped it into his chest pocket. He patted it, just to make me mad.

"No spats, now," he said. "I would like to enjoy this cigar."

"Then what?"

"Then I might kill you. Or I might not." He shrugged his shoulders. "I can give you good odds, one way or t'other."

CHAPTER 7

ORINDA
1898
WE WORK OUT A SONG AND DANCE—THE PARASOL NUMBER—A
WARNING IS GIVEN

Monday days at The Paradise were not the relaxing holiday the mornings promised. After a few bits of peace and a strong coffee, the girls lined up outside China Mary's private rooms at the rear of the first floor to await their weekly pay and receive their health checkup.

Pip went first, as she always did; I didn't go at all, as I was not on the squeaky-bed payroll and did not require a health checkup. China Mary took my tips as rent and said I cost her more than I was worth.

Afterward, the girls returned to their rooms to strip the Sunday night linens and drag the mattresses to the back yard for their weekly airing. But most gave a penny to Tommy Gee to do that, and to bring up stacks of clean sheets from Mr. Wu Lin's laundry. Pip gave Tommy triple what the others did, and she had the nicest room that faced north-east and avoided the worst of the heat.

Pip and I used the remainder of the day to choreograph and

rehearse the next week's show, then climb to the attic to sew the costumes. She had a clumsy hand with thread and needle, which left me as head costumier after all. She took her new free time to peek out the front window and pace, and fool around with a few of the new steps I'd given her, as I had seen the latest in dance while down in Tucson.

"It's ball-change and two snaps." I knotted the thread along a corset stay and set it on a crate. "Like this."

"Flip my head back like that, too?"

I repeated the move. "Just a small come-hither look, not too much." I held the position, my foot pointed teasingly out from my invisible skirt, as we were both in camisoles and drawers to keep cool. I tapped my bare heel like a flamenco dancer and arched my back so my tits faced the ceiling. "You could add in another snap and sigh. Like so."

"What's wrong with your eye?"

"What? Nothing."

"You look like you got a shard of glass in there."

"Ha ha."

She smacked my bottom and waved me aside. "Let me do it."

There was no doubt she could twist, turn, tease, and trouble any sort of man. Graceful as a butterfly, virtuous even, in her choice of lines. She knew when to hold them, until her arms quivered and she took in shallow breaths to stretch and hold the pose that one second longer. Then with a spin and smirk she was nothing but pure sin.

I pierced my finger one too many times, my attention on her hips and shimmies instead of repairing a velveteen hem.

"Come over here." She waved her hand for me to step to her left. "I want to practice the Tally Ho number. You were late on Friday with the crop."

"You were in the way. I didn't have room to spin it. It's a great big stage; you don't always have to be in the center of it."

She took my arms, moved me back a few inches. "Now strut." She hummed and started the routine.

"I am five feet and a drop of water; how come I am playing the man?"

"Because I got the better breasts for baring on the last note."

There was no argument to that. We shared any coins thrown our way, and her tits, to be honest, were more valuable than mine.

I hooked a crop under my arm to walk like a gent, kicking my toes out just so and tipping my head as I passed her.

She curtseyed and simpered and counted under her breath. Then, she straightened and set her hands to her hips. "Stick your chest out and give me a wink as you pass."

A wink seemed a smallish effect, so I added a good lookaloo up and down her figure. To which she gave me a funny look and stopped humming.

"What?"

"Is that your I-am-extremely-attracted-to-you look?"

"It's a brush look with a wide eye." I moved my hand as if I was painting a wall.

"Just wink. The other looks like you have gas."

IF A MAN WANTED A SEAT IN THE PARADISE DANCEHALL, HE HAD TO run a gamut of obstacles, all of which had been calculated to withdraw funds from pockets. The miners, having come clean-shaven and short-nailed from the barbers, dropped ten cents in the box by the door and received a token and a paper ticket to reserve a seat. The token then could be used as partial payment on a whiskey or single dance with one of the girls. If a patron wanted a closer seat to Pip's and my frills, trills, and bums, two tickets could be purchased from Maggie Hallo-ran, bartender and flirt. Three more tokens gave a fella entrance to the Paradise parlor and all the intimate hoopla that came along with that.

A long mahogany bar ran the right wall of the room, its silver-backed mirror reflecting the card tables lined opposite. Access to the poker tables cost a dollar to show your seriousness in the game. Faro seats were on the house, but that was because the house always won. China Mary softened that losing blow with the choice of one drink and one dance. She herself sat queenlike in bombazine silk on a raised velvet chair set within the cashier's cage, her view unobstructed from the front leaded-glass door to the painted backdrop of the stage.

The whole of it smelled of kerosene and after-shave and, on that Tuesday night, of head spinning lavender soap, which Pip had shaved in curls into her bath water. She also exuded Bohemian Malt Tonic, which she had imbibed throughout the day.

Her eyes worried me greatly. They had a sparkly sharp edge—the green one more pronounced in its anxious anticipation than the copper. The hiccups that afflicted her the last hour threatened to return; she swallowed over and over, then bent down with another small beer glass and took a swig. She popped up straight, stretching her back. "He's here."

"Who?"

"That son of a bitch."

"Who?"

"Cullen." She pulled her lips back in a feral way and said nothing, instead pranced onto the stage, making small curtsies, and blowing kisses hither and yon.

Pip, being the Paradise's star draw, opened the show with a solo act —a dance of startling contortions. I watched from backstage, my riding crop in one hand and her costume change for our routine in the other. I had a shiver of pride at the efficacy of the design I had created, for the dress could be shrugged on and tied down in a matter of seconds, thus keeping the show going at a gay clip.

She raised and stretched her billowy leg, frowned at the twirl of a red stockinged ankle, then shook her head at the parasol balanced on a slippered toe. She grabbed two more parasols from a stand near the upright piano, and somehow lost a petticoat along the way. She slid her eyes across the rough audience of men and sprung into a back flip. The parasols twirled and floated above her, then descended and were caught—one, then two, then three—between her waiting knees. I do admit it was some trick to go from a backflip to such an arch of the body, her hips thrust from the stage, her silks slipped up her thighs.

I took a quick peek at the house. I didn't know who she was referring to; all the men looked alike, shiny heads of just-been-to-the-barber oily locks and foam mustaches atop the real ones. The only one I recognized was Joe Harper, who sat at the bar nursing a sarsaparilla and not at all interested in Pip's earthly delights.

I sighed and rolled my eyes. Four nights in a row the fella had been in, and truly, the outrageous clapping at my performance had embarrassed even China Mary, who threatened to cut off his root beer and force him to sit outside.

Then I saw Cullen. He sat up front, rangy and narrow faced, with long black hair oiled to keep the curl and a neat mustache that exaggerated pouty lips. He took a sip of a gold-hued liquor from a miniature wine glass, swirling the drink around his mouth as his eyes roamed the room. They were the same honey color as the liquor. His suit had creases where it had been folded. He crossed a leg, and his shoe shined too bright in the flicker of the lights.

Not someone I would think twice about; a two-bit dandy showing off his expensive aperitif.

There was something about him, though: how his eyes caught on Pip as she strutted and bowed, as if he ogled and owned her at the same time. He took a small sip of liquor and turned to talk to someone at the table, but I could not see who he addressed from my angle.

His eyes glided around the room, slowing on a table of men involved in a friendly shell game involving three silver thimbles. He gave a nod to Verna, who tucked her neck into her shoulders like a tortoise and hit the wrong key in the next chord. Darby dropped her eyes to the floor when he looked to her. Maggie nearly tipped her tray of drinks when she saw Cullen's attention turn to Darby. Then he lazed his gaze back to Pip and took another sip of his foppish drink.

Verna plunked out a ragtime. Pip crawled on the piano top and fondled one closed parasol between her thighs. She pursed her lips, licked them. Slid one hand up and down the parasol. Fluttered her lashes and wiped her brow. Her feet soon tensed, and her toes turned out in a quiver. And poof! The parasol floated open, the fabric a riotous mess of red poppies and yellow daisies and green glass beads.

A few gents lifted their arms to toss daisies and assorted wildflowers they'd plucked on the way to the show, the blooms a cascade of color that fell and tumbled on Pip's corseted curves.

Verna played the introduction to a popular song, old and familiar to all.

Pip opened her mouth with the shine of tongue and teeth and let out a first warbling note—*Ohhhh...*

The floor shook as the men stomped boots, releasing the smells of sawdust, shoeshine, and leather, and swayed as they joined her in a booming *Ohhhh...*

...he floats through the air with the greatest of ease...

The boom rolled around the dance hall and saloon mirror, bounced off the low ceiling and got stuck in the wings. I was deaf save the barreling of voices and stamp of feet, and overwhelmed with the commingled stinks of stale beer, whiskey, and crushed mint.

Pip swung her arms around like a conductor, her ruby-tipped nails glittering, palms spreading open to grasp the coins that flew around her and stuffed them quick between her breasts and bodice. "Sing it out fellas." She gave a great big smile. "*...once I was happy but now I'm forlorn...*"

Then she gave a big wave and flounced to the wings.

I held out her dress. She gripped my elbow. "Don't let me go with him."

She shoved her arms through the sleeves, turned for me to button up the back, then took the blue straw hat I'd hung on a hook. Her hand trembled so that I took the long pin from her and set the hat myself.

"Damn man." The words came out through clenched teeth.

Verna thumped the intro, signaling our cue. I started my trills, and we skipped out.

Pip tripped and took tiny steps to keep herself from bowling over the lip of the stage.

"What the hell, Pip?"

She gave me a quick smile and a dip of her head, as if I needed such an apology. What I needed was for her to get her shuffle step in gear.

A single red rose arced in the air. It landed at Pip's feet.

She looked down at it, not moving, not scooping it up as per normal and sticking in between her teeth. She curled her hands tight against her sides.

"Pip..."

Verna riffed a bit on the piano, her shoulders hunched over the keys.

"You gonna dance?" Cullen crossed a leg and leaned back in his seat. His eyes drifted to Pip's tits. Then he knocked his knuckle to the table, in time with the music. Loud and hard and mean.

China Mary's head swiveled. I paraded by Pip, trying to entice her back into the song and dance. But she was stone still. Her face looked like a chip of granite.

"Come on," I whispered as I pulled on her shoulder and did a wiggle to tease the crowd. The men were growing restless; the room took on a dull thrum that most often preceded the throwing of bottles and rocks.

Verna cut a look at China Mary, who rolled her hand for us to move the show along. I smacked my crop on Pip's bum, which got her to jump and say "Oh!" But did not garner another move.

I removed my derby, flipping it down my arm to catch in my fingers.

"There once was a fellow from Essex,
who knew not at all about Sessex.
A maid came along with a wink—"

"At his dong!" Verna called out and I did want to kiss her on the lips for the rescue.

I slapped the bowler over my nether regions and lifted a finger to quiet her. "With a wink and a *song*. This is a family establishment. We don't speak of dongs and dingles and pickles and pipes."

Pip snapped to life with a shuffle-step and a toss of the rose back Cullen's way. "Nor willies or winkies or widdlers."

"Say that thrice." I rolled the hat back up to my head and popped the top like a drum.

And we continued the show.

Pip proceeded through the act as if a pole had been shoved up her ass. She crowded me in the exact same stanza of the exact same song she always did and did not apologize for stomping my foot during the last pas de deux. She was mad as hell, and only took two stiff shallow bows before prancing off stage.

We sat in the smidge of space behind the muslin backdrop, keeping our voices low. It was Darby's turn to sing, and any loud noise set her crying and off-key.

Pip humpfed and tugged at the ribbons and buttons of her bodice. I whacked her hand to keep her from ruining it.

"That's the last bit of lemon silk." I smacked her hand again and unbuttoned it myself.

I switched from my duds to a skirt and blouse. She sat in her chemise and garters, knees struck out and an elbow to her thigh.

"You mind giving me a hint as to your sour demeanor?"

She swung her gaze to me. There was something forlorn in it, I dropped my costume to the bench and bent to grab her in a tight hug.

Her jaw clenched and unclenched against my cheek. "What are you doing?"

"Giving you a hug."

"Well, don't." She wriggled and pulled herself free. "What the hell is wrong with you?"

"Is he your damn bastard?"

"Don't make me sick."

And thus, I had my answer.

"Let's sneak on out to Pascoe's, get drunk, and watch the sun come up." I thought a night sitting out with Big Henry might bring her spirits up.

Her fingers picked at the back of my shirt. She rested her forehead on my shoulder and a great shudder traveled through her.

"He's damn ugly," I whispered. "Ogrelike."

Pip's head snapped up and she smirked. "He has his moments."

"You're not supposed to go with him."

"What?"

"You told me to tell you that, so I am. Damn bastards bring damn problems. Now let's go get drunk."

Out front, Darby hit a high note that made me wince.

Pip shuddered and clapped her hands to her ears.

"I hope she has other talents."

I stuck a boot to the fence at Pascoe's Livery, slung myself up, sat on the top board and keened a look down Broad Street. A smattering of people idled near the entrances, ambling from the 638 to McQueen's, zigzagging their way to the Eagle and The Cabinet. The Paradise had all its lamps blazing and a crowd of men sitting along the wooden sidewalk chucking dice and smoking.

Big Henry chomped a carrot, happy to be out of his stall and free to roam the paddock. He did one roundabout, giving a headshake and prance by a little filly in the corner stall, before ambling to me, and nuzzling my neck with those soft whiskers. But I wasn't Pip, so he took to yanking a tuft of grass that shot up near a post and masticated and ground his teeth.

"I believe I am drunk." I determined this by the half empty bottle of whiskey I swung in my grip, and the way the other half sloshed in my belly. I held the bottle to the moonlight and squeezed an eye shut. "And I've been stood up."

A sharp prod to my left hip forced me awake. I tepidly opened an eye, blinked, and thought better of it, so closed it up.

"You drank all the whiskey."

I waved a hand in Pip's direction and patted the straw under my head. "You just let me sleep."

She poked a finger to my leg.

"I am paying no mind to you." I hadn't the energy to tell her that, in the pecking order, friends and horses came before lowlife two-timing bastards, so I wrapped my arm around my head.

This did not stop the poking and prodding and tapping on my forehead.

"Stop it."

She tapped once more. I cranked open my eyes.

Pip tilted her head and crouched down. She wore her riding duds and silver trimmed boots, which was a common sight. It was the ring she flapped in front of me that wasn't.

I grabbed and held her hand steady and pressed my thumb to the gemstone.

"It's a garnet," she said.

"Am I supposed to give congratulations?" I let out a small belch. "For that bitty thing? That's just a piece of glass."

Pip chuffed a breath and shook her head. "I know you don't like him."

"I did not like his tone with you tonight. Other than that, he's a blank to me."

"You're going to ruin this one moment I got something nice."

"I don't understand you."

"What's to understand?"

"Are you leaving the act for him? Because if you are, I'll ask Verna to join me. It's no skin off my nose if you go off with the damn bastard." I rolled onto my hands and knees, then stood, knocking the muck and dirt from my skirts. "It's your funeral."

"Who said anything about leaving the act?"

"You did."

"No, I didn't. I just wanted to show you the ring."

"All right then. You did. I'm going to bed now."

The sun was on the brightish side when I clomped from the stall to the paddock. My stomach churned a great deal when I stumbled to the street. I thought Pip might follow me out, to show off the bauble and maybe apologize for leaving me to spend the evening in conversation with her horse. But she didn't, so I made my way to the Paradise alone.

I stopped once, holding a post to keep my balance as I turned back around to her. "You got some worthless taste in men."

She was too far away to hear, already near the tack room and swinging her saddle to her shoulder, that damn cut glass ring catching the light.

CHAPTER 8

KANSAS
1905
TRAIN TROUBLE

I knew what sorts of odds Boudreaux gave me. Neither of them was good. Either he had come to shoot me dead or keep me alive for Cullen to do it later.

Endicott let loose a pickle-smelling burp behind me. Ernice kicked the back of the seat and no doubt had continued to chomp her hair. I grimaced at the snow of ash that drifted from the brass ashtray hanging from the ledge of the window sash, watched it land in a line on my skirt as Boudreaux reached over to tap his fancy cigar.

"We could switch seats, you know."

"Ladies should be given the view."

"Can you tell me the time?"

He took his watch from his vest pocket, opening in the case with a flick of his thumb. "Eleven thirty-five." He tilted the face towards me.

"Actually, it's eleven thirty-seven. You shouldn't approximate time when you're on a train. It can cause a mess of problems when you need to transfer lines."

He let the watch twist and spin from the fob before stuffing it away. It was gold-plate, too shiny for the real thing, engraved on the inside cover with a single name: LORETTA, which struck me as being somewhat odd.

But the mysterious Loretta and her no doubt untimely demise had to take a step back. I had fifty-nine minutes to figure a way out of this and catch up with Pip.

There were only two ways to get to First Class, as far as I could tell: through the cars themselves or up top of the train. Both cases involved jumping the couplers, though it would take a leap of faith and a big "Hail-Jesus-and-Mary" and loud "Sonofabitch" to jump the gap from one roof to another. One small slip and I'd be a tragedy printed in the *Paola Times* and telegraphed to other papers for page four or five filler. My sister Rose would read it and say: "It's what you always had coming, Ruby."

She'd probably frame it, put it above Emma's bed as a warning of what happened to miscreants who didn't follow the Church and the law.

Boudreaux put out the cigar. "You got ash on your skirt." He pulled a matchbox from his chest pocket, took one out, and picked at his teeth. "Game of cards?"

"I thought you said you sold Bibles."

"One activity does not preclude the other."

"So, you're not lying? You do sell Bibles?"

"King James leatherbound pocket size or a tabletop version customized with family name and crest-tooled on the cover. Both can be purchased in French Morocco or American Levantine and paid over time."

"Well, hell."

"Yessirree." He sucked on the matchstick and smoothed his mustache with his thumb. "Yessirree."

"Where are those?"

He chucked his thumb towards the back. "I got a case in the baggage car. Also in red leather to show off the quality of the wares."

"What if I want to buy one?"

"You'll have to wait until Paola, at which point I can sell you one."

"We're getting off at the Paola depot, then?"

"There's a nice diner close by with Coca-Colas and egg salad sandwiches that I am fond of."

"Then what?"

"Then I'll get your Bible."

"Hm-mm." I nodded and looked out the window, forcing my breathing steady. I needed a diversion in Paola, something to warn Pip so she wouldn't step into the center of this. Or maybe she'd figure a way to get us out of it. Since I put the whole of it down to her damn fault.

I pulled in a big gulp of air, clambered around on the bench and slapped Ernice's leg. "We're going to get Bibles, children."

"We ain't—"

I kneeled forward, the seat cutting into my stomach, and pinched the girl's cheek. "Ah, yes, you *are* deserving, don't you be so humble."

Endicott stared at me. He had a rivulet of spit that had dried from the corner of his mouth and down his chin. "I don't want a Bible."

"You're going to get a damn Bible, anyway." I twisted Ernice's cheek until she chirped, then let go and drew a circle in the air. "We are getting off this train in Paola, and this kind man is going to buy you each an egg salad sandwich and a Coca-Cola."

Ernice rubbed her cheek. "I like root beer."

I glared at her. "Your aunt Ruby is going to give you both a lovely red leather pocket Bible. How much are those, Mr. Boudreaux?"

"You're neck's all funny red." Endicott pointed then wiped the spittle from his chin.

"Mr. Boudreaux?"

Barnabé pulled the soggy match from his teeth and narrowed his eyes at me. "Ninety-eight cents each. But we can round those to a dollar for ease."

"Why would we want two?" Ernice asked. "It's the same words in both." She scooted forward, resting her skinny elbow on the railing and stared at Boudreaux. "Don't you think one will do? My brother's so dumb he barely knows his alphabet, so two sets of Elijah and Esau and —what's the one who turns into salt?"

"Lot's wife," Barnabé and I answered together.

"That one would cause him apoplexy. The best thing would be one Bible then you can give me the other dollar." Her lips curled in a smirk. "Auntie."

"I suppose that could be—"

"There won't be time, *children*, to get you your Bibles. It's an unfortunate thing, I know, but Mrs. Calhoun and I have an appointment we must attend." Boudreaux smiled, if you could call it that, his lips stretched so wide both his gums and two missing molars showed. He stared at Ernice who glared right back.

"So, I won't get a sandwich?" Endicott asked.

"I'll get you one, I promise. There'll be enough time for me to feed these poor young kids, won't there?" Or enough time to run like hell while he ordered the food.

Ernice scrunched her nose and squinted. "What's your business with this lady?"

"None of your concern."

"My mama said to make it mine. If I smelled a skunk." She chewed on the tips of her hair, then twirled a piece on her pinky finger. "Let me tell you what I think, Mr. Fat Man."

Endicott poked her shoulder. "You shouldn't—"

"I think you've got dark designs on her."

"Like Black Bart—"

"Shut up, Endy."

"I have no designs on this woman, little girl."

"Don't call me little."

"If the shoe fits," he said.

Her eyes rolled up in her head and she pinched her lips. Her voice came out in a whisper. "My mama got beat to death by a man full of smarm like you and that man happened to be my daddy. You know what happened to him?" She pushed onto her tiptoes and cupped her hand to his ear.

I had no notion what she said, but Boudreaux's face went gray then chalk white.

Ernice sat back. Boudreaux curled his hand to her arm and pulled her so her ear was against his mouth. He cupped his hand and whispered something back.

She swallowed hard, staring at me with eyes that grew wide then closed them tight.

He let her go, rubbing her arm before giving it a pat. "We understood?"

She nodded and dropped back down.

"What'd he say?" Endicott shoved her, trying to get her to look at him. She wiggled away, squeezing against the wall.

I reached for her knee, but she rebuffed me with a backhand slap to my arm.

"What'd you say to her?"

"Turn around and sit proper." Boudreaux's voice was low.

"Tell me what you said to her. She's just a little girl."

He pulled at his shirtsleeve and admired one of his cufflinks. He smoothed the front of his coat, picking off bits of lint from the collar. "When we get off in Paola, you're going to keep your head down and your mouth shut, you understand me? Because I will do what I told her I'd do to her if you make one little noise."

Across the aisle, the failed Gibson Girl's head bobbed as she napped. Her *Ladies' Home Journal* slipped from her lap to the floor.

"I will have my meal in peace." Boudreaux wiped at his opal ring with a silk handkerchief and, after he was content with its shine, folded the fabric neatly to his chest pocket. "You can't run away, Mrs. Calhoun. No sirree, you can't. You have ash all over you. Clean yourself up."

The train whistled, though there was no crossroad I could see. Just flat acreage, green and yellow, the sky tilting away, cornflower blue at the crest, a bruised purple as it curved to the horizon. It was beautiful, and made me cry in the way things do when you're aware it might be the last you'll see of them.

"Do you mind if I use the ladies' room? To clean up and all."

"Are you crying?"

"Why would I be crying? I got to pee."

He glanced back at the narrow door that held the toilet and maybe a mirror. "Two minutes."

"You do see that I am dressed as a woman? There are multiple layers involved."

"Three minutes, then."

"Four."

"All right." He stood and sidled into the aisle to let me pass. "I'll keep accurate time."

"You do that, now."

The lavatory had enough room to squeeze in, turn around, and sit. Which I was not there to do. I stared down the drop chute toilet, watching the rush of tracks and railroad ties, then stared at an advertisement for The Egyptian Pile Cure, allowing myself a moment to get calm and think.

"All right, then." I blew out a long breath and turned in a tight circle. "Think think think."

I took my pencil and the train schedule from my pocket, palmed the paper to the wall and wrote: *IMPERATIVE. Give this to woman with scarred face in 1st class.*

I turned the schedule to the next margin:

CAUGHT. Will be in diner.

On the left margin: *Ernice, take this silver dollar for good keeping and write Calhoun's Cigars 304 4th St KC of your safe arrival in Lomax. PS–Stop talking to strangers on trains.*

On the last margin, for good measure should things come out awry: *Next life, Lord, I'll be better.*

I took out a dollar coin from my drawstring bag, folded the paper around it and upon reaching my seat, dropped the missive to Endicott's lap with a jerk of my chin to give it to his sister.

"All done?" Boudreaux stood up, and I squeezed into my seat.

I gave a side glance at Ernice. She had not moved from staring out upon the fields and knocked Endicott's hand away when he tried to give her the paper and coin.

I sunk to the bench, dropped my head, and screwed shut my eyes. My mother said it was a method she used to keep her calm, so I tried it as I often did, and just as many times it led me to seeing nothing but an airless, grim black void.

※

THE CAR WAS A RIOT OF MOVEMENT AS WE PULLED PAST THE WATER tower and into Paola proper. The depot, a dinky brick thing with a sloping black slate roof and a single cupola, was empty, save for a postman waiting for the mail bags to be delivered. Steam and smoke slipped along the train and around his body as the engine passed and came to a stop.

As if dropped from the sky, the platform filled as those in the train cars up front clambered down the stairs to stretch their legs and get a quick bite to eat.

My throat closed down in panic. I had not written down the name of the diner. And there, past the depot was a real town with many blocks and, no doubt, more than one purveyor of food. "Where's the diner?"

Boudreaux looked at me, his eyes blank.

"Coca-Cola and an egg salad sandwich. Your favorite. What's its name?"

"Let's go." Boudreaux grabbed my arm and pulled me up with a smile, that dimple bright and innocent. "You look peckish. I think I will buy you a sandwich." He reached for my case, with a "pardon me" aimed at the woman behind him. He caught sight of her magazine on the floor and, like a gentleman, procured it and handed it to her with a flourish.

"Thank you kindly," she said and flushed. She was not immune to that dimple, either.

"Are you Wichita bound, miss?" he asked her.

I grabbed my bag, rolling the strings around my wrist, making to stand and exit. Making to run for it when I could. Behind me, Ernice sat alone.

"Where's Endicott?" I whispered.

"He's on the john." She shook her head. "I don't talk to strangers."

Boudreaux turned his attention back to me. He had not once let go of my arm, and now his grip tightened. "It's our stop."

My foot slipped on the platform step as we descended. I clamped a hand to the rail, my hip swinging hard against the metal. "You could slow down a bit."

"Places to go, things to do."

He shouldered us past a group of men in shirtsleeves, coats slung over their arms, waiting by the baggage window for their trunks and luggage. A woman's laugh came from near the front of the train. I tore my gaze along the cars to find its owner stepping from the parlor car, her hand out and waiting for the porter to take it and hand her down. All along First Class, green and white awnings had been unfurled, shading the glass black so I could not see inside.

At the edge of the station, two buggies and drivers waited for fares. The harnesses jangled and one of the horses stamped his hoof to the packed earth.

Boudreaux skirted around the building, and I gave one last look for Pip before he pulled me away from the depot and into an alley that ran behind the squat brick of Paola's businesses. Potholes ran the course of it, each filled with the blues and browns of broken bottles. All of it stunk like rotten food.

"If the diner's down here," I said, "I'd have to question the freshness."

He flicked a look at me. "It's just a ways up."

"How're you going to do it?"

"What?"

"Kill me? How're you going to do it? Just so I know. I don't like surprises. So, how're you going to do it?"

A door swung open at the end of the block. A man slung a bucket of entrails onto the ground, then turned the bucket and shook out the pieces that stuck. When the door slammed shut, a couple of cats slid on their bellies from behind a stack of barrels and lapped up the free lunch.

My legs wobbled. I yanked with all my weight, trying to pull free. My shoes skidded in the gravel and muck and my bag swung around my thigh, banging my knee.

Boudreaux twisted my arm until I thought it would snap in two and shoved me into the brick.

I kicked out, which made him drop my suitcase and dance around.

It only took one smack of my head against the wall to get me to stop.

His breath was hot on my cheek. "You going to calm down?"

"No, I am not. That is the last thing—"

He smacked my head again. The pain was white like a firecracker gone off in my skull.

This was it. Death in an alley that smelled of last week's meat and a sewage leak.

A pistol hammer clicked. "Let her go."

Boudreaux moved his hand down to my neck, loosening his grip. His eyes cut around, then he blinked a few times and seemed to contemplate the cats. "You wouldn't shoot a man in the back, would you?"

"Only ones who deserve it."

I scraped my fingers to the brick in an effort to remain standing. For it was Pip, and she had come, standing off to the side with her arm raised and her aim true. "Oh, Pip. You're here." I let out a ragged sigh and slumped to the ground.

Boudreaux spun fast, gravel flying from his heel as he lunged towards Pip.

And stopped dead when he came forehead to barrel with her pearl-handled $33.50 Colt.

Pip raised an eyebrow. "I have very good aim at this distance."

"He was going to kill me, Pip." I grabbed at my head, lifting my hands away to check for blood.

"You work for Cullen," she said.

He kept his arms stretched wide but lifted a shoulder in a shrug. "I am an independent contractor who has been hired as such."

"Other times he sells Bibles."

"You tell Cullen he should watch his back, you got that?"

The train whistled. Pip cut her eyes down the way. "Get your case, Ruby."

I scrambled up. "The train..." My head was fuzzy and I could not get my hand to connect directly with the case's handle, so I lifted it to my chest and stumbled to her side.

Boudreaux lowered his arms and reached inside his jacket, pulling out my derringer and aiming at Pip.

The Colt went off. The brick past his head puffed as the bullet hit.

"Stop shooting." I shoved into her before she could get a better bead on his forehead.

She glared at me. "What are you doing?"

"The train, Pip. Let's just get on the train."

Boudreaux walked forward confident as could be. He pulled the tiny trigger, which did nothing at all. He eyeballed the pistol before lengthening his pace to a run. He raised it for the second shot.

"Well, hell," Pip said. She never took her sight from him and the gun never wavered as we turned heel to run.

"Come on."

We skidded on the platform and my heart fell at the sight of Ernice and Endicott waving as the car passed us by. "You still want Wichita?"

I peered down the train cars, then clattered down the steps to the rail bed and pointed three down the line.

The rattle and roar of the wheel pistons made any more talk impossible. I pointed again, then ran.

Pip was much longer legged and naturally athletic, and she passed me. She grabbed the handrail and swung her foot to the step, crawling into the car. I hefted my case to her, but she missed, and it skittered on the floor.

The train picked up speed. Soon it would be too fast to catch, and I ran the risk of tripping on the rail and getting caught underneath.

I grabbed my skirts and pumped my legs. Pip lay on her belly reaching out, yelling something I could not hear.

Her hand clasped mine and I got my foot to the step. She hooked her arms under my shoulders and wrestled and pulled.

Then I was in. Flat out on top of her and both of us out of breath.

I gasped in air. "What'd you just say?"

She glared at me. "You didn't load the gun."

I blinked. "That'd be dangerous."

I rolled onto my back, gazed at the heavy beams and the scrapes to the walls. "But thinking upon it from another way, you could say I saved your life. Because if it were loaded, well." I gave a click of my tongue. "Where would we be at, then?"

Out the window, the sky had turned yellow gray, readying for a rumble and rain.

"How much did you give that little kid?" she said.

I sat up, crossing my legs and rocking with the train. "I gave him a dollar."

"A dollar."

"I did think it was a fair trade. I still have three more." I reached for my drawstring bag. Which I did not have at all. My shoulders deflated. "Had."

She rolled her head and regarded me with her mean green eye.

"Never mind." She moved over to sit by me, her knees hitched up and her arms crossed on top.

"Your hat stayed on."

"It did, didn't it?"

"Good to know your head hasn't grown too big. I always was aware of your ego."

She swallowed, drew her mouth down, rested her head on her arms and looked at me.

I reached out to touch her scar, but thought better of it, so crossed my arms and stared out at the flat land. "Thank you."

She followed my gaze and pointed at the gathering black. "That'll be a big clapper."

"Or two."

"Or three."

"You never know."

"No, indeed. You never know."

CHAPTER 9

ORINDA
1898
JOE HARPER COMES CALLING

L ike most houses of assignation, the Paradise sported a deceptively simple interior design. China Mary had added a private entrance for the good mayor and other biggedywigs to join the girls for their evening partakings. It was down the main hall from the parlor, before the kitchen, hidden behind a swath of velvet curtain and a painting of an Albino brahmin bull. This led to a set of stairs which led to the tunnel under The Cabinet, Our House, 448 Kentucky and came up in the barber shop, to the right of its sink and a full-length mirror.

In addition, she had installed spy holes to keep an eye on things, and open piping between the walls, so if a girl had trouble at all, she could yell down and hope to hell someone on another floor heard it. Outside of the architecture, the girls had their own codes to warn or compliment the men. Say a young miner came into the parlor, wet behind the ears and not sure yet of his prowess. A quick double rap of a knuckle to a table or to the curved wooden of a sofa gave the signal:

VIRGIN. Three raps and a tsk meant to beware of boredom and that the john liked to blubber on and waste a lot of expensive time. A whistle and request for a fancy whiskey sour—code for a rough kind of man but over in a flash. Fingers tapped to the piano top meant the man had breath that'd turn Medusa from stone to mud. A pinch to the shoulder—watch out. Verna knew the worst of them, and she and Maggie made sure Darby wasn't anywhere in sight when they called.

But Joe Harper didn't garner a single code. He stood in the parlor soaked with cologne that permeated two floors and no doubt the next three buildings, and whatever girl happened by called up the stairs. "Hey, it's Joe." Or "Harper's here." Or if it was China Mary, "It's two bits every half hour to stand there. This isn't a charity house."

If it was Pip, "Ruby isn't here." Because, though Pip had no compunction in ruining her own life, she was adamant about me not ruining mine.

"He's a nothing," she said. "He's all mustache."

It was true Joe had a marvelous mustache that swooped down and proudly out. It was also true he wasn't much of an anything, having been a mule drover, a camp cook, a petty thief, a janitorial assistant, and a prospector with a claim more rock than dirt—none of which lasted out more than a few days. He liked to tell people some hoo-hah about how, one Sunday, he rescued me on the mule line coming over the mountains from Mammoth, though he never could come up with a reason for why I would be up there. It was a story Joe concocted and seemed to make him feel good about himself, even though it was a load of turds and beans.

I had no fuzzy yearnings and feckless hopes about Joe Harper. He had come to the show one night, then another, and on the third had requested an evening stroll. One thing led to another. He brought flowers, was generous with his affections, liked to walk about the town and hold hands afterwards, and when I said I was done for the day, he went off to do whatever else it was Joe Harper did.

One afternoon, I noticed Joe had on a new necktie, a brilliant red with gold diamond patterns threaded throughout. He held out a fistful of daisies and dipped his head for me to take them.

"What yard did you find these in?" I plucked them from his grip, stuffed them in the vase I had brought down with me, and set it atop the piano.

"I didn't...well, maybe one or two from Prinie Weiss's but she doesn't ever go out to enjoy them." He picked at the knot on his necktie and stretched his neck, showing off the chicken white skin under the collar line.

Darby hovered near the top of the stairs. She wore her hair straight down, and her dress was a plain cotton. She held her hands still against her sides, half-hidden in the dress folds, but I spied the red angry skin around her nails. I wondered what father gave up his daughter in a bet, and guessed she chewed her nails to the nub wondering the same thing. She wasn't more than fourteen, and already she seemed like a coffee cup that had been cracked a few times and mended badly.

I had a brief stab of guilt over making fun of her wobbly voice and thought I might remember my Christian vows to be kinder.

"Hi Joe," she said.

Even he gave a small wince at the nature of her voice.

She cleared her throat and smiled before running up the stairs.

Joe, being a good three seconds behind the rest of the world said, "Hello, Darby." He cleared his throat, smiled, and smoothed down that necktie.

"Joe," I said.

"Yes."

I noticed how long his lashes were as he fluttered them at me.

"Ruby," he said. Then he took me in his arms, squeezed me to him, and planted a kiss.

"What the hell have you been eating?" I flinched and struggled away from the noxious smell.

He pursed his lips. "That's just not nice to say."

"That's just not nice breath. I can't say it any other way." I opened a large silver box set next to a settee, scooping out some hard mint candies. I thought better of it and handed him the box. "Eat them all."

The mints snapped and crunched. He eyed me, first narrowing his gaze to take in my hair, which I had braided up and around my head, then down to my yellow poplin dress I knew showed him just enough of what he liked. Then, he stared down at my slippers. "Bet you I can eat every single mint in here."

"I'd lose that bet."

"May or may not." He rolled a handful of mints around with his paw. "If I win, I get a dozen kisses. If I lose? You get a dozen more. Both ways, we're rich."

◈◈◈

"WELL? WHAT DO YOU THINK?" JOE BIT DOWN ON A FINAL MINT and gave a wave of his arm in the direction of a pile of rocks and a couple barrel cacti.

Being October, the day was not as hot as Hades but more a temperate sort of perdition, which precluded my blaming my loss of words on heatstroke. I twisted my parasol against my shoulder, then swung it down, pulled it shut, and poked around at the ground.

Joe had hired a small buggy and horse to take us part way to this location. I squinted back east towards the gulley we'd had to abandon them in before the climb to this particular patch of soil. Joe left a leather water bag tied to the nag's head, and I wished he'd thought to bring such a kindness along for me.

I ran my tongue over my drying lips and kicked a stone. I smiled at Joe. "What am I looking at?"

His face drooped then chipped back up. "Why it's my claim."

"Claim to what?"

"Copper. This is my piece of copper."

He stuck his toe down and drew a line from one short stick to another. Then he repeated it until we were both standing in the middle of a ten-by-ten-foot area.

"How far down do you own it?"

"Why, far enough, I suppose." He shuffled around in his vest pocket and picked out a much-folded piece of paper. "It's all written here."

"That's an awfully short contract."

"It's enough."

I tapped the parasol against my leg and surveyed the land. Joe's claim, as it was, encompassed a hunk of dirt just flat enough to stand on sober. It was a steep little canyon of sharp ridges and every so often a post tied with a piece of white cloth to mark someone else's claim. My eyes traveled back towards Orinda way and set on the tops of the smokestacks and rooflines of Old Dominion.

"How deep do you own it?"

"Three hundred feet." He pushed the paper at me.

"That's a long ladder."

"You do it in stages, Ruby."

"Don't get mad."

"I'm not mad."

"I am just interested in your planning with this said claim. You got a pickaxe?"

"I got two."

"And a shovel?"

"Of course."

A shiny black beetle flew at his cheek and he swatted at it.

"A trough, a wagon, a burro, a tent to sleep in so no one claims your claim, a good cookstove and lantern, and a few barrels of water in which to wash and to sluice the rock?"

He stared at me, then set his hands on his hips and kicked his own stone.

"As I thought."

CHAPTER 10

KANSAS
1905
We Learn the Truth of Mr. Boudreaux—Good Deeds Done

After the Paola disaster, Pip and I had nothing to our names but the clothes on our back. And they were in bad shape. The thunderstorm had come like a whipsaw and not one corner of the box car escaped the deluge of rain. For though we had pulled shut the doors, the storm knew all the crannies and cracks and used them to devilish intent.

We huddled in a corner to wait out the worst of it, then collapsed flat to our backs when it ended and the steam and heat stole our bones and strength. My head pounded a great deal, so I kept as still as I could with the nauseating sway of the train.

Pip pulled a door open to catch any breeze and plopped down to watch the scenery. "What's the next town?"

"Osawatomie."

She took off her hat and fiddled with the crown before rolling the sides of the brim. "We should switch trains."

"The next is at five fifteen but their watchmen aren't as casual as those on the local route."

"And you know that how?"

"I shall not willfully incriminate myself." I pressed my thumbs to the walnut that had swelled up on the back of my head and breathed out. "I got an awful headache."

"We need to get you another gun."

"I don't want a gun." I dropped my hands to my stomach and closed my eyes. "I want my shop. I want to be worrying about Willie desecrating my Indian. I want Olaf to bug me until I am raving mad. I want—"

"You should want Cullen dead. Then you can have all of that. As small as it is."

"Are you judging my life's desires?"

"Why would I do that?" She folded the front of the brim and put the hat back on. "I want a smoke. That is my desire."

"My life may seem dull to you, Pip, but it took a great deal of effort to make it."

She stood and rubbed her face before walking over to me. "That effort's worth nothing unless we finish this."

I peeked open an eye and looked at her. "Then I guess we keep going."

OUR BOXCAR JOURNEY CAME TO A SWIFT AND ABRUPT END. FOR NO sooner had we settled down, and my head had improved from a ringing throb to a steady ache, the train pulled into Osawatomie. Pip sneaked a look out station way, then gave me an urgent wave to take a leap out the opposite door.

My head was not up for such a rattle of a landing, and I bent over, clutching it and waiting for the rails to stop wavering into sets of three. Before this had all settled, Pip jumped down, took my elbow and we hightailed for the willows and sycamore.

Two train men uncoupled the boxcar then ambled along the rail timbers, every so often crouching to look beneath the train cars until they'd gone along to the engine and called something to the engineer.

The rest of the train rolled forward a good twenty feet, leaving a clear view of the water tower, which proudly sported the name of the town in bright white capital letters.

"Osawatomie," I murmured.

Pip slapped a bug on her neck. "Where's that?"

"Thirty minutes past where we were." The wind rustled the trees above us, then decided that wasn't enough and bent them all one direction then the other before shaking off half the leaves. A small creek flowed at our backs, just over a lip of red rock. It was narrow enough to hop across most of the time, but I feared the impending boomer would swell its banks and cut us off from any escape were we to be spied upon by the train officials.

"We needed that boxcar," Pip said, and slapped at her cheek.

I felt the sting of a bite on my neck, then another on my chest and scrambled away from the water and the cloud of mosquitoes that had not been noticed on our run to the tree line.

Pip took off her hat and flapped it every which way. She shook her head and glared at the boxcar, as if the force of her stare could couple it back on up and we'd be comfy cozy on our way. "Now what?"

"We get right back on," I said. "I have a ticket. It isn't as fancy as your Pullman, but it will get us to Wichita. So come on, before he blows that whistle and we miss it altogether."

A dollop of rain splat on ground, then another. I gathered my coat and skirts and plodded back towards the car.

But Pip did not choose to follow.

"Come on. My head feels split and it's going to rain cats and donkeys."

"I don't have a ticket."

"What?"

"I wanted to see the reclining chairs." She lifted her arms then dropped them to her side. "They're not as comfortable as advertised. It's just Pullman pulling the wool. I bet the sleepers—" She dropped like a stone behind some bramble.

I turned to the train to see what had caused her reaction and my eye caught on a nice straw hat being flipped to and fro from a window. *My* straw hat, with the striped blue ribbon. I rolled to a crouch and snuck along until I was directly below. Ernice leaned out.

"They're looking for your friend," she hissed.

"Who?"

"The watchmen. Say she tried to kill a man and train hopped."

"Well, hell."

"They're asking about you, too, but I told them you were long gone in Paola. I guess there was a kerfuffle and shootout back there."

"There wasn't a shootout."

Endicott snaked under his sister's arm. "Are you an outlaw?"

I bit my lip. "No, sir. I am reformed."

There was not a movement or peep from the brush and bramble behind me.

I peered at the two. "Give me my hat."

Ernice dropped it to me.

"Now look out the other side. Is everyone on the platform?"

Endicott slipped out of sight, then popped back. "Yeah."

"All right. I want you to count to thirty then let out a scream or two and point to the creek and holler some more."

"What're we hollering?"

Ernice rolled her eyes. "'*There they go,*' that's what we're hollering."

"That's right. You start counting now...One. Two..." I stayed close to the train, so close my shoulder rubbed against the wheels and pistons as I retreated towards the last car. I slowed as I came upon the spot Pip had ducked down. "Let's go steal some luggage."

She stood, ready to sprint.

Endicott must have stopped counting. He pointed right at Pip and shrieked.

Ernice clamped a hand to his mouth, but the alert was out. "There they go—"

"Point *that* way. At the creek, not at me. Jesus, Mary and damn it to hell." I turned on my heel and took off.

The sky let loose the rain in sheets, plunking the ground and leaving divots in the dirt. My poor hat soaked through until it was nothing but a wad of straw, so I dropped it and kept running.

I took the ladder to the platform between the caboose and baggage, stopping to catch my breath. The air was heavy as bathtub water. I heard voices off afar and took a chance of climbing down the other side. My luck had turned for the better since my morning fright and near death. The platform was mercifully empty of anyone or anything, save the baggage cart half-full and the baggage door left gaping open in the melee.

One black pressed board valise flew in the air and skidded across the wooden boards. A second, this one red leather with brass studded corners, twisted over itself before landing. Pip jumped down, her own satchel crossed over her chest, and without missing a stride grabbed up both bags and took off towards the water tower.

I gulped down rain and lunged forward, my shoes squelching and heart knocking my chest. "You know, the mosquitos are the size of rats under there."

❧

WE TUCKED UP BEHIND A RIOT OF HONEYSUCKLE AND SOME SORT OF thorn bush and did not move until night. The storm rolled on past, leaving a low moon and enough light to find an old shed out on the edge of the town proper. There was no door and most of the slats had rotted and hung from their nails. One corner of the roof had given up hope, meeting the ground in defeat. But it was dryer than our previous hiding place and I had not one more step left in me to take.

I scuffed aside a couple rusty cans and dropped down, resting my head against what was left of the wall.

"I guess I'm an outlaw again."

"You were an outlaw for all of a minute."

"It was enough."

We shut our eyes for a bit before opening the cases. The black valise held men's clothing and shaving kit, all neatly packed with a portrait of the man's wife—or mistress—tucked in the pocket of the suit. I believed it was the wife, but Pip said the woman had a glint in her eye that promised more than a home-cooked meal.

The second was Boudreaux's. I do not know why he left it when we departed at Paola. Maybe he *was* just after that egg salad sandwich and I had annoyed him to no end. But there it was, a hefty leather with a lock that took Pip ten minutes to jimmy with her knife.

The sample case sat right up top. Pip flipped the lid to show me the contents: ten pocket Bibles and four tabletop size that were tooled with names.

"Look at this." Pip tossed me a leather folder.

I opened it to find a listing of names and addresses, and a note as to who had recently passed in the family. "Thank you, Mr. Boudreaux." I flipped a page. He was quite organized and he took care with his handwriting. "I'm going to sell these, Pip. There's three of these people right here in this very town. I'll double the price and we'll be in the parlor car, won't we? I just need to clean up a bit and...what's all that?"

My eyes roamed the materials she had pulled out of the case. A length of rope. Two boxes of bullets, .32 caliber by the label. A wrench. A rubber sheet.

"Ah, no." My throat closed up.

She flipped a card, so I could see.

The same coffin. The same X.

"Number three," she said. "Verna."

I rubbed the folio's fine leather and turned my head in the direction of a rooster crowing good morning. "I'm too hungry to think on that."

"We need to find her."

"Burdick. She's in Burdick." I pointed at the line in Boudreaux's list of address. I stood, wiping dirt from my coat. It wasn't of any use; the mud had ground its way in. One of the pockets had torn; I'd have to tell Olaf to check the stitch. I slung the folder against the shed wall.

"We'll need to warn her." Pip yawned. "If she's alive."

"If she's alive? We have the card right here," I said. "He hasn't got to her yet."

"Or he keeps it. Gives it back to Cullen with some evidence he's done the deed."

"Like what sort of evidence?"

Pip shrugged. "I don't know. A toe. Maybe an ear."

"If that be so, why did he not cut us to pieces at the cigar store? He's meant to bring us to Cullen."

"Then why take you off the train in Paola?"

"I'm too hungry to think about that, all right?" I rubbed my nose and paced, regretful about the loss of my string bag and money. "There isn't a body part of Verna's in that inventory, is there?"

"Maybe he keeps it in a box. In his chest pocket."

"How many dime novels have you read?"

"None. None, Ruby. It's Cullen, remember?"

***

"My husband said, 'Don't ever let in a Bibleman.' But he didn't say a thing about a Biblewoman." Norma Croft clapped her bony hands and pushed open the screen door. "Come on in and settle your feet a bit."

"That's kind of you. As the Lord knows, a good sit down is manna for the soul."

I followed Norma into the parlor of Croft manor, which consisted of two rooms, a lean-to kitchen, one spindly tree and a yellow mongrel who barked without cease from the end of his tie-down.

The entire room could be crossed in five good steps, but it would take triple that to maneuver the amount of furniture stuffed within the whitewashed walls. I took a seat on the blue-tufted chair she offered, keeping the sample case on my lap.

She perched on a horsehair sofa, leaning forward to take a good close look at me. Her eyes were a light blue and the skin crinkly at the corners, no doubt from squinting out at the godforsaken emptiness around her. She wore a shiny black percale wrapper with a braided collar and ruffles along the shoulder flaps. I suspect it had come recently from Sears & Roebuck, for it was a dress I had eyed and admired last spring, though I would have purchased it in blue. She had altered the garment, adding skirt flounces as lacy as the curtains and the doilies that adorned every surface of the room, all eyelets and shell-patterned borders. She showed it off by dipping her shoulders so the sheen caught the light.

"May I bring you a lemonade?" She popped up and shimmied around the other tufted chair and the piano bench before stepping to the front door and pushing at the screen. "Shut your racket!"

The dog stopped and started again.

"I have some rhubarb pie, too, if you'd like a slice?"

"Both would be a blessing, thank you."

She nodded and went outside, walking around to the kitchen, passing the front window then the tall one on the side of the house.

"Shush, dog." She gave a sharp lunge at it, but I could not see the cur's reaction from my position on the chair.

I thrummed my fingers atop the sample case. The dog's bark grew odd then became a whine and whimper. Norma passed by, shushed it again, and stepped onto the porch.

I heard her clear her throat. One time, then again.

"Are you all right?" I called.

"You wouldn't mind getting the screen door, would you?"

"Well, aren't I being rude." I set the case down and wound my way over to hold the door, as she held a tray covered, as per the décor, in doilies.

After the fuss of pouring the lemonade and making sure I enjoyed the pie, she took the empty plate and glass and returned them to the tray.

"My Caleb does like his rhubarb," she said, wiping a napkin to the bottom of the glass. "Not strawberries, he doesn't like those at all. I think it reminds him of our youngest."

"Oh, yes?"

"Poor boy choked on a strawberry. An early spring one, you, know, when they're little bitty things. And he—John James—got both his grandfather's names, he just..." She folded the napkin and set my plate on it. "I'm sure you saw the stone. Over by the turn to the walk? We had his shoes bronzed, did you see those, too? I imagine it gives him comfort to see who's coming and going."

I glanced past her shoulder to the window. "You get a lot of visitors this way?"

"Well, not many. No, not...but you're here."

I took the sample case. "May I?"

She nodded and moved the tray to the piano bench. I rose and joined her on the sofa, placing the box between us and snapping it open.

I rested my fingers atop the holy book, thanking the Lord Mr. Boudreaux had maintained a list of recent obituaries, weddings, and engagements, including aforesaid poor little John James. Mrs. Croft was the third and final Osawatomie griever on my list. I had not realized John James was a child, and I thought Boudreaux could have doubled his business had he made note of such as that, as he could have sold pretty frames for the final portrait.

"I do think I have something of comfort for you, Mrs. Croft. It's a special edition, and, as you can see, small enough to slip into your apron pocket." I fanned the Bible open. "As you can see, there are two silk ribbons, so, if you find a particular piece of Scripture you return to again and again, you slide the ribbon in thus. Then the other can be moved to mark your place in your regular reading."

"It's a pretty red."

"Italian Morocco Levantine. Custom for this edition. And only a dollar ninety-eight, but we can round that to two, for ease of payment. The other two cents go to a fund I have set up for undertrodden and homeless women."

She said not a word. Her lower lip quivered, and right eye drooped. She gripped her skirts and shuddered a breath. "I..."

The dog barked, his bay straining each time he yanked at his collar. I wished I had a whiskey-soaked steak I could throw at him to shut him up.

"Will you pray with me, Miss...?"

"Mrs. Luft." I lowered my lids and sighed. "Marigold Luft. I am a widow."

"Then let us pray together for comfort, Mrs. Luft."

She ordered two Bibles. One for her and one for Caleb to keep next to his heart while tilling the fields.

Norma rounded up to four dollars and gave an extra nickel for the "fund." She insisted I take a ham sandwich for my walk, and when I demurred, she insisted I take two. We stopped at the gate to pay tribute to the boy and his bronzed shoes. Held hands and prayed once more.

"Mrs. Croft," I said, "you have done more than you could possibly imagine. My heart is full. I believe it will burst if I say but one more word."

"You just keep to the good work, Mrs. Luft."

"Marigold. Please."

"Marigold. You keep the good Lord close."

I made my escape to the road and hurried down it. I could not look back, for I was certain Norma would be standing there by the grave of her dead child and wishing me well. I felt a shiver of guilt. Then I thought of the nickel and four pennies extra, and the sandwiches tucked in a bag. I had hurt nobody. Indeed, I had done a good deed. Two good deeds. Norma could rest her mind a bit, and Pip could eat. That counted on the plus side for heaven, and that made me sing right out loud.

My song, which had few lyrics and a lackluster tune, soon petered out and I was left to clomp to the crossroad and take the evasive long way around Osawatomie to our hideout shed.

The sun was bright and bore down upon me without reprieve. I sweat profusely, all the way from my armpits to my shoes, and my step turned to a limp as the chafing caused a blister to grow and bubble and threaten to burst. Which made me mutter a few dozen "To hell with Kansas" curses.

But that brought neither relief nor succor. I was certain that Kansas had countered with a few "To hell with Ruby Calhoun" retorts

I transferred the sample case to my other hand. My fingers had grown numb and swelled, so I shook them until they tingled back to some form of life. At the crest of the single hillock, I stopped to give my foot a rest.

A shadow crossed over me. I leaned to its shade, covering my eyes to see who had disturbed my short reprieve.

"Why are you here?" I unbuttoned my boot and slipped it off, giving a great sigh at the relief of it.

"You sell some?"

"I sold four. Which gives us eight dollars. And a nickel extra because Mrs. Croft took to me."

"You do have your charming moments."

I pulled the boot on again, never minding the way it rubbed. "You're checking up on me."

"No, I'm not."

"You are." I stood, hefting the sample case. "Yes, you are. Which disappoints me. It truly does. I brought you ham sandwiches. I could have eaten them myself, but I thought: no, Pip has not eaten since her strenuous trip in First Class, I'll bring these to her."

"Is there mustard?"

I glared at her, then unclasped the box and took out the sandwiches Mrs. Croft had wrapped so neatly in a square of calico. "Here."

Pip's stomach growled. She pressed her hand to her belly, then untied the cloth and curled back a thick slice of bread. Her mouth twitched in a little grin. Then she took a big bite, chewing away and staring at me as she swallowed.

After both sandwiches had been consumed, she wiped her mouth with the rag and strode down the hillock. "Come on."

"You didn't need to check up on me."

She didn't answer, just kept on walking, though she was thoughtful enough to slow to my gimping gait.

We continued on, cutting through a fallow field to make the creek and the shade of the trees there.

I yanked off my boots and stockings and waded into the water. My feet curled over round rocks, toes digging into the silt. I stood, head back, skirts rolled over my arms, and let the creek rove around my legs.

"I'm staying right here," I said. "I will never ever leave this very spot. This spot is a panacea. This is manna in heaven."

"I saw a wanted poster hanging at the train depot."

I swiveled my gaze to Pip who kneeled at the shore edge, splashing her face, then dunking the calico to the water and wrapping the cloth around her neck. "There's a bounty on my head for one hundred and eighty dollars."

"The fine for shooting in the street's only fifty."

"The bounty's for attempted murder."

I sunk down in the creek. "What the hell—"

"You're up there for stealing those Bibles."

The fronds of creek grass tickled my wrists and fingers. I crossed my arms and stared at a few tiny fish darting around my ankles. "That's just not right."

"But that's what it is."

"Why?"

"To make sure we don't turn tail back to Kansas City. We'd run smack into the law."

"Will Boudreaux go on to Verna?"

Pip stood, shaking the water from her hands. "What do you think?"

"There's no possibility he got to Burdick already."

"He could have taken the next train."

"There's only one to Burdick and it left KC an hour before we did. At nine thirty-seven a.m. and it's a slow-as-marmalade local." I stood and slogged my way to the shore. "Where are the suitcases?"

"Just down at the turn under some ivy."

"We need to get to Burdick," I said. "And I don't know how to get to Burdick without a map. You know what I know of Kansas, Pip? The Missouri Pacific, the Union Pacific, and the Atchison, Topeka & Santa Fe. Which does not serve our situation at all."

CHAPTER 11

ORINDA

1898

A RENT IS UNPAID—I MEET CULLEN WILDER—I HIRE A SPY

It had been weeks since Cullen had left town (thirteen days and a couple of hours if you asked Pip) and her heart was less in our act and more taken to brooding by the window. I couldn't determine what charm he had over her, but she was like a cobra swaying to Cullen's whistle.

I thought back upon my time with Frank, looking to see if I, too, had ever acted such. I had, at least a couple times early on, even after he busted my arm. I drank up his apologies like healing wine. Rose had sent a letter during that period saying our momma no longer understood me and to stop upsetting her with my news. That made me defend Frank ever more greatly, as I believe Rose and her righteousness had poisoned our mother against me.

Pip begged off rehearsals with all form of excuses, from headaches to sore teeth. She stopped riding Big Henry and left the horse to get ungainly fat. Though maybe it was the extra grain and apples I took him, as he and I liked to sit around while he chawed.

"There are women, Big Henry, that have not a modicum of sense when it comes to the harsher sex."

He let out a long sigh and with it some apple bits.

"I do think I need to get her on another track that has a worthwhile goal."

Outside the stall, Matteo Pascoe slouched by. His shoulders drooped and the paisley shirt he wore drooped along with them. His cheek bore the red creases of his pillowcase. He looped a lead rope over a gray nag that had spent a good chunk of the morning circling alone on a four-horse walker.

I leaned my elbows on the stall door. "Mr. Pascoe, it's nearly Thanksgiving and Christmas."

He buckled the leather halter on the horse and patted her neck. "That it is."

"Since I'm a new resident here, I wondered if there were to be festivities."

He rounded the nag with a hand to her rump and unclipped the lead from the iron pipe. "Last year the firemen and all the girls had a to-do. It didn't end well."

"Why not?"

A sharp whistle cut through from the street. He turned to look, gave a tired wave, and mumbled something about burros.

"I don't—"

"Your friend's three weeks late on stall rent and feed."

"Big Henry looks fed enough."

"You keep feeding those treats, you're heading for a mess of colic. He needs roughage."

"Hay."

"You tell Pip Quinn I'll give her another week. Got a waiting list for that stall." He raised a burly eyebrow and looked me over. "Of course, I'm amenable to a few trades."

I gave Henry a scruff on his head and pulled at his forelock. "We'll bring you money, Mr. Pascoe. Coin's going to be the only trade you get from me."

❧

PIP DIDN'T ANSWER MY KNOCK.

"Pip Quinn your horse is about to be homeless." I put my ear to the wood. "I hear you snoring in there."

"Move your lily ass down the hall and leave me alone."

The door behind me clicked open. Verna leaned out, her satin robe swaying. "Shh."

"This isn't nothing about you, Verna."

"Some of us need sleep."

I flicked my wrist at her, much as I would a fly. "Then close your door and get it."

She made to slam it shut but thought better and at the last moment closed it with a soft click.

I bit at my thumbnail and stared down the hall. It was afternoon siesta, and the only bumps came from the mayor going about his business with Maggie Halloran.

"Pip." I rapped a knuckle to the wood. "Pip, come on. You missed two quick turns last night and I nearly fell off the stage." I held up my knuckle. "I'm going to knock again. At the count of three, I will smack this door. One. Two."

She opened it before I could properly knock, grabbing onto my fist to keep me from pummeling her chest. "I should have left you out with the javelinas."

"How come you haven't paid your stall fee?"

Her eyelids and neighboring areas were both puffy and purplish gray. But her eyes gave away the real truth. She had got hold of some opium and was about as high as a kite could fly.

"When's the last time you slept?"

"I believe I was sleeping until you woke me."

"We've got to practice that section."

"No, we don't."

"Yes, we do."

A low whisper came from the end of the hall. I caught the back end of the mayor as he slipped down the rear stairs, his coat flapping behind as he stuffed one arm in then the other.

I thought he might be one to talk to about the Christmas activities and made a note in my head to stop by Maggie's door next Thursday when he came for his appointment.

I looked back at Pip. "What's the story with the burros?"

She didn't hear me. She glanced over her shoulder, then back at me. "You got a visitor in there?" I asked.

Her lips curled up, lazy like they do after flagrante activities.

"Ah." I said. "When did he get here?"

She slid her hand along the edge of the door, ready to close it. Her robe slipped down her arm, showing off a four-finger bruise. She didn't need to turn her wrist for me to know there'd be a thumbprint on the other side.

☙❧

THE SHOW THAT NIGHT WENT ALMOST AS EXPECTED, EXCEPT FOR PIP missing three pirouettes and her left bosom popping out two bars before it was meant to.

That's because Cullen Wilder caught her eye and lifted his tippler of gold liquor to her.

I smacked her tail with the crop I carried and that got her back on track.

☙❧

I MET CULLEN PROPERLY WHEN ON MY WAY TO BREAKFAST THE NEXT morning. I often woke early, as I appreciated a bit of silence and a smoke to myself at that early hour and made my way down to the kitchen to get an apple and a cup of strong coffee.

He was down the hall, leaving China Mary's parlor-slash-boudoir, and I did not hear what he said to her. But she followed him, or rather leaned out and touched his arm. Then she spied me standing at the bottom of the stairs. "What are you looking at?"

"Nothing."

Cullen brushed past. "Pardon me." He was fully dressed in a suit and hard collar, as if he were heading out to a funeral. He settled on one of the settees, stretching his legs out and crossing his ankles like he owned it all. His eyebrows raised as he took in my nightdress and tangled hair.

I clutched my cigar and lighter to my chest. "There's no men allowed in the parlor until eleven a.m."

"There isn't?"

"If you're going, you should have left Pip's room last night at one a.m. On the dot. If you're coming, you can't be in here until eleven and those are the rules."

"Why?"

"Why what?"

He smiled and leaned forward, a hand to each knee. "Why eleven? Why not ten? Or two? Or eight-thirty?"

"I don't make the rules. You'll need to take that up with China Mary."

"That so?"

"That is so." I started for the hall. "Well, you have a good day."

"You don't like me."

I stopped and turned back to him. "No sir, I do not."

"You should give me a chance."

"There's a lot of rumors going around about you. You hold grudges."

"I keep promises."

"You shot a man for giving you the wrong change."

"That's a flat out lie. He cheated me."

"You're a fancy man with a silver tongue. I've known enough in a similar vein to you, so I know better than to like you."

He shrugged and sat back. "The viper's tongue is sharp."

"And honest. What's your game? Besides stringing Pip along? Cards, rustling, bank robbery, got a line of cribs somewhere outside of Florence? Because I don't see you having a proper job of anything."

"You have a mouth on you. Whores should keep their lips closed unless paid to open them."

My gut boiled and I took a step forward. "I am offended by that remark."

"No offense meant." He stood up, and I cringed, though he made

97

no move to come closer. In fact, his face brightened and he smiled wide. "Fire insurance."

"Beg pardon?"

"I am in fire insurance. And other pursuits." Fire insurance was code for extortion: pay me a nice fee or watch your shop burn down. Frank toyed with going into the field himself, but the possibility of burning up an innocent person was too much even for him. "Some men like it too much, Ruby," he said. If he could think an inch further than his nose, he'd realize he wasn't much different from them, except he didn't take money for the injuries given.

Cullen strode to the piano, took one of the daisies Joe had left, and held it out for me to take.

I let it dangle between my fingers, the water dripping from the stem onto my cigar, effectively ruining it.

"Say thank you."

"You just handed me a rotten flower that was given me by my own beau and now I don't have a working cigar and I still don't like you."

Pip swooped down the stairs, dressed in a bright checked top and simple skirt, her hair pulled up and pinned like a lady's under a hat sporting three feathers and a lace overlay. She even wore a pair of lace gloves, a fact I noticed as she remained holding the newel.

"Who in God's name are you?" I asked.

She ignored that, instead swinging her hips and twirling just so to land right by Cullen's side. "You two have met properly now?"

"We certainly have," I said. I wanted to add that it was her I hadn't met before.

She pressed herself close to him, and I saw two things: a wince as he reached to tuck her hair over her ear, and the press of his thumb against her jawline. He turned to the front door, and she lifted her chin and smiled at me before swooning on out. But I saw that red thumbprint. And I saw the telltale bruise at the edge of her lace collar.

"You need to come back early, Pip."

"I'll be back when I'll be back."

I was left to the empty parlor and the residual stink of Cullen's cologne and Pip's lack of common sense.

THERE WASN'T MUCH FOR ME TO DO WHEN CULLEN WAS AROUND. Pip chose to put on blinders and I chose to ignore her idiocy. I spent some hours in the attic mending the wears and tears in the costumes and working out a few new steps I wanted to add to the umbrella routine. When the attic grew too hot to continue my brooding, I went for an ice cream thinking it might pick up my spirits and take up some of the time until the evening show.

No one was in the parlor; the thumps and bumps upstairs gave me a clue as to the girls' activities. I tied on a straw hat and stepped out onto Broad Street, thinking I would treat myself to vanilla ice cream with cherries and a dribble of chocolate to spice it all up. Tommy Gee passed in front of me, carrying his ubiquitous water buckets.

"Hey," I said.

"Hey yourself."

"You seen Pip around? With that oily fella?"

He shrugged. The empty buckets swayed.

"What do you know about him?"

He squinted until his eyes were a line of suspicion. "Why're you asking?"

"Curious is all."

"He gives me a silver dollar every time he's in town."

"Generous of him."

"That's right."

The sun beat right through my hat. "You want an ice cream?"

"Sure I do."

We took seats at a little table by the window so Tommy could keep an eye on his yoke and buckets.

He ate three scoops and four dollops of whipped cream.

"You know what you are Tommy?"

"What is that?"

"You are the Mayor of Broad Street."

"I am?"

"Sure you are. You know the comings and goings and I bet you don't let one thing escape your eagle eye."

"Such as you're jealous of Mr. Wilder."

"What? No, sir, I am not. I am merely curious as to his intent. At any moment. Because I am curious as to how it affects my friend."

Tommy squinted at me and sucked in his upper lip. "You want me to spy."

"I want you to perform your duties as said Mayor."

"I'm not the mayor, lady."

"Two silver dollars."

"You don't have two silver dollars."

"How would you know?"

"Cause you wouldn't be hanging out at China Mary's and sticking your ass out for all and sundry to see. You would be a shop woman or—"

"Do not judge, lest ye be." I dug in my purse and held out two silver dollars.

His eyes went wide, which made me think Cullen only passed on a nickel or two and I had been had by a child.

He plucked the silver from my fingers, bit down on each then stuffed them in a pants pocket. "He's got a girl here and there and down in Florence and over Mammoth way."

"Does he have a wife on the side?"

"You don't know nothing, do you?" He slipped from the chair, kicked one heel against the other, then stuck out a hip.

"That's a nice little move."

He burped, then shuffled outside, picked up his buckets, and trundled away. I jumped and charged out after him.

"Tommy Gee. Tommy." I hopped from the sidewalk to the street proper to follow him, but he picked up his pace. "You stop, you damn little flea." I swiveled around a baby carriage and the mother pushing it and jumped onto the walk by Owl's Cigars. Tommy wasn't anywhere at all.

I screwed my eyes tight and smacked my hand to my thigh in frustration. "If I don't know nothing, then what am I supposed to know?"

Which made me mad, so I stomped my way into Owl's to purchase a pick me up and stomped out madder because I'd given my two dollars to Tommy Gee.

CHAPTER 12

KANSAS
1905
CRIMES AND RUMINATIONS—D.P. LaPlante

Pip did not leave me to mope about the Burdick problem for long. She let me pace—or mostly limp—around, due to my blistered foot. She herself stretched out on the rubber sheet from Mr. Boudreaux's luggage, used her satchel as a pillow, sighed and waited me out.

I thumped up the bank to her new "Eden Under the Cottonwoods" and kicked at her leg to get her to stop daydreaming and counting the clouds. "Hey."

"Hey, what?"

"We have a dilemma. In fact, we have a multitude of dilemmas. And you're lounging around like a cat who's drunk all the cream."

"I'm thinking." She put one hand behind her head and rested the other on her belly. "And I want a nap."

"This is not a time to nap. And frankly, that rubber sheet was meant for more frightening experiences than shut eye, and I'd prefer you weren't laying upon it."

I swiped at a mosquito buzzing around my nose. "We need to get to Verna."

"If she's alive."

"One way or the other, we need to know."

"To warn her or to bury her?" Pip said. "That is the question."

"What'd you do with our coats?"

She pointed in a lackadaisical way to the next stand of trees. "I washed them. They're drying."

I spied the jackets, looking for all purposes like two men who'd just made friends with a noose. "Where's your hat?"

"Over there."

"Where?"

"Mmmph." Which she followed with a burble and her eyelids sinking down.

I bent over her and assessed. Then smacked her cheek. "Hey."

"What was that for?"

"You stole my special medicine." Another smack, this time to the other cheek. Then I yanked her satchel from under her head.

"Hey!"

I stomped out of her reach, my toes squelching in a mud-hole. I flung her bag open and dug through the contents until I found the evidence. "Ha." I held up the bottle. "This is *my* bottle of Doctor Kate's Speciality. You are a thief."

"The ginger's a good flavor choice. It's...a very spicy sort of flavor." She flapped her bottom lip with her middle finger, then her arm went wobbly and dropped to her chest. Her mouth yawned open. I gave a quick wish for the mosquitoes to take up residence on her tongue.

"You get one hour, Pip. Then I'm dunking you in the creek."

I rolled the bottle between my palms, remembering how recently my life had been one of normality. The pang in my stomach was sharp.

I set the bottle to the side and pulled Pip's bag to my lap. It was soft from use, the leather thick, crisscrossed with scuffs and scrapes, dark cuts that held on to the oil. An odd bag for Pip; not a silver doodad nor fine tooling to show it off.

My hand itched. I tried to ignore it and stared at the knee-high stalks of corn in the field across from the creek. But my curiosity over-came my meditation on the crop. I glanced at Pip.

"I'm going to look in your bag, Pip. For my other bottle."

She made a lumpy noise, then clamped her mouth shut and snored.

"This is not snooping. Let's be clear upon that."

I riffled around—only for the bottle; I did not care in the least for the rolls of cotton drawers and undershirts, nor the cardboard box and the bullets that rolled and clanked within. I pushed aside a knit wool sweater, a bristle toothbrush, and wood comb. My hand caught on a small leather case. I pulled it out. A photograph case. Frank had given me one with our wedding picture, the oval portrait set to velvet and sealed in glass.

It was finely tooled, the burgundy leather well-rubbed at the corners, the clip that opened it shiny from use. Maybe Pip had a fella now and he gave her this as a keepsake. I remember the one she carried of Cullen, until the hinges broke from her staring at it and emitting ridiculous long sighs before slinging it at a wall or two.

I stuck my nail to the clip. The case sprung open.

Not a fella.

An infant in christening clothes, surrounded by sprigs of wildflow-ers. Dark curlicue of hair, mouth open in slumber.

"Get out of my things."

"I was looking for the other bottle."

"Get out of my things."

"All right, then. I heard you the first time, I won't say another word." I pushed the case back. "I'm a little surprised, is all."

"Well, don't be."

"What's her name?"

"Olive. Her name is Olive."

"She's alive?"

"Of course, she's alive. Why would you—"

"Olive's a pretty name." I cut Pip off. There was no need to let on the photo made little Olive look dead as a doornail. "Was it your mother's name?"

"Grandmother."

"I was named after my grandmother on my daddy's side. She fell ill from the yellow fever long before my time, I think my father was twelve, but don't hold me to that. She was six feet two in her stocking feet."

"Huh." Pip scratched a twig and twisted it around. "Things you don't know."

"And now you do."

"Six feet two. Huh."

"Where's your girl now?"

"I left her with the nuns. In Albuquerque. I'm not any better at motherhood than you are."

The twig rolled from her grip. Doctor Kate's bottle did pack a clobber. If Pip had asked, I might have warned her of the effect. But she hadn't.

I lay back myself as the air had a comforting warmth, weaving my hands behind my head and staring at the tree limbs. They stirred and swayed. A couple tiny birds flitted in and around, one turning its black bead of eye to me before tearing off along the creek. A rock dug into my buttock, so I shifted a bit and pursued my thoughts.

First, I thought of Pip's last comment, but that made me sad, so I refocused my thought on the situation at hand. One: the money in my purse belt. I had sold four bibles to three people within the space of a two hours, three pocket size and one deluxe, and thus had earned eight dollars and the extra nickel from Mrs. Croft. Next, I thought of provisions we might need such as toothpowder and a couple apples and some jerky. I allotted thirty-five cents to that and hoped the next town we came to had a general merchandise and that it had reasonable prices. Then my stomach cramped.

How dare Boudreaux accuse me of stealing his Bibles? I should walk into the next sheriff's office and accuse him of slamming a poor woman's head against a brick wall. I still had a walnut on my skull and the edgy threat of a headache. The remaining Bibles were of no use to me: they carried the taint of his accusation and the stink of fraud. All it would take was one phone call to the police from the next poor grieving soul I tried to impress the Lord on, and all the biddies, grannies, and snoops that kept their ear on the party line would spread my crime across this county and into the next.

We were fugitives. Though unjustly accused, this put a damper on waltzing into Lane (which I knew from my timetables) and ordering up goods and materials. Even if we weren't recognized, someone was bound to ask, "Where are you from?" and "Where are you heading?" and no matter if I said we were headed to my aunt's two streets over or taking a tour of the Panama Canal, four more questions would follow and darkness would set in and the nice sales lady would go home and, while serving her husband broccoli, mention the two traveling gals and he—being a deputized sheriff—would drag us by the collar to the town jail.

Maybe the conversation in the store should be more honest:

"Where are you heading?"

"We're heading to Burdick to see if a friend of ours is alive or has been cut dead. Can I have a red ribbon while you're near the display?"

"You'd look better with the yellow."

"Then I'll take a yellow."

She'd poke at the register and pluck out the change. As she handed it over, she'd squint and suck a breath through her front teeth to keep her curiosity about Pip's disfigurement all stuffed inside her. "Have a safe trip."

Then there was the matter of Olive, and that revelation. But I decided that was a matter for a different time, perhaps to discuss when we were thrown in that jail by the sales lady's husband and needed to wile away a few hours until they brought breakfast.

I sat up, shoving my skirts under me in a bunch, and drummed my hands on my thighs.

For on top of this, there was the matter of Cullen Wilder.

This was a predicament.

PIP DID NOT APPRECIATE ME DRAGGING HER OVER TO THE CREEK and dunking her head in the water. But I had grown tired of her snoring and could no longer abide monitoring the minute hand on my watch, nor count one more bitty stalk of corn. We needed to get a move on. One way or the other, I did not exactly know. The creek flowed to the Marais des Cygnes which in turn rolled right through Osawatomie. This made up my mind we should follow it in the opposite direction and hope we found another town far off the train line that had not yet heard of Pip's supposedly murderous deeds.

"Wake the hell up, we need to move on."

Pip spluttered and pulled my hand from her collar. She spit out a stream of water, snarling and stalking off to get her coat from the hanging tree. She folded it and shoved it to her bag. "I was having a good dream. You interrupted it."

"Tough luck. Get my coat, too." I rolled down my shirt sleeves to button them, then opened Boudreaux's suitcase to put away the coat and the sample box. I had thought it would be right to rid myself of the extra Good Books at the steps of the next church.

"Where's this creek go that we're walking?" Pip picked up the other case and slipped on some wet river grass. Her boot sunk into the muddy water. "This will be quite a joy."

"Least you've got real cowboy boots," I said. My own little city boots pinched badly. I slurped a breath as I took a step. "If you stay up here by these roots, you'll get out of the waterworks."

She gave a go-to-Hell gesture and forged ahead.

After some walking went by, we became aware that a road ran the other side of the trees. But Pip was too easy to identify, what with the scar and the fancy hat, both of which she said were prominently displayed in the Wanted poster. She added that the picture of me was not so accurate.

"You look like a drunk chipmunk."

"But they've got photographs of me from before. They might drag one of those out. You never know."

I hoisted Boudreaux's case with both hands. It knocked my shin then swung around and knocked my thigh. "How come I have the heavy case?"

"It's your penance for waking me up."

"That's just fine. Always happy to be your Sancho Panza."

We slogged along another while. Pip huffed and grumbled. The sky had turned a pink like a puppy's belly, the clouds lumping around along the sidelines holding in the steam.

The creek rambled around, and the cottonwoods let loose enough cotton it looked like it had snowed. I bent to wipe the flax off my mouth and spit it out.

The knock and backfire of a vehicle's engine sounded. Pip and I sank down and listened, waiting for it to pass. But with a grind of gears and a clang, it stopped dead. A man hummed. A twig or two snapped followed by some more humming.

I looked at Pip.

"Peeing," she mouthed.

There was a rustling and the strike of a match to a shoe.

"Smoking," I mouthed to her, then sneezed. And sneezed again, dropping the suitcase to itch my nose and dig out the damn cottonwood.

Smoke drifted through the bushes. "If you are a robber, I am armed."

I pinched my nostrils and bent over to bury the next bout of sneezing in my skirts. I turned my head enough to watch the bush line.

Pip gave a melodious girly laugh, one I'd heard her use many times in our acts, and a couple more to assuage Cullen. "He thinks we're robbers, Sister Mae." She made a big sign of the cross on her chest, then cupped her hand to her mouth and called out. "We're not robbers, sir."

"No, sir." I stepped forward. "We are with the WCTU. We are just taking a moment to pray for temperance to cloak this world."

Cigar smoke came in round puffs. A five cent *Herco* by the smell of it. The man himself followed, bending aside the small limbs and brushing white fuzz and leaves from his green and black cheviot suit. His straw fedora was pushed far back, and his hair stuck against his forehead. He had thick lines that must have been dimples when he was younger. He wore no collar. His gold silk tie peeked from his jacket pocket.

"I am a temperance man, myself. It is an honor to meet the likeminded."

He took in our luggage and stared hard in Pip's direction. Then he puffed his cigar and peered up and down the creek.

"Have you come from Osawatomie way?" I asked.

"No, ma'am. I had business in Lomax."

"Are you heading in the direction of Osawatomie?"

"I'm heading west then south. Garnett, Le Roy, Mont Ida, and Vernon."

I clapped my hands. "There's a tent meeting in Mont Ida on Tuesday."

Pip screwed up her face like she would cry with the joy of Jesus. "You know how much I want a souvenir Carrie Nation hatchet."

"Yes, I do, Sister LuLu."

"Mont Ida is a long way to get with just your feet." He stuck a thumb in his vest pocket and rocked. "I'll escort you to your tent meeting."

"We couldn't—" I tried.

"But you must." He held up his hand. "And I am remiss. I haven't introduced myself, and I must in order for you to think well on me and my offer of assistance." He pinched a card from his vest pocket and presented it with a curt bow. "D.P. LaPlante. Olathe Oil and Gas."

I read it and it said what he said it said.

"What do you think, Sister?"

But Mr. LaPlante picked up Pip's case. "I will get you to your tent meeting, sisters, if it's the last thing I do."

"I can't say no to chivalry." I handed him Boudreaux's heavy case. "Come along, Sister LuLu. We shall get you your hatchet."

❧

"IS THERE NOTHING YOU'VE SEEN ANY FINER?" MR. LAPLANTE stood at the front of the automobile, hands to his hips, one leg slung out, chest stuck out and boastful though it lost its impact behind the belly.

I moved to touch the brass headlamp.

"No, no...Don't touch that."

I curled back my hand. "A Winton."

"Two cylinders, twenty horsepower, four-seater." He tugged on his kid driving gloves and put out his hand for me to take it.

I stepped up to the passenger seat, rubbing my hand over the fine black leather.

"I had the surrey roof specially designed. Open air and shade, you cannot do better than that."

Pip circled the machine, her head tilted like it all puzzled her. Perhaps in her wanderings she had seen few automobiles. She ran her fingers over the wicker baskets tied with leather to each fender and yanked the straps securing our luggage to the spare tire.

"This is a fine car," I said. "I haven't seen many finer. And none quite so red. Well, the Oldsmobiles are good lookers."

"And like a good-looking woman," he said as he fiddled with some engine-type things, "she's fickle in her affections. Ha. Ha ha!" He closed the trunk and patted the metal again.

"That makes no sense," Pip peered at him over the engine. "There are plenty of ugly women who are fickle."

"I'm sure there are, Sister. And I mean them no disrespect, none at all."

"How fast does it go?" I asked.

"As fast as twenty horses. Can you imagine the speed of twenty horses?"

"And that makes no sense," Pip said. "Twenty horses can only go as fast as the slowest. If one went faster than the others, it'd snap the traces or drag half the team. That would cause a horrible accident."

Mr. LaPlante blinked and crossed his arms. "Well, you have me there. Ha. Ha ha!" He held out his elbow. "Let me assist you to your seat. I guarantee you this is not an old plug but the swiftest thoroughbred. You'll need to keep a tight hold of your hat once I've let out the throttle. Indeed, you'll see, girls. Ha!"

❦

THE CAR BOUNCED AND JERKED, THUMPING INTO RUTS AND grinding its way out of them. I held tight to the wood on the front dash, worried my nails would dig permanent marks into the varnish.

Pip was sick within minutes.

Mr. LaPlante stopped along a fence line and helped her down so she could get her legs. Then he wisely put her in the front seat, and I stepped through the rear door to the back. Which did give a grand view, in my opinion, for I could see far across the fields.

Kansas is a state much maligned. This is, I think, on account of its stubborn determination to remain a dry state, not allowing the slightest tipple or relaxing share of a glass between two friends. Many say this has made Kansans a brittle and stern lot. It also makes a lot of money for the illegal operations that loosen them up.

Others say the horizon of Kansas never stops. Just keeps teasing and running off, so nothing stops or starts, and that causes a reverse cabin fever and that, in turn, drives a man mad. Keep out the illegal liquor and the whole state might erupt in a tremendous row of violence and whoever's left would have run for the hills. Which they'd never find. Because Kansas is flat like that.

Carrie Nation can try her damnedest to get the citizens to follow their constitutional laws, but it's the barkeeps who keep everyone in line.

It's what I've heard, and I have no doubt as to its veracity.

I found the scenery calming if a bit numbing. The sky curved, from pink right on down to a dusty line as it touched that limitless border. A stand of cattle grazed. A white barn gleamed bright. We passed a farmhouse with red checked curtains in the window. A woman hung laundry, stopping midway to placing a pin to watch the car roll by. I waved and smiled, then had to grab the back of the driver's seat when we swerved to avoid a tortoiseshell cat. It jumped straight up, hissing and screaming before disappearing into a clump of wild mustard on the roadside.

"The horses are worse." LaPlante turned the knob on the steering wheel and pushed the foot pedal.

Pip gulped in some air, her cheeks expanding to hold it before blowing out.

"How can you be so sick feeling, Sister?" I scooted forward so I could converse.

"How can you not?"

I refrained from mentioning the recent slug of medicinal she'd imbibed. "So, you're an oil and gas man, is that correct, Mr. LaPlante?"

"You have that right."

"What brings you out on these roads?"

"I check the pipelines. We've got a gas line all the way from Olathe up to Nebraska. I check the pipe. Then I check the tanks."

"So, you're a pipe and tank man."

"Yes, I am that."

"And a temperance man."

He shifted in his seat and stretched out his leg as best he could.

"Got a cramp?"

"Falls asleep sometime. War wound."

"Really."

Pip side-eyed him. "What war?"

"A few skirmishes here and there. Down in Indian Territory." His eyebrows needed a good trim. They rose and fell and he sighed. "Got it in the knee."

"How?" she asked.

"I do not feel comfortable telling the story to ladies."

Which meant there'd been no skirmish except maybe with his wife and a rolling pin.

I rested my elbow on the seat and my cheek on my palm. "My husband joined on up for the Mexican War."

"Is that right?"

"Unfortunately, he came back."

"Is that...oh, ha!"

"Yeah, that's a big ha ha."

"Will he be joining you at the tent meeting?"

"Oh, yes. He's a preacher."

Pip coughed and turned her head to watch the fields.

"Is he, now?"

"Why yes. Did you know—and I do not like to brag—however, did you know we met Carrie Nation?"

"Did you?"

"In Peoria. Have you been to Peoria, Illinois?"

"I have not had the pleasure."

"Maybe your pipeline will end up there. It's a fine city, I could give you some pointers on the sites."

"That's kind of you."

He slowed the car and turned onto a narrow two-wheel path that would have been easy to miss. The car hit a bump and we all bounced and grabbed onto the brass rails.

Heavy brush and a few gnarled trees encroached on the road. Globes of sweat rolled down Mr. LaPlante's forehead and stopped on the ledge of his eyebrows. Every branch that swiped along the car caused him to wince and his mouth to move in silent, but well-formed, curses.

"Where are we going?" Pip asked.

"Got a well to check."

"How far is it?"

"Just down a bit."

She flicked a look at me then looked at him. "What do you check when you check a well?"

"I take measurements. I check to make sure there's been no vandalism. Or thievery. There's a lot of competition wishing to see Olathe out of the market and they are known for their underhanded methods. As senior partner, I take it upon myself to personally oversee the health of—"

"You talk too much."

He took his eyes off the road and stared at Pip. There was a long scrape against the side of the car. "What in the—"

"Aw, Pip, put the gun away."

LaPlante took his foot from the gas and stomped the brake. "I am offended, madam."

"You get out here, go do what you need to do and get back in."

He glanced at me. "Your friend is not a tent person, as we are."

"She has a rugged relationship with the Lord."

"I have a rugged relationship with liars," Pip said.

"I am not a liar, madam. Well, I'm really more a regional manager than a senior partner. And it's not really a war wound."

"Get out."

He scrambled about, his foot slipping on the running board. Once on the ground, he turned to open a wicker basket on the fender.

"Don't."

He flinched and lifted his hands up. "I need my tools."

"Get his tools, Ruby."

I climbed over to the front seat and hopped out. Mr. LaPlante shook like a leaf.

I unbuckled the basket. "It's just notebooks and a couple measuring sticks, Sister LuLu. Which ones do you need, Mr. LaPlante?"

"The two sticks and the blue ledger. Not the light blue, the dark blue with the deckles."

"I apologize for this poor turn in affairs." I handed the book and sticks to him. "How far is the walk?"

"Another twenty minutes or so."

"Then you best get to it. We'll be waiting right here."

The sweat dripped down from his eyebrows and stained his shirt. "I've never been held up before."

"Oh, no. This isn't a hold up. We're not going to steal from you. You go on and take your measurements and we'll be right here. Go on, now. Everything's going to be fine, just check that tank."

He stumbled and jogged down the road. I waited until he was out of ear shot then shoved in next to Pip.

"What the hell on earth are you about?"

"I didn't have a good feeling."

"That's on account of your stomach." I smacked the dash. "Did you think we'd steal this car? Do you know how to drive?"

"He could have done anything. He could have done whatever he wanted." She made a circle with her hand then rested it on the pistol. "Look around, Ruby."

"You're the one who made up the game. Calling me Sister Mae. He nearly pooed when you stuck that gun at him, I don't think he's someone who'd cut our heads off and stuff us in an oil tank. I believe he'd buy us tickets to that imaginary tent meeting."

She sat like she had a board tied to her back, her eyes glued to the road, acting righteous. But I saw the tic of doubt at the side of her mouth.

"He's taking us part way to Burdick," I said. "Once we get to Burdick, we get to Verna, and once we've taken care of that, we get on the road and achieve your goal of killing Cullen."

"*Our* goal."

"It's *your* goal. Now, put the gun away. I am sorely in need of a drink and a cigar, and that piece of weaponry is not helping."

She did as requested but kept the satchel on her lap and her hand holding the grip.

I chewed my lip as we watched the clouds and waited upon Mr. LaPlante. My eye followed a black wire that cut across the sky, paralleling the road. I pointed. "Telephone line."

Pip leaned across me to stare at it. "Yep."

"Think he made a call?"

"Yep."

I scrambled over her to the driver's seat and grabbed on to the wheel. But my foot did not reach the pedal. "You're going to need to drive. It's just a couple of pedals, a wheel, and a pull clutch."

"And the oil thing he turned."

"Yeah, that, too."

We climbed around each other and switched seats. A long shadow came from the end of the road, then split in two. LaPlante was not alone.

"Hang on there you good for nothings." LaPlante ran towards us, waving his ruler.

The farmer came right on his heels. And he had a shot gun.

Pip set her jaw and glared. "Son of a bitch."

"We gotta go."

"I'm aware." She pushed one pedal, pulled at something else and the car lurched forward, bearing down on the two men.

"Get the brake, Pip. Put your foot on the brake."

I do not know what got into her at that point. She half-stood, as if she rode atop Big Henry, knees soft to absorb the bounce, hands upon the steering wheel like it was a pair of reins. "What are you doing?"

I pulled at her arm to get her to sit down, but it was like tugging an iron bar. "You're going to hit them."

The farmer aimed his shotgun skyward and let off a warning shot. LaPlante dove into the bushes.

I dropped down to the car bed and grabbed Pip's ankle, then pulled and swung her leg with all my might, trying to get her foot to land on top of the brake. She tried to kick me off, but I wrapped my arm around her calf and got her toe to hit gold. The tires shimmied in the dirt and bounced up a rut. We spun halfway around, so we were sideways on the road.

The farmer, gun tucked under his arm, jumped on the running board, and pulled the gear. He stared at Pip, then stepped back to the ground. "You're in a whole heap of trouble, ladies."

LaPlante clambered his way from the bushes and clumped over. "What have you done to the car?" He ran his fingers over a headlamp and winced at something on the bonnet. His face went grayish, and he pulled his lips into a thin, rageful line. "You're going to pay for that. They're going to have to pay for that, Mr. Tate."

"Oh, they will. You can count on that." Mr. Tate pinched the crown of his fedora and pushed it back. He gave a nod and lifted the shotgun. "You both show me your hands and get on down to the road. The sheriff'll be here in no time."

Pip took her hands from the wheel. She gave me a quick look. "In for a nickel, in for a dollar," she murmured. "All right?"

"Well, hell..."

She raised her arms, clamped her hands to the bar of the surrey roof and kicked Mr. Tate square in the chest.

The gun dropped from his grip. He stumbled back with a grunt, sucking in gasps of air. LaPlante rushed forward to catch him.

I grabbed the Colt from the satchel and cocked it. "You just stop where you're at."

Pip hopped down and took up Tate's shotgun. "Now, put your hands in the air."

My skin broke out in a mess of sweat. I raised my arm to wipe my face, and LaPlante took the opening to grab for Pip.

She stopped him dead flat with a push of the barrel into his stomach. "And step back."

He did as required with a blustering breath. "You ladies are no ladies at all."

Tate looked Pip up and down and smirked. "Who dragged you behind their wagon? You ain't even good for a hog crib."

Pip's shoulders tensed and she tipped her head. "I think I'll shoot you for that."

I squeaked something, then swallowed and regained my poise. "She'll shoot you for that."

"Sheriff's going to be here in a matter of minutes."

"Take off your trousers." I put my other hand to the gun as it was heavier than I'd expected. "Take off your trousers and throw them and your wallets in the car."

The men slid off their suspenders, unbuttoned and dropped their pants, showing their spindly white legs and stockings held up with garters. Men are, in general, sorry things to look at once unclothed.

"Mr. LaPlante?" I pointed the gun at him. "Is this the reverse pedal? It's all right, you can step in close to look."

He hesitated from coming near, instead craning his neck and giving a nod.

"And that's the oil?"

His next nod came with a long weaselly whine.

"There's no need to cry, Mr. LaPlante. This is a robbery, not a murder." My forearms started to quaver, and I sent a prayer that we could end this all and be on the road.

"I took you for a temperance woman," he said.

"There are mornings I think I should be; I will give you that."

Pip slammed the butt to his head. He went down like a rock, arms and legs splayed and a fine fountain of red squirting from the split of skin on his scalp.

She turned to the farmer and smacked the barrel to his nose.

My chest went tight. "What in the...Jesus Christ."

I scrambled out of the car and skidded over to LaPlante. Blood spurted from his head and sprayed across my shirt. I pushed at the split skin to stop the flow, then crawled to his side and patted his cheek until he groaned. "You're going to be all right, Mr. LaPlante. You'll soon have a terrible headache, that is the God's honest truth."

I glanced at Tate who had gone down on his rear end. He rocked like a baby, cradling his poor face in his hands. "You have an ice box, Mr. Tate?"

Pip tossed the shotgun to the rear seat and jumped to the cab. "Get in."

I lowered the cock on the Colt and stood. "This is entirely uncalled for."

Her gaze bore into me like knives. "In for a nickel, in for a dollar. Get in the car."

CHAPTER 13

ORINDA
1898
I Trace My Ruination to Little Sure Shot—The Hair Raiser
—Verna Rolfe

Dear John and Emma,

I miss you greatly and hope your Auntie Rose takes it in her heart to tell you that. Every night, after my ablutions and prayers, I lay my head to my pillow, close my eyes, and send on to you via the moon three hundred kisses and a mighty hug.

Your momma is coming home to you soon. I am on a great adventure which I will share once we all meet again. I can tell you that I have met a world-famous trick rider and she was kind enough to sign her name to an old photograph of herself. I am enclosing it here for you, Emma. You may consider it my early Christmas present. Remember: ambition and hard work make a man (and woman), and thus you see the benefits and prize of doing so right here in this one photograph.

I am enclosing a javelina tusk for you, John. You must be a very good hunter to outsmart a javelina. They are known for their cleverness and are as ornery as you.
Your Daddy sends his love and affection. Though he is far away in Mexico fighting a war, do not worry about him. He is cleverer than John and that javelina combined. I am certain he will write you himself sometime, though I would not hold my breath too long.

Well, that's it from here in the desert wilds. Here are three hundred more kisses—

Your Momma

I folded the letter, took a sip of sarsaparilla, and stared out the window of the 368 Saloon. It was cool and quiet in the mornings, and the bartender left me to myself. Pascoe's sat across the way, and Pip loped Big Henry around the ring, her bloomers bright sunny yellow, hair flopping on her back, and her smile wide as if she'd been discussing the weather with Jesus.

I did not yet know the full story as to her downfall from trick rider to the turning of tricks, but my assumption was it had something to do with a man. I wondered if she had been dazzled by another trick rider and their daredevil ways, her thinking, *yep, this is a life for me*. Only to find the show as phony as the dizzle dazzle man who pulled her into it. Because if Pip had an Achilles heel, it was for the slick-oiled promises of the stinkier sex.

Well, who at one time or another didn't have that problem? Maybe nuns. Maybe not. I thought it might be interesting to interview one or two to see if theirs was a true calling or an evasion of impending disaster.

<hr>

I TOOK ANOTHER SLUG OF MY SODA AND WASHED IT AROUND MY mouth. Then I took the pencil to another piece of paper.

Dear Rose,
This time give the kids my letter. I know you didn't last time nor the time or ten before that. I promise I am working very hard to return to K.C.

ME

PS - I would not be averse to you sending me a few extra dollars for the trip.

I pondered upon the turns my sorry life had taken to here. For a long time, I thought the worst turn had been marrying Frank Calhoun. He whispered in other girl's ears, and I could not blame anyone but myself when he abandoned me in front of the Dairy exhibit at the Columbia Exhibition.

"I am a man of the river." He'd brushed his felt hat and wiped his boots on the back of his trousers before sauntering into the crowd.

"You're a damn snake," I'd said. Then took myself to the beer pavilion and drank to his immediate demise.

I was escorted out at a later point; the two barmen giving me a heave-ho for good measure, so I landed rear first into the crowds.

The Columbia Exhibition in Chicago boasted many wonders and untold number of whatnots. Frank had bought us tickets as an apology for busting my nose the month prior. I would have preferred a ticket to see my child, but Rose declared baby John off limits and my desire to visit both selfish and unhealthy.

I remembered blinking past all the buntings to the purpling sky. "What the hell, God?"

And found myself staring at a two-story poster of a woman in leather skirt and beaded jacket, a rifle slung over her shoulder and a mass of curls framing a pretty face.

Annie Oakley.

Little Sure Shot herself.

Star of Buffalo Bill's Wild West.

The fast-riding sharp-shooting wonder of the world.

The true cause of my life's turn for the worse.

If I'd not gone in to see that show with the whoops and hollers and wild chases and arrows flying one way and cowboys shooting from the other. But I did. And my heart had stopped. Annie Oakley had entered, standing calm as could be atop her galloping horse, gun held to her shoulder, not once missing the glass globes tossed to the air.

She might as well have stepped right up to me and handed me a ticket west.

Now, she made me angry. There were many times I'd paced my room and had an imaginary conversation with her to let off some steam.

"You," I said to her, "are a corrupter."

To which she'd shake her curls and twirl her six-shooter on her finger and drop it into the holster. "And you, Ruby Calhoun, are a two-bit nothing."

"You are a two-bit fake."

"A n-o-t-h-i-n-g. I know it and your sister knows it. And she is not turning any letter over to your children. For their own good sake."

Which sometimes made me madder and sometimes led me to sulk, for she was right.

With a last swallow of sarsaparilla, I stuffed the letter in my skirt pocket, took my leave of the saloon, and crossed over to watch Pip and Big Henry run through their paces. She gave a wave from the far side of the ring, then patted Big Henry's neck and smoothed a strop of his mane.

"Take a look at this move," she shouted, and heeled Big Henry.

As he cantered by, she placed a hand on each side of his withers, scooted her feet up his back then pushed herself into a handstand. This was a wondrous feat and other people had gathered around the ring to watch and whoop.

She went one dangerous level further, lifting one arm straight out to the side, and dropped her legs into midair splits.

The Hair Raiser. One of her trademark moves. Particularly as it let her legs show in their bare glory.

I clapped and jumped on the rail to cheer her on. Someone

bumped my shoulder. I looked around to see Verna climbing to sit on the rail. She gave me a nod, then settled her hands to her legs and watched as Pip moved into *The Scissor.* Even old Pascoe smacked his hat to the dirt at its magnificence.

"Look at that." I backhanded Verna's arm.

"Riding around and showing off for nothing," Verna said, her eyes following Pip. "It's a lot of show and effort, but it's still round and round and never getting anywhere at all. Just..." She made a tiny circle with her finger like water going down a drain.

"Did you know water drains one direction on the east side of the Rockies and goes round the other way on the west?" I asked.

My guess is she did not know that fact but hid it with a strange shrug. "That is about as meaningful as dirt."

"It's an interesting fact, you do have to admit, and my guess is you'll be curious next time you pull the toilet chain."

"I have no response to that."

Without warning, Big Henry locked his front legs and slid to a dust-strewn stop. Pip spun over his head, landing on her back with a loud wallop. She lay still as a corpse, mouth open, eyes considering the heavens.

Henry pawed a hoof at her side. He gave a soft nicker and lowered his head to touch his muzzle to her cheek.

No one in the crowd moved. My heart clanged and dread thunked in my stomach but I did not move, either. Maybe we were all waiting for her to jump and take a bow, that this, too, was part of the act. Maybe it had a name, like *I Seen Death and Lived* or *The Dead Drop.*

Big Henry trotted to the fence, shook his head, and chewed on a sprig of grass. We all watched him, then it seemed to dawn on us we might need to pay some heed to the heap called Pip.

Matteo, closest to her, slipped under the rail and jogged over. Verna jumped down and I followed right on her skirts, then was lost in a bunch of shouts and "Hey, she alive?" "Get the doctor!" came next. I bent low and shoved through to crouch next to her.

Verna kneeled on the other side, waving her arms to keep the gawpers back. "Leave her some room, you damn idiots."

"She looks awful pale," I said.

"It's just the breath knocked out and a conk on the head. Give her a minute."

Upon hearing this, the small crowd lost interest as crowds do when the thrill of imminent tragedy and possible gore is denied them.

Matteo took Big Henry out of the ring and back to his stall. Verna thumped down cross-legged and set her elbows to her knees to wait. I held my hand above Pip's nose and wished I had a mirror on me. But it'd probably shake like my hand did and I'd end up seeing the fog of my own breath or some bug crawling by. "She might be dead."

Which would leave me in all sorts of a terrible situation, as she was, in fact, my only real friend in Orinda. Without her, China Mary was sure to make me join the fold or worse, make me do the act with Darby and I did not think my eardrums could survive that.

Pip sucked in a big breath, her mouth flapping open like a fish stuck in the sun on a pier. Her eyes went all wild, roaming for nothing except another lifesaving influx of air.

A string of expletives flew out on the exhale and even I winced as to the nature of them. She smacked her fist to the dirt and rolled to her knees.

I reached out to help.

"Don't touch me."

Verna grimaced and shooed me back. "You don't want to touch her."

Pip stood and swayed. She rubbed the back of her head and checked for blood. She looked about, peering at each building, the post nearby, Verna, and me, and then checked her head again.

She kicked the ground with her bare toe, winced, and staggered towards the stalls.

❧

WE FOLLOWED PIP, STAYING FAR ENOUGH BACK SHE WOULDN'T BITE and close enough we could catch her should she take a spinning fall.

"I see you behind me." Her shoulder bumped against the wall. A bridle and reins slithered off their hook and she looked like she was contemplating how to get around them without tripping or being caught in the leathers. She picked her way past them like one does on the edge of a muddy lake, clapped at her accomplishment when she reached the other side, and continued towards Big Henry.

"I think she may have hit her head," I whispered.

"You don't say."

"I heard that." Pip pushed her hair back, letting loose a swoosh of dirt and straw, and stumbled on. "Big Henry and I would appreciate some quiet."

Then she burst into tears.

Verna took a step back and squinted. "Oh. Well."

I stepped back, too, as I had never seen Pip cry and the sight had a disconcerting edge.

"You're just in a slump," I said. "Tomorrow you'll do better. Then the day after that betterer than better. Why, by June you might be ready to join a rodeo tour."

Pip wiped at her face. Her eyes glistened and nose brayed red. "The door to that life closed long ago."

"I suppose you're right," Verna said. "Good to look at life through a realistic lens."

"I think you were wonderful, Pip."

Pip looked at me like a puppy not sure he's done the right thing, but wishes desperately for a treat and a pat. "That was one of my best *Scissors*."

"And you saw the crowd. Stunned and agog."

"What are you on about?" Verna asked. She took a big breath as if she were about to repeat her desolate "round and round" theory. Which would not serve Pip at all.

I elbowed her and gave a jerk of my head for us to leave.

She sighed but obeyed, and we made it all the way to the livery door before she had to open her trap. "Useless dreams bring despair and heartache."

"I don't think that's a useful sentiment right now, Verna."

"Despair and heartache." She pointed a finger to the air and swung it around as if she thought that would poke the point home.

I pushed her to the street. We blinked against the sun's devilish glare.

"You, Verna, are a bouquet of doom."

"I am a realist. That's how I keep from crumbling." She squinted and chucked a shoulder. "Look around, Ruby. Everyone here's on the edge of it. One day you're going to walk out the door of the Paradise and all you're going to see is dust."

CHAPTER 14

KANSAS
1905
BETWEEN HERE AND THERE

We drove from one farm road to another, staying far from grain elevators that gave notice of a town boundary. South and west we went, keeping an eye on the curve of trees along a meandering creek and ever careful to follow the lowering western sun.

I kept watch behind us, sure the sheriff had a faster car, certain the telephone lines that ran for miles carried our names across county lines.

Pip puffed on one of LaPlante's cigars. I had refused the offer to join her, because I did not like to smoke with those who made me angry or whom I feared.

The fuel in the Winton gave out just after dusk. We came to an ignoble stop, somewhere between neither here nor there. On the left, prairie grass bent and caught the first slip of moonlight. On the right, the trees grew dark and merged onto a wall of black. The dirt road rolled silver before us and dipped into emptiness behind us. Out near the horizon edge, one speck of light glowed.

"We need to put the car in the creek," Pip said.

"You do it." I got down from the automobile and wiped the dust from my mouth and nose. "That man," I said, "he's got a family to look after. How's he going to do that without a nose?"

She clenched her jaw and raked her gaze over the tree line. "Fine. I'll push it myself."

"You do that, then." There was nothing more I wanted to say to her, so I took to the rise in the middle of the road. When she honked the horn, I covered my ears until it stopped.

There wasn't a sound then, save the swish of grasses and the crunch of my footsteps on the earth.

I didn't know where I was going. I guess towards that bright tiny light. It could take an hour or a week, but I would get to that light and sit down in that house. I would sit and say, "I am woefully tired." They'd bring me a slice of pie, maybe lemon meringue.

But as I'd lulled myself from my anxiety, I caught sight of a spatter of blood on my sleeve, and black spots of it set into my skirt. I had nothing. Not a stitch to my name beyond these ruined togs. Everything remained in that car we should not have stolen. I wished fervently that time could be rolled into a ball and knit a whole different way. But it couldn't, much as it couldn't the last hundred times I'd wished it so.

The light snuffed itself out.

I turned around and trudged back. Pip's satchel and the shotgun lay in a heap on the side of the road. She struggled to move the car, putting her shoulder against the door, throwing so much effort into it I could see the glow of her teeth as she grimaced.

"Half those men's money is mine." I shoved her shoulder. "You hear me?"

"I hear you." She dug her boots into the dirt and gave another push.

The Winton rolled down the decline to the trees, picking up speed as it went. Pip jogged next to it, then jumped in the steer it into a gap. A high pierced wheezing came as it barreled toward the creek.

"She's going to hit the trees." I grabbed Pip's satchel and the shotgun and leaped from the road to the field, angling myself across the slope. "Turn it left! Pip, you're going to kill yourself. You gotta turn—"

Then they were over the bank, the rear tires spinning in space as the car tipped and dove into the water.

Everything went back to quiet. I slipped on the bank and grabbed at a root to steady myself, then slung off the satchel and dropped the gun before wading into knee-high water. The car wobbled on a ledge, its front end submerged.

Steam gurgled around the chassis. I waded over and peered underneath. "Pip. Damn it, it's too shallow to drown here, so I know you're just playing with me."

The moon was bright across the trees but cast the river in darkness. I reached into the water. Searched along the ledge for anything, but my fingers caught only long grasses and sand. The front end was buried in silt. I feared she might be crushed under the front tire. I may have hated her at that moment, but it is a true terrible thing to die with an automobile on your chest and river water in your lungs. I clawed at the fine silt, but no matter how much I dug I made no progress. The silt slipped and pulled at my wrists like quicksand. It could have swallowed Pip whole, out of my reach. My teeth chattered and I gulped in air. "Jesus, oh please, I swear to you I will give up all sins right now. Just bring my friend back to me."

A metallic groan stopped my words. The Winton slid further into the water and twisted to its side. I flailed my arms to move from it. A wicker basket flopped open, releasing ledgers and papers that floated around me and soon sunk.

"What the hell am I supposed to do?" I could no longer see; my vision blurred and streaked. I pressed my palms to my face, grit and silt mixing with tears. "What am I to do now?"

"You might come on out of that water before you catch some sort of disease."

I dropped my hands and stared. There on the bank, her clothes soaked and water dripping from the brim of her hat, stood Pip.

"Did you see me do that *Layout Fender?*" she asked. "I had a wobble on the vault—"

"You no good, trick-riding, sorry ass son of a whore's bitch damn..." I slapped at the water. "Mule-faced jack-handled mother of a shit-eating demon-breath..." I did not know where else to take the words so pursed my lips and screamed into the crook of my elbow.

"Are you done?"

"I'm done."

"Then would you mind unbuckling the luggage and handing it to me?"

I glared at her. "You have some gall."

"It's all right," she said. "I'll get it."

⚜

WE STRIPPED FROM OUR SKIRTS AND SHIRTS, EXCHANGING THEM FOR pieces of dry clothing we picked out of the luggage. Pip chose a worsted outfit of LaPlante's. The trousers' waist bunched under her holster belt, which she decided would never leave her person again. She admired the celluloid collar he had packed, and the mother-of-pearl button that came with it, so rolled those back in the luggage for future use.

I pulled on the suit of Mr. Cuckold, which fit as could be expected when one is five feet and nothing on a good day. I cut the legs with the straight razor from his shaving kit, then folded the new hemlines and sat on them to create flat cuffs. He was slim as he was tall, and that made for a tight fit at the hips and a loose one everywhere else. I tucked the shirt tails in and pulled the suspenders to my shoulders. Pip stepped over from where we'd spread the luggage contents to help tighten my suspenders so the pants wouldn't sag off.

"Why is it men don't carry sewing kits?" I asked. "It's not as if they don't get rips or loose buttons." I stretched my neck one way and the other to loosen it, then braided my hair tight for convenience sake. "I could fix us up right now if we had a kit. You remember when we did that Promenade number? That was a fine set of suits, wasn't it?"

"Sure it was."

"I took in the sides a little differently, you remember that? With the four tucks and an arrow?"

"I finally saw you had breasts."

"Well, to be honest, I addended my brassiere." I pushed up my breasts, winked at her and sang.

"There was once a little maiden, quite
original was she,
For she never did the same thing twice:
And her hair was so lovely, to describe it puzzles me.
For she never wore the same hair twice."

We were in bare feet; our stockings hung on a low branch next to a map I spied among all the sinking papers and books. Both our boots waited for us to scrape off the clay mud of the creek bottom. I did admire the brogans LaPlante packed, and Boudreaux's wingtips shined. But neither of us sported elephant feet, so we set those aside.

Pip sat cross-legged and took apart the Colt, cleaning all the pieces with a torn bit from one of the undershirts and sang along the harmony as I strutted.

"She was such an original girl,
She was nice;
An angel minus wings—who did a lot of things,
And thank God, *she never did the same thing twice."*

The moon continued its climb. I sat to watch its cool rays glint off the brass rack on the Winton and the white spokes of the rear wheel that remained above water. Pip tossed me my coat to use as a blanket. Her own looked as worse for the wear as mine. To think so much could go to tatters in the matter of a few days.

I lifted my watch for the twentieth time, wishing the glass case had miraculously healed itself between viewings. Then I shoved it to my vest pocket, where it cuddled up with the photo of Mr. Cuckold's girlfriend whom I named Marie Latrelle because she had a French look about her.

Pip, who had finished cleaning both guns, crouched by the luggage and scratched the top of her foot. "We can't carry three cases."

I fiddled with the cufflinks on the shirt and decided to remove them and roll up the sleeves. I reached past her for the wad of our old clothing, twisted it all and slapped it to a suitcase. "I think we're near Waverly. With all your turns left and south and right, though, I wouldn't be surprised if we're down by Garnett." I closed the case, pulling the buckles tight before lifting it.

"What are you doing?"

"What do you think I'm doing? We can't carry three cases. I'm going to throw this in the river."

"It'll just float downstream."

"Exactly right." I stepped over her legs and headed for the bank. "And we're heading upstream." With my toes dug into the mud, I slung the case. "See, Pip, I thought this all through. That case is going to bob itself all the way down river. It'll be headed that way and we'll be going the other. That's called planning." I tapped my temple and strode back to her. "That's called thinking through to the next step and assessing the outcome before you take it." I put a finger to both temples and made a screwing movement. "Thinking things through. Not stealing cars and breaking people's heads open just because you feel like it."

"Now you're going to school me on planning things out? You, the expert. You with the prison record and two years locked up in Tucson."

I crossed my arms, digging my fingers into my ribs. "There wasn't time to plan much of anything, was there? You know that as well as me. I wouldn't have done any of it if you hadn't—At least I had some sort of plan. I highly doubt you have any such for Cullen. He may not even be in Hutchinson, you think of that? He could be in Kanapolis. He could be in Borneo. And what are you going to do when you find him?"

"One: *you're* going to shoot him in each leg so he can't walk. Two: *I'm* going to take a knife to his face like he did mine. Three: *I'm* going to gut him. Four: *we're* going to leave."

"That might be slightly—"

"Look at me, Ruby. I have spent the last five years on my stomach with my face shoved into a pillow or brick wall by whatever man couldn't look at what Cullen did to me. I've had plenty of time to think. So, don't tell me I don't have a plan."

"What if I miss? What if I only hit one leg?"

"You're not going to miss."

"It's a very large possibility."

She tumbled that around a bit, and her eyebrows lifted and dropped as she saw the chink. "But you won't."

"We need to mull over variables such as that."

She sneered. "Like you did with the suitcase."

"Just as such."

"Just as you did with the chipboard suitcase that's going to sink like a stone at the first bend. Just like that."

Regret rolled through me like river muck. "Maybe not like that."

"You won't miss." She dusted the lapels of my jacket. "You want a smoke?"

"No, thanks."

"All right, then."

She left me to myself and sat a ways away. I watched the glow of her cigar and tried to keep out thoughts of the Paradise and that whole sad situation. I barely remembered what was real and what wasn't. I didn't want to look too hard. That was the naked fact of it. Because if I did, I'd remember that I'd had a chance to stop Cullen once, and I didn't. I ran.

❧

IN THE MORNING, I BRUSHED COTTONWOOD SEEDS FROM THE MAP I'd spread on the ground, then pointed. "I believe we're somewhere between here and—" I slid my finger along the turns of a creek. "Emporia. I think that's the next town."

"How far?"

"Oh, it's a good day's walk. Maybe more if we keep to this creek."

"And Burdick?" Pip paced behind me, chawing on an unlit cigar.

"Another day. Maybe more. We can go north up the Neosha River —see? And then cut west on farm roads."

"I think we should stay low during the day. Move on at night."

"I think we should get to Emporia and send a telegram. To Verna. Maybe she can come get us."

"You're going to walk into the Western Union and send a note. 'SOS. If you're alive, come get us.' Is that before or after the man behind the counter recognizes your face from the poster?" She waved in dismissal.

"You pick a route then." I pushed the map towards her. "I'm hungry."

"Don't have a tantrum."

"I'm not having a tantrum."

"You know how you get."

"I don't get any way." I stood and shook the dirt from my trousers. "I am not waiting until Burdick to have a bite to eat. We have money. Between the wallets and the Bible sales we can afford to stop and get a meal. We just need to find a place that'll turn a blind eye or two."

Pip pushed the cigar to the chest pocket of her vest. "You look good in men's clothes."

"Don't start."

We each hefted a case.

She leaned out over the water and patted the Winton's bumper. "Goodbye car." She jogged up next to me. "It's much more fun to ride a horse. You know if we found a barn—"

"No. We are not going to steal one more thing until I have had a proper meal. That consists of a pork chop, a few greens, two baked potatoes, a slice of pie, and a beer. Then, and only then, will we discuss horse thievery."

CHAPTER 15

ORINDA
1898
Pip Aims to Put Me in My Place—China Mary Refuses My Request

P ip and I smoked and shared a ham sandwich and watched Wu
Lin at his tubs. I pulled my shawl tighter around me. Just the
day before it had been hot enough for knickers and a chemise.
At noon the temperature dropped and all the leaves along with it. And
thus, fall had completed its cycle which is how seasons occur in the
desert and Arizona mountains.

I squinted at Pip. "You pay Pascoe's yet?"

"I will."

But I knew she had the same empty wallet as me.

"We have been paid minimally for three weeks straight," I said. "All
that money coming in and none of it heading out. So, where's it go? Is
it all under China Mary's bed? Down some old mine shaft?"

Pip spit a bit of tobacco and took her time blowing smoke rings.
She lounged in the chair, knees spread under her skirt and head lolled
back so her hair swept on the ground. I envied her wool skirt and

jacket, for she seemed content and didn't crowd into the square of sun with me. "Cockfights."

I squinted at her. "What?"

"And dogfights. And fan-tan when she heads over to Mammoth every once in a while."

"But it's our money she's gambling."

Pip shrugged.

"That's all? You're just going to shrug? She's stealing our money."

"You going to confront her on that issue?"

"I just might."

"You're dumber than I thought."

"Don't call me that."

"Then don't be dumb."

"You're the one that's dumb. I'm just here temporarily."

She made some humph-humphy noise.

"Why are you like this?" I asked.

"Like what?"

"So laissez-faire. Those slips of paper she waves around. She can put anything on them she damn well pleases. We pay board and food and anything else that needs replacing, like that silk ribbon I ordered for your swan costume. She says I owe her for that. And she says I'm ahead because I broke even this week, and she was generous and didn't charge for the extra pillow I took from the hall closet when I had my monthly and wanted some extra comfort."

"You took two."

"She does not value our act, Pip. And we have a good act." I swiped at a fly that tried to batter my head. "She'd be sorry if we left."

"And where would we go?"

Wu Lin lifted a heavy soaking pile of sheets and slapped them onto a table. Then he leaned the pole to it and took something from a long pocket on his cloak and tossed it near the ocotillo fence. A rush of birds exploded from the limbs, jostling and cawing at each other as they fought for some of the seed. Then it was gone and so were they. Wu Lin returned to squeezing out the sheets and Pip picked at a callous on her palm.

"You're in a funk," she said.

It appeared to me Pip was more interested in ripping at the callous with her teeth than remarking upon China Mary's penurious ways. I folded the wax paper from the sandwich and crushed my cigar in the dirt.

"Where you going?"

"It's practically snowing out here."

Pip kept gnawing at her palm and narrowed her eyes as she watched me. "You got any aloe?"

"You keep chewing, you'll end up with a hole in your hand. And that might go septic. Then you might die." I took a step to the kitchen door. "And no one will be at your funeral because Verna will have murdered me in my bed prior to your demise."

Pip snorted. "Why are you afraid of Verna?"

"It's that look she has."

"She gives that to everybody. She's eternally resentful of the world."

"Well, what'd the world do to her that wasn't her fault to begin with?"

Pip twisted in her seat to stare at me. "Her husband died in a mine fire at New Atlas and left her next to nothing. Was that her fault?"

"She married a miner, so, yes, I would say she had an inkling of that outcome."

"And Maggie won't tell anyone anything about herself, and that means something so dark and awful happened she can't even speak it."

Wu Lin clipped a sheet across a laundry line, then threw out some more seed for the birds.

"Darby's dad beat her so bad as a child she's deaf in one ear."

"So that's why she can't sing."

"Stop blaming and throwing around fault." Pip gave a sharp glare and turned back around. "Verna's allowed to be mad. It's better than despair, isn't it?"

A match flared as she relit her cigar.

"Well, I don't need to be the recipient of it. And she does not have to be spread-eagled and taking it from every direction." I pulled the shawl so tight I stretched it round my waist. "She could be a schoolteacher or a, well, not a dancer, she's terrible at that, but maybe a clerk over at the dry goods or a—"

"Shut up, Ruby."

"I'm just saying—"

"And I'm just telling you to shut up."

I clenched my teeth and ground them. "That's not very nice."

"Your self-righteousness isn't very nice."

"We all have choices."

Pip's shoulders raised and lowered with a big sigh. "Grand choice you made singing at a whorehouse."

I wheeled in front of her. "I'm going to get back my kids. And it was *my* fault I got on the wrong train that landed me here, and it was *my* fault before that to keep taking back my sorry husband and it was *my* fault that I was mesmerized by Annie Oakley because the Wild West is nothing at all like she and Buffalo Bill presented it. I can go all the way back through every situation in my life and I know what I did. I'm planning to get out and I'm planning to make it right. You're just going to molder waiting around for Cullen to sweep you off to the nameless valley he claims he owns. You'll still be here, bloomers half down, with boos from the audience to get your aged, talentless, drunken ass off the stage. And your damn horse is going to starve."

Pip sat stock still, her eyes boring in me, the cigar dangling in her hand and the ash flecking on her skirt and the ground.

"You're going to catch your dress on fire, Pip."

She flicked the smoke between us and reached a boot tip out to crush it flat. "You are a self-righteous little shit."

She spun around and made sure to slam the kitchen door hard enough that it shook in its frame.

I rubbed my neck and blinked, wondering how we'd gone from a nice sit down in the yard to this. I kicked the dirt and went back to my chair, swiping the cigar I had stubbed earlier. I dug around in my pocket for a match, scraped it across my shoe and held it up.

Across the yard, Wu Lin had stopped midway from slinging out another sheet. It balanced in a lump on the edge of the pole.

"What are you looking at?" I threw the match down and stomped to the opposite end of the shared yard, disrupting the sleep of the lone chicken. "You could fly over this fence, you know."

The couple puffs I took to settle my nerves did not settle them.

Instead, I felt as if I were strung onto wire, so taut I might split in two. I shut my eyes against the whole wild country between me and my Emma and John. I had failed them thinking I had saved them. But I was going to get the money China Mary owed me and get on a train to Kansas City. Walk right on up to Rose and say: "Hey, those two kids are mine, so you give them here, sister."

I took another puff, then coughed. My throat felt ragged, and I realized I was crying. "Well, hell."

A window wrenched open behind me. "I've got plans, too, you know."

I wiped my nose on my sleeve and peered up.

"Are you crying?" Pip asked.

"No."

"You are. I can see you are." She leaned on her elbows. "You're going to look like hell by tonight's show, so I suggest you reel in the tears. I'm not going on with someone looks like they got run over by the fire brigade."

"I'll cry as long as I want."

"Then you do that." She pulled at the window to close it.

"Hey."

"Hey what?"

"What are your plans?"

"I said I got them. I didn't say I was going to share them with you."

I rubbed my eyelids then blew my nose on my handkerchief. "I'll give you five dollars to tell me."

"You don't have five dollars."

"Well, you won't know because I am tired of listening to you and am rescinding my offer." I lifted my shoulder. "I want my earned money. I am going to get it."

"Now?"

"Yes, now. There is never a time better than now. And then I will have five dollars and you will be out of luck."

At that, she slammed down the window.

China Mary pushed herself back in her chair until its ribs squealed. She drummed her hands on the slip of paper that somehow added up to my net wages for the week. "You want what?"

"I want to see that paper." I stood at the far end of the dining room table.

"Why?"

"Because it's my money, and I want to see how you add it up."

She rolled her lips from one side of her face to the other. Then she picked the small glasses from her nose and rested them carefully to the tablecloth. "Come see it."

This, of course, was a dilemma. I could not trust my safety at that point. Verna had a bruise on her cheek that matched the precise location of China Mary's rings. "You can just slide it across."

She tilted her head. Her skin took on a mottled, lizard-like hue. "All right."

"All right?"

"Yes, all right, you can look at the receipt." She slid it closer with her index finger.

I reached to grab it. She was quick; her claw dug into my wrist and she pulled me around the table, right up close so I could see the gray hairs in her eyebrows before she pummeled my head. My vision went blotchy, then white.

Next I knew, I was flat on the floor, staring at the tin ceiling. I rolled onto my side. Dust and dirt stuck along the baseboard. The bottom of the wallpaper didn't quite make it all the way down, leaving sections of plaster and horsehair.

It all went blurry.

I wiped my eyes with the back of my hand and blinked in surprise at the tears. They were pink with the blood that had decided to ooze from my head. I'd be docked for the stains it made on the carpet. That made me cry even more.

The door opened and a pair of button-up boots stopped in front of me. Their owner squatted. A handkerchief fluttered before being held to my head. "You really are dumb."

Pip took me by the shoulders and helped me sit up.

"She could have killed me."

"Well, she didn't."

"Lucky, I guess." I pressed my palms to my lids. "What am I going to do?"

"We're going to fix that shiner." Pip swatted my arm and stood. "It's going to take a good hour and a whole jar of powder, but that's what we're going to do."

CHAPTER 16

KANSAS
1905
THE RIVER MAN—THE KINDNESS OF STRANGERS

First came the empty tin cans. VanCamps Baked Beans, mostly, though my foot kicked an empty tin or two of King Oscar Sardines. Some tins stuck halfway up from the sandbar, others floated and bobbed against the riverbank. A few still held their labels, and some sat in rings of rust. My eye caught on one with a picture of fancy plums. I kicked that extra hard, it having caused my mouth to water. It bounced off Pip's leg, but she didn't make a scene about it.

We had made it to the Neosho, as far as I could determine. It wasn't what you'd call impressive, though my guess was it swelled and flooded every few years. Now the river did its meandering thing, leaving sandbars to bleach in the sun and the cottonwoods to invade the shore. It was fickle in its design, curling in on itself then twisting itself out. I thought if stretched it out, it would cover the distance from this speck of Kansas to somewhere on the other side of the moon. Thus my plan that we might make Emporia within five or six hours was denied. Not that I'd figured out the time. I had looked so often at my poor twisted watch, Pip scruffed it away from me and dropped it into the pocket of her trousers.

It was somewhere near abouts another dusk. Breakfast and lunch had consisted of scoopfuls of river water followed by a shared puff of cigar. We knew the smoke might give us away when it drifted above the trees, so we hunched over, our hands cupped above the cherry and took but two tokes each before putting it out and moving along.

Most of our travels had been uninterrupted, though we heard the chatter of little birds, a jangle of traces on a mule, and the lows of cattle. When a bird cut out singing and tucked its beak in all quiet, we shrank against the shore edge in case a sheriff or bounty man had taken up our trail.

Pip stopped amidst a tin can graveyard. She removed her hat to wipe her brow, flapped the brim against her thigh, and squinted upriver.

I took the time to drop Boudreaux's suitcase and rub my numb fist. Both my feet throbbed and swelled in my shoes. My blisters had grown other blisters and this made me churlish. "I thought you said we should travel at night. This has been a day of hell."

"You're the one said we'd be in Emporia by lunchtime."

"By the trash, we're near there. Or somewhere. I'd give my right tit for a good steak right about now."

She plopped on her hat, shifted her satchel, then switched the shotgun from one shoulder to the other. Her fingers touched the knot of the strap, which she'd made out of her chemise. She turned, looking me up and down. "What'll you give your left tit for?"

"Two perfectly cooked eggs. Over easy and smothered in bacon grease. How about you?"

"You remember that chocolate flambe with the pepper sauce Verna made for my birthday?"

"I do remember that. She had those sparklers and burnt that settee and the curtain. I don't have your sweet tooth, but that sure was good. That's a runner up for my right tit."

I picked up the case and hefted it onto my head.

Pip swung LaPlante's by her side and I had a spike of resentment at that.

"I think we should switch luggage."

"Why?"

"I've got the Bibles and wrench and all the other doodads, and you've got a case of men's underwear and socks."

"That is a heavy suitcase you carry, I'll give you that. All that leather and brass." She crawled over a tree trunk that lay on its side. "That chip case was a good ten pounds lighter, would be my guess. Shame you chose to get rid of it."

"Well, I did."

"Let's just take a few Bibles. That'll lighten your load."

I dropped the case and unhooked it. She had a point. We each took four little red leather editions and stuffed them to various pockets in our coats and trousers. "How come men get all the pockets?" I asked.

But she didn't answer and instead rested the sample case against a trunk.

I closed the luggage and scrambled over a log to trek along behind her. "What else?"

"What else what?"

"Your other tit choice."

She shrugged and held up a branch so I didn't have to duck as I passed. "I don't know." Her eyes got hazy as she thought. Then she lifted a corner of her mouth. "To have my little girl back."

"Ask the nuns to return her."

"What would I do with her if they did?"

I couldn't answer that.

She let go of the branch and kept herself to herself.

The cans gave way to flotsam—beer bottles and a boy's lace-up boot, a wheelbarrow missing a wheel and the handles swelled with water, shiny pink silk panties pasted to the rocks, a crowbar Pip grabbed and stuck in her satchel.

Then everything started to glitter. Rainbows of light, blues and oranges and pinks and yellows shimmered and spun on the water, the trees, across our clothes and skin.

"Would you look at that," Pip whispered. Bottles of all shapes and colors hung from the limbs of trees.

The bank narrowed to a thin steep strip, forcing us to tread halfway in the water. Colors caked across the surface like beads of sugar, splitting and reforming around our splashing feet.

We came upon a trestle bridge hung with hundreds of bottles; the sunlight bounced off the glass, spinning sharp blades of light. I guarded my eyes until we stopped in the shadows. The brick smelled musty and bore telltale signs of high waterlines. A dead catfish floated near a clump of red cloth.

On the bank opposite, three fishing poles were stuck in the muck and arched over the edge, the cat gut lines idle.

The bottles tinkled above us. I glanced up and caught sight of a hand fanning its way through them so they swayed out over the water and clinked back. The canopy of trees around us sparked with darts of light.

A man peered over the iron railing. His jowls hung down like two turkey wattles, with his lips pursed tight between. His hair was black, a wild muss that grew low on his forehead and curved around into two fluffed-out sideburns.

"Are you crossing under the bridge or over the bridge?"

Pip gave me a questioning look, as I was in charge of the map.

"We're Emporia bound," I said. "So whichever way takes us there will be the best way."

"Emporia bound." He weaved his fingers together and wiggled them. "That would be that way." But he didn't point any which way, just stared down at us. "Are you duck hunting?"

Pip reached to touch the barrel of the shotgun. I prayed she wasn't going to drop to her knees and shoot him.

"We're just traveling," she said.

"Selling Bibles and spreading the Lord's good work." I lifted Boudreaux's luggage and thumped the side. It rang hollow, so I stopped.

He blinked. The bottles swung around as he disappeared from view. He thumped along the wood to the end of the bridge. His step crunched in gravel. Then he stood directly above us, hands clasped to his chest. His suit—if one could call it that—was a patchwork of materials. His jacket sported both flour sack and silk. A bit of calico wrapped the shin of his right leg, a brown moleskin circled the knee of his left. His toes, blackened with many months of grime, curled over a root.

My nose wrinkled from the stench of him, a mixture of old urine, old fish, and rotten teeth.

"Three dollars to cross above and one to cross below." He tapped his tongue to his upper lip, smiled, and flattened his hand for the toll.

Pip clambered up the slope and stood in front of him. She flicked her jacket and hooked a thumb on her holster belt. "How about you let us cross for free?"

"A fee's a fee. This here is my bridge. Three dollars to cross atop and one to cross below. That is the market price."

He poked his finger to her chest, then turned his palm over for the money.

"We're not paying a cent," she said. "This is a county bridge and public property. I pay my taxes the same as you."

I didn't think Pip had ever once paid a tax, and I could see the river man was suspicious of that, too. His eyebrows rose until they were one with his scalp. He stuck out his chest and bumped her. "You pay me the money for this private property or I'll cut the other side of your face, then where will you be? Still here on this side of the bridge."

I do not know where the boning knife came from. It wasn't there and then it was, the tip pushing Pip's chin.

She dropped her suitcase. It tumbled down the slope into the reeds.

"You got fish in this river?" I asked as way of distraction.

"Fish?" A dot of red hung on the thin blade.

"Yes, fish. See?" I pointed to the three fishing poles under the trestles. "Those are your rods, aren't they? Because they aren't biting, as far as I can see."

"They're napping."

I peered down, then looked directly at him, as if there was nothing out of the ordinary in the situation as it stood. "You got catfish?"

"Yeah." His fist tightened.

"Got crappie, too?"

"We got crappie."

"And bass?"

"Largemouth."

"Those are good eats." I shook my head. "Too bad you don't have any loudmouths. Those are the creme of the creme. I'd give my left... I'd give anything for a loudmouth bass."

"You don't say."

"I do say. But one can't have everything one desires in this world and lord knows there's only an iota more in the next." I took in a great breath, and screwed my eyes shut, as if I were conjuring the greatest fish fry imaginable. Then I dropped my shoulder, ran the rest of the way up the hill and rammed him as hard as I could.

He let out an oomph and stumbled a few steps but did not flail and fall as I had planned he would. I clamped my arms about his waist, and kept shoving, thinking he would surely fall over. My nose was pressed against his back. I dug my fingers into his jacket, driving my nails between his ribs. He spun around in circles, dragging me with him. As he thrashed the knife about, I had two truths come to me in rapid succession:

One: The Kansas countryside was a degree worse than hell.

Two: Pip wasn't coming to the rescue.

She stood stiff as my wooden Indian.

"Pip!" But the fabric muffled my yell, and when I swiped my nose and mouth clear to yell again, the river man grunted and called me a tiny whore.

Neither of which I took kindly to.

I let go, gulping in air, long enough for him to swing around with that knife. I crouched. The blade whizzed by my head. I lunged forward, catching his ankle and yanked. He hit the ground with a hard thud. The knife skittered to the lip of the bridge.

Pip's eyes followed it, then she sparked out of her funk and sprinted for it.

My arms stayed wrapped around the man's skinny ankle. He wheezed, digging his fingers into the dirt, the breath knocked out of him.

I patted his shin and crawled to my knees. Pip's shadow came over us as the shotgun slid across my side vision and pressed against his chest. My heart jimmied around; I did not want a repeat of the previous experience, and hoped the man had enough reason to let us be. I stood, brushed off my hands, and took baby steps backward, one eye on him and one on Pip.

"Check his pockets," she said.

"What?"

"Do it."

"No."

His chest heaved as he pulled in a good breath. Pip kicked him in the ribs.

I trotted back to her and pulled up the gun barrel. "What the hell is wrong with you?"

"She kicked me." The man sat up, gripping his ribcage.

"You called her a tiny whore."

"This is my bridge and you owe me three dollars." He rolled forward, pushing himself from the ground.

A third truth came to me.

Pip was going to shoot him.

She had the gun to her shoulder, eyeing him.

"You're not really going to do that," he stuttered.

"Pip—"

He covered his face with both hands. "Oh, please don't. You can go on across. I won't charge a cent. Please don't."

"Pip, stop—"

Her finger curled on the trigger and pulled.

But there was only a click.

"Huh," she said.

The man blubbered and fell forward, his head to the dirt. "Thank you, Lordy God. Oh Lordy..."

We turned to the river, our shoes clobbering across the bridge, past milk bottles and dead catfish and a blubbering man. We kept running up the road until the trees gave way to fields that stretched on either side, and the moon came up, its light slathering everything gray.

Far ahead, though whether a mile or ten I couldn't tell, specks of lights floated. Emporia, maybe. Maybe someplace else.

My lungs felt so hot I thought they'd burn and char my skin. My legs cramped and gave out. I crumpled to the road.

Pip slowed. Her shoulders rose and fell as she took in air. The lace on the chemise gun strap fluttered as she turned in circles and came towards me.

"I can't run any further." I lay on my back and put my hands to my stomach.

"Come on." She nudged my leg with the toe of her boot. "I'll buy you a T-bone steak." She gave a lopsided smile. "Two if you want."

A train whistled. She turned her head towards the sound. I watched her. Saw the smile drop away and the hard lines take its place. Her scar glowed a rage of white against the tan of her skin. Even in the moonlight, I saw it. Maybe it set the scar off even more.

"You were going to kill him." It wasn't a question. It was something I knew was a fact.

She dipped her head but didn't answer.

"We could afford the three dollars." I stood up. Took the shotgun from her. She didn't fight to keep it, nor did she chase after it when I threw it into the field. "Unload the pistol and give me the bullets."

She kept her eyes to the distance, to where the train had called and continued on. Then she removed the gun from the holster, spun the cylinder, and opened the loading gate. Pulled the hammer back to half-cock and worked the plunger until each bullet ejected from the chamber into my open palm. I stopped her after the fifth bullet.

"You can keep the one." I pocketed the rest. "In case."

She slid the Colt back, metal against leather, and buttoned the suit jacket. "In case of what?"

"Cullen. In case he gets to us first."

⚜

LATE THAT NIGHT, WE CAME UPON THE EDGES AND DREDGES OF Emporia, trudging past the grain silos and feed lots that lined the train tracks. Pip wagged a thumb to the tracks, and we walked foot to heel on one of the iron rails, looking out for the wafts of cigar smoke and slits of light that announced a welcome illegal establishment to settle ourselves for a bit.

Pip took a dainty leap, landing on one foot with her arms spread out like a swan. She grinned and took a low bow before rolling into a cartwheel. This did not have the same grace, as her satchel thunked her head as she spun around. But she didn't grouse, just slung it off and handed it to me so she could carry on her gymnastics routine.

It did give me pause to watch and think that this Pip doing a whirly jump had not much earlier been dead set on making a man deceased. I wasn't about to point out the inconsistencies, however, as I much preferred this Pip to that one, so I applauded at the appropriate opportunities.

"You still have that good balance," I said.

She wiggled her ass and winked, before realizing it no longer had the desired effect. She shoved her hands in her pockets and hunched her shoulders. We went back to our search for repast and relaxation.

A wink of orange caught my eye. "Right up there." I pointed down the empty tracks to a long line of loading docks.

Sure enough it came again. Another joined it, bouncing around before arcing out of one of the storage sheds to the railbed.

That was enough for me. I picked up my pace and pushed right by Pip.

I blinked at two men sitting on stools and jawing. "Hey."

They didn't look one bit surprised to see me and Pip.

Both wore good linen suits and straw hats. Their aftershave wafted into the night and slapped me upside the head. They were either about to attend to some business or had finished their business. Neither of which would be discussed with the wife.

The one who'd tossed out his cigarette took a step towards us and leaned forward. He peered down the tracks and spent time taking stock of us. He worked his lips, causing the thin moustache to dance around like a worm with a case of the flops.

"You keep on walking," he said. "Damn hobos."

His friend leaned back, causing the crate to creak. "Get along, little doggies." His laugh, raggedy and strangely high-pitched, garbled into a cough.

"It's dangerous to smoke and talk at the same time," I said.

He crushed the cigarette under his shoe and pushed himself up. "Come on, Artie, it's between late and later."

"Wait."

"What?" Artie took off his hat and fanned his face.

"Never mind, I..." I crushed up my face and pressed my fist to my mouth. "We haven't eaten in days, sir. Not since my husband..." I swayed into Pip and grabbed on to the front of her shirt.

"He's got it in for her," she said.

"Yes, he...well, he..." I closed my eyes and shook her a bit. But I couldn't think another word to lie. I turned around. "My feet hurt, I haven't eaten in a day and a half, and I want a beer. If you could pinch one Christian thought out of your heart and help us up and purchase us a beer, we will be ever grateful."

A bell went off in Artie's head as he stared at us. That set the moustache to stretching out. "Why, you're two girls."

The dim bulb raged.

"Timbo, these are two girls."

Timbo came and rolled a look over us. "Those are two girls."

"Are you in trouble?"

"Loads of it," I said.

Artie snapped his hat back on. "Well, let me help you on up. You should not be out here in the dark at night."

"As opposed to the dark during the day," Pip mumbled as she took his hand.

Timbo pulled me up with a palm to each of my armpits and set me to rights in front of him. "You are a bitty thing."

"I am also a biter, so if you love your nose, I'd shut your mouth."

"It was just a comment. Sticks and stones and all." He pulled at the ends of his vest. "You don't have to take such umbrage at a simple observation."

Artie put his arm around Pip's shoulder. He was a good three inches shorter than her. "What are you doing in men's togs and walking the line?"

"I'm on my way to kill a man," she said.

"Well, that's..." He dropped his arm. Then picked at the sleeve of her jacket and smoothed the fabric. "Guess if he's done something, that's all right."

"He did this." She ran her finger down her cheek.

Artie leaned in to truly look. Then scowled. "He deserves two deaths for that. And you two look like you need two beers, so come on and Timbo'll buy us the rounds."

❧

THE RESTAURANT, IF ONE COULD CALL TWO RUSTED CABOOSES SUCH A thing, offered tin can style seating and a limited menu of ham and beans, ham without beans, and beans sans ham. I ordered a bowl of each, as did Pip. Artie and Timbo were good as their word, providing us with two beers each, with a couple more to follow.

There were two other customers, though they were more interested in each other's tonsils than our raucous group. The barman kept an eye on his timepiece and the door.

I scraped up the last of my bowl, chewed on a square of ham and watched. "What's he waiting for?"

"He's got a nervous condition, is all." Artie lolled his head against the planked-up window. "Had a run in with the sheriff over in Council Grove. He won't say what happened. Spends his Sundays at the Lutheran church though. All day Sunday." He lifted his glass to take a swig, but it was empty, a dollop of foam along the rim. "Where's this fella you're trying to kill?"

Pip, who had her head rested on her arms, yawned. "Hutchinson."

I kicked her shin. "She's joking about that. You know how us girls joke about such things." I pushed my bowl away and sat up straight, giving Pip one more tap of my shoe to stay quiet. "Tell me about Emporia."

"Well." Artie's voice went deep and he elongated the word as men do when they're going to gas on and boast about nothing much of anything. I pasted on a smile, batted my eyes, and stared at his forehead. "We have our library."

"There's one thousand seven hundred and twenty-eight books in it." Timbo pointed a finger directly at me to punch up the point.

I turned to him. "That's a lot of reading."

He chucked his chin and whistled low. "You could say so."

"We got cattle. And a Methodist church and a Baptist church."

Artie's eyebrow peaked and fell. "Catholic, too, but we take the long route round that one."

"As one does." I eyed Pip's bowl. She hadn't finished it and I thought it a shame to waste, so pulled it over. "You got kids?"

"Got four." Artie held up his fingers. "All girls."

"I got a boy, a girl, and a baby." Timbo tsked and shook his head.

"You are blessed men," I said.

The barman's rag squeaked against a glass. We turned to the sound. He balanced the glass on a pyramid of others. Looked at the clock. Looked at the door. Looked at us. Then picked up the same glass and wiped it again.

"That sheriff did a number on him," Pip said.

"I'd avoid Morris County if I were you." Artie leaned around Pip and took his hat from the hook at the end of the bench. "Ladies, it's time for me to retire to my hearth and home."

Pip slid out to make room.

Artie took her hand and gave a small bow of his head. "I wish you the best in your quest. I can see you were a great beauty." He lay a peck on her cheek. "Come on Timbo, Maddie'll have a fit if I don't get on."

"I meant no harm calling you little bitty." Timbo took my hand and slobbered a kiss on it, dug a few bills from his wallet. "Don't you stay at Magnolia House. They call themselves the Petals of the Prairie, but they'll rob you blind. You go down to The Bartholomew, that's two turns and a block. Right by the bank. That's the respectful place. You tell them Timothy Wilcox, Jr. sent you. They'll set you up in the best room. Tell you what." He licked his thumb and pulled out another bill. "You ask for the suite. It's got real feather pillows and hot water to boot."

My eyes watered and I felt a smidgeon of love for Timbo. "You're a good man, Mr. Wilcox."

Artie waved his hat at the bartender. His gaze stopped on the couple in the corner, who were as far past the tonsil stage as two can get while fully dressed and within the letter of law, then he popped his hat on and swung open the door. "We also have a fine cabinet manufactory. Finest work north of Wichita."

Once they'd left, Pip slumped in the seat. "How much did he give you?"

"Six dollars. They were nice men. That gives me a better feeling for this part of the state." I rolled the bills and stuffed them in my pants pocket. "What'd you get?"

"Three dollars and a picture of his kids."

She tossed the photo to me.

"The girl's already got his mustache." I set the photo to the table and sighed. "I am tired as a drunken tick." I rested my head against the back of the bench and closed my eyes. "Feather pillows, Pip. I'm going to ask for four. Plump them all around my head and stick my feet in a bucket of Epsom salts that I'll order from the front desk."

Someone cleared their throat. I lifted one eyelid. The bartender hovered at the table.

"We don't want anything else."

He pulled a folded newspaper from his apron pocket and switched it out for our empty bowls. "Stay at Magnolia House."

Pip swiveled the paper so she could read it. Her sunburn paled to a greyish pink.

I kneeled on the seat and cocked my head to see what pained her so.

WOMEN ON RUN
DANGEROUS AND ARMED
WANTED IN TWO COUNTIES

OSAWATOMIE, JUNE 7—Penelope Quinn and Ruby Calhoun, police say, are wanted for Bible theft, attempted murder, and robbery. Wanted in both Miami and Franklin counties. Miss Quinn is tall and disfigured; Ruby Calhoun is a small woman, once infamous as a stage robber in the Arizona Territory. Reward.

CHAPTER 17

ORINDA
1898
I Tell Joe No—The Dreamland—Chaos Blooms at the
Paradise

There were only so many things to see in Orinda, though Joe did not give up trying to impress me with its charm. We were on the third time round the town, and even the old chestnut nag had started in on grinding her teeth.

"If you go down that path—" Joe pointed into the scrub and cacti. "There's some ancient Indian ruins."

"Is that so?" I glanced at the seat between us. Joe had brought me a bottle of rye whiskey and a box of cheroots wrapped in a yellow bow. I gave him credit for realizing that these held more value to me than flowers. It also gave me a twinge, as it seemed to be a prelude to a question I did not want asked. I peered in the general direction he pointed and spotted a mound of red rubble and some old tin cans. Just to keep the conversation on rubble and decay rather than what came with the gift box and bow.

"There's a lot of legends about that spot," he said. "Some say it's haunted by a chieftain and his half-coyote dog."

"Who says its haunted?"

"People."

"You seen the ghost?"

"Well, no. But Gusty over at the barber says he's heard plaintive howling many a night."

"Gusty's is three doors down from the Paradise. He could've been hearing Darby sing that last hymn that makes no sense."

"Could be. But I doubt it." He jiggled the reins. The nag groaned and kept the same plodding pace. "How about we get an ice cream? We can go sit on the rocks and listen ourselves for the old dead dog, then take off our clothes and have a romp around."

"As you wish." I gave up on the fan, dropped it to my lap, and thought how Joe was generous if not very bright.

He enjoyed the ice cream—two scoops of chocolate with a drizzling of strawberry jam. He didn't mind that it was too hot out to do much but lay back in the shade of some rocks and take a siesta. He did not complain when I requested two feet between us so as to leave room for the movement of air. I rested my hands to my stomach and he did the same. A few wisps of cloud hung above us. I plumped my bonnet under my head. The quiet here, just a tick outside the town and away from the monotonous rumble of carts dragging slag and ore in and out of mines, was dense enough to hear my own heartbeat and the nag ripping a hank of grass from the soil.

Joe noodled around then rolled over to face me, his head resting in the crook of his arm. "Ruby?"

"I'm sleeping, Joe."

He shuffled closer and poked my shoulder.

"What?"

"I been thinking—"

I sat up and smacked my knees. "No. Absolutely not."

"You don't know what I was gonna—"

"I do, too."

He sat up. "I do not think you do."

"You were going to ask me to marry you."

"No." But his cheeks glowed red as he denied it.

"Yes."

"No." He swiped up his hat and stood. "You're a damn woman."

"That would be true."

"And I'm a damn man."

"The answer is still no."

"Why?"

I rubbed a sprinkle of vanilla ice cream from the corner of my mouth and licked it from my finger. I took my bonnet and tied it under the chin. "Let's go."

"We're not going anywhere until you tell me why."

I stood and brushed off my skirt. "You don't get hitched just because I'm a damn woman and you're a damn man."

"I love you, Ruby."

"You're going to ruin your hat if you keep twisting it up like that."

He gave it a gloopy look, untwisted it, and slapped it on his head. "Fine."

He stomped over to the horse and pulled the reins from where he'd tucked them under a rock, then fussed around with the buckles and lines. "Come on then. I pay for this rig by the hour."

"Joe."

"What?"

"You're one of the finest, kindest men I've ever known. You don't cheat me, you don't hit me, and you don't take me for granted. Only about one percent of the world is like you. But I am still saying no."

"Truly, no?"

"Joe, Orinda is a temporary stop for me. I want to get on home. Back to Missouri. Back to..." I let that trail off, as he was not aware I had two kids, and was technically still married to a two-timing son-of-a-donkey's-ass. "Know I am grateful for your proposal."

"So, you'll think about it?"

My patience in Joe's dumbery wore out. "This conversation is closed." I smacked his shoulder and tramped over to the surrey. "You going to help me up?"

Which, of course, he did because he was Joe.

WE WENT BACK A DIFFERENT ROUTE THAN WE CAME, WITH JOE veering off on an old road heading east.

"Why're you taking this long way?"

He shrugged and fiddled the reins. "Just giving you time to change your mind."

It did change my mind, but not in the way he hoped it would. His proposal made me realize I'd settled like a canker sore in this sorry place. I had meant it as a stopping over, not a place to gather proposals or even good pals, but there you go: I had gathered both and this irked me. If I stayed much longer Joe would try to wear me down, much as Frank had once done, with flowers and reasonableness and reminders that a wedded wife had much more of a comfort in life than a spinster without means. Of which argument I tired, as I had found neither to be all the way true nor all the way false.

The more he wandered, the more I stewed on this and how I needed to get out of Orinda somehow and some way and soon. But I had only a few pennies to my name. China Mary had made sure of that. I tucked my arms to my stomach. "I need to get out, Joe."

"We're almost back."

It wasn't what I meant but I let the matter rest.

We rolled over a wash and up the other side to the flatlands, passing a few beat-up abandoned lean-tos, a church naked of paint, and a squat building of adobe and boards. On its corner, a sign hung down from a chain, the letters close to unreadable. I twisted my head to spy them out, but too many had given up the ghost.

"That's the Dreamland."

"Huh."

"It was a fine theater. Miners from over at the old Prosperity used to come here. Even listened themselves to opera."

"Did they?"

"Something to do."

I leaned around as we passed the building. Once it held people and song. Now the wind whistled through the gaps where boards were missing. The whole of the place had succumbed to dirt and ash, much as Verna said Orinda would—and all of us along with it.

"I want to see."

"There's nothing to—"

"Just let me down."

DUST AND DIRT COVERED EVERYTHING INSIDE, CRUSTING THE TOPS of seats that had once been a fine green velvet, and clinging to ripped brocade curtains that hung on the sides of the proscenium. A single wide aisle ran up the middle to a stage I did not expect to soar so. I squinted at the walls, making out the undulating forms of mermaids and strange-shaped whales.

I closed my eyes and listened. Maybe everything didn't run to ash as Verna so firmly believed. Maybe the trickle edge of a song or someone's laughter lived on, rolling around on the swirls of the paint seas.

I heaved a sigh. Nothing.

Joe waited in the shade of the surrey. I stepped out of the gloom, but it followed me right through the door. Everything around here held a tinge of brutality and disintegration.

"What'd you think?" he asked.

"I think the rental time of this nag is nearly up."

"There's a fine view of—"

"No. Again."

"All right already."

By the time we returned to the town proper, my mood had become a sour grape. Perhaps it was seeing the dead theater. Or how I had no means to leave this swill of dirt and heat. Or the mournfulness in Joe's gaze, which gave me no untold amount of guilt. And that mixed with annoyance that he'd asked in the first place and nearly ruined our friendship by doing so.

Joe slowed in front of the Paradise and gave a sullen nod. "Ruby."

I gathered the box of cheroots and the bottle of rye whiskey he'd brought along for his ill-fated marriage request and hopped down.

"You'll feel better tomorrow. Rejection runs its course same as dyspepsia."

He took off without another word to me, which was just as well.

⚜

A FLASH OF SILVER CAUGHT MY EYE ACROSS BY McQUEEN'S AND I would not have given it one iota of attention had it not, first, belonged to the silver buckle on Cullen Wilder's hatband and, second, had he not held the door and, third, had his hand not been on the small of Darby's back as he guided her inside. She gave one small look back. When he said something in her ear, his hand drifted lower.

A horse and rider passed by. The door to McQueen's closed tight again.

"Well, hell."

Maybe he was only taking her there for a steak. The cook had a reputation for his rib eyes and flanks. Or perhaps he wanted to show her their new felt blackjack tables. Maybe play a game or two to show off.

An upstairs window of the Paradise exploded, sending shards to the awnings. This was followed by a brass spittoon, which was a ringer for the one that sat at the top of the stairs. It landed in the street and twisted around like a top.

I darted to the front door, pushing aside a few of the saloon regulars who'd come out to see the show.

I didn't make it more than a step inside before Pip barreled into me, knocking the cigar box one way and the whiskey the other. She flew through the parlor door to the street, her silk robe trailing out behind her. "Cullen Wilder," she yelled.

She stood stock still in the street, never minding the calls from drivers to move her ass. "Cullen Wilder!" Her voice had a shaky edge to it, like she might next choose to scream like a banshee and roll around in the dirt.

"You need to stop, Pip." I rushed to the roadway and held up my hand to keep the traffic from running me over.

She shook and trembled, gathering herself for another grand holler.

I reached for her elbow, catching it to drag her back. She spun around, teeth bared. I had never seen eyes so filled with fury. And emptiness. Like her heart had been hollowed out.

"Get out of the street, Pip. You're acting a fool."

"I can act any way I wish."

"He's not worth it."

She lunged for me, both hands fisted up. "You know nothing about it."

"Yes, I do know something about—"

I didn't get another word out. Cullen bounded past me and grabbed her up like a sack of flour, not even stopping his stride.

I thought she might fight such treatment. Give a kick or two. Let go the rest of the fire she had in her. But she didn't. She hung there, arms and legs swaying. "I'm sorry," she whispered. "I'm sorry."

It wasn't to me. It was to him.

I got myself out of the flow of vehicles and into the shade of the Paradise awning.

Verna stepped from the door, fanning herself and pulling at her collar for some air. "I got your cheroots. And the whiskey."

"I don't care about those."

"She's pregnant."

"She can't..." My legs gave out all of a sudden and I slipped down the wall. My insides churned. "Jesus. Why didn't she tell me? I just thought she was getting fat."

Verna considered me a minute. Her lashes were tipped with silvery powder. "Last girl who got in the family way was on her ass in the middle of the street by noon."

"Where'd she go?"

"Who knows? It's a big desert." She threw a look to someone inside, lifted her chin, and took a step back.

Cullen strode to the walk, not looking at me or Verna. "You all need a leash." He stepped off to the street and headed for McQueen's.

VERNA ROLLED A STRAND OF HAIR AROUND HER FINGER AND PUT HER ear to Pip's door. "Honey, you need something for your pains?"

I gave a good solid pound. "Pip?"

"Go away."

Maggie slunk out from her room down the hall. "She okay in there?"

Verna gave me a look. I knew from it that Maggie had no knowledge of Darby leaving the premises.

"Damn son of—" I kicked the door. "I got some stinky cheroots from Joe. The ones you like. I promise I won't speak ill of your boyfriend if you let me in."

"I said to get away."

"I have a new routine I want to run by you."

"Get the hell away."

"But we have a show tonight."

Verna eyed the cheroots. "I can hold on to those for you."

"No. You'll just smoke them and blame Maggie." I tapped the door with my elbow. "Pip, please let me in."

"Mr. Wilder took her to see—" Maggie stopped herself and took a quick look over her shoulder before mouthing the words. "The midwife." She mimed drinking from a tiny bottle.

The floor down the hall groaned. China Mary waddled her way to us, a stack of towels to her bosom. She shouldered us aside, dropping the towels to the carpet. "One day."

Her nostrils flared out and sucked back in as she waited for one of us to answer back. Then she swung her head to stare at me. "Maggie will go on with you tonight."

The door swung open. Pip gripped her stomach and took in sharp breaths, her face seared with pain. "Over my dead body."

"It looks kind of dead right now," I said.

"I do an excellent snake dance," Maggie offered. "You've never seen someone writhe so."

Pip slammed the door and locked it.

"Get your sorry asses downstairs and earn your keep. There're customers in the parlor. And someone go out and get that spittoon."

China Mary lumbered back the way she came. She turned back, glared at me, snorted, and continued down to the parlor.

Maggie sauntered down the hall, tying her robe around her waist. "You all seen Darby?" She cocked her head and her eyes, an opium-glazed brown, rolled from me to Verna. "Oh, well."

Verna crossed her arms and looked me up and down. "You know that routine you do with the boa feathers coming out between your breasts? And then Pip does that—"

"I know which one."

"It's very dull. We'll cut that and let Maggie do the Aztec Slither."

"Is that her specialty?"

"Watch yourself tonight. She's a stage hog."

The three of them sauntered downstairs. I kicked a toe at Pip's door. She had had ample opportunity to discuss her "family way" with me and didn't. Which meant she didn't think much of me at all. That cut deep and made me angry in all directions.

Muffled voices floated up as the girls put on airs, flirting and fawning over the waiting clientele. Someone banged at the piano, hitting the same wrong keys, and starting over on a song I did not recognize.

I set the whiskey and cigars on the towels. "You could have told me, Pip. I thought..." It felt foolish talking to a door, so I swiped back the whiskey and gave up. "Never mind. Do whatever you want."

CHAPTER 18

KANSAS
1905
We Meet the Petals of the Prairie—The Mule

We sat in the front room of the Magnolia House, with a waifish girl staring bug-eyed at us and an awful picture of baby Jesus and the Lambs hanging over a radiator that clunked and hissed. If they stole stuff, as Artie warned, I saw no evidence of their ill-gotten gains. It felt more like a waiting room for an enema treatment. It held—beyond the girl and baby Jesus—three spindle chairs, a single-bulb light, and a corner glass front cabinet that held objects of fascination.

"Is that a rattler jaw?" I queried.

"Mm-hm." The girl did a three-fingered drum on her chair leg.

I crossed to take a closer look. Besides the jaw, I counted three glass thingums and two whats-its, one in leather, the other in vulcanized rubber. "You sell these?"

"Those are just for show and tell. We got a small store down the hall. Leathers and feathers and a lot of whatnot."

Pip joined me, resting her hand on her knees as she peeked at the shelves.

"You two are *those* two, ain't ya?" The girl clamped her hands to her knees and wiggled them back and forth. Her dressing gown, diaphanous and not leaving a sight unseen, draped down to her heels. An electric light flickered in the hall; she cut a look to it, leaned sideways and said, "Yeah yeah."

I jerked my thumb at the hall light. "Does that mean we're getting the grand tour?"

She shrugged one skinny shoulder and thrummed the chair leg again. "It means nothing. It's just a short."

"That's a fire hazard. Pip you remember Ma Doyle's..."

But Pip wasn't paying any attention to me. Her eyes were trained on the hallway. She shook her head slow. "Minnie DuBois."

I turned around. A woman lounged against the doorframe. She was lanky, with a lost tired look to her, eyelids drooping and discolored, cheeks sunken and the skin clinging along the bone. Her hands fluttered to her throat, big-boned hands that didn't fit the rest of her. She smiled, or something like it, her lips twisting and hesitant. "I never thought."

"I never thought, either."

Then, this Minnie took a step and wrapped Pip up in her arms.

Pip stiffened, her arms bolted to her side and hands fisted.

Minnie arched back so she could get a good look at Pip. She cupped her face. "My God..." She dropped her hands to her hips. "Candy Doll, get a room ready for my friend Pip and her friend...?"

"Ruby."

"Ruby. Get a room ready for her, too, and set us some champagne in the back parlor."

"They're the ones, Minnie. From the paper. Artie—"

"Never you mind that, Candy Doll." She waved her arm. Her bracelets slid down to her elbow with a clang. "This is Pip Quinn, and we were once the finest twosome in Spokane. The finest." She splayed a hand to her chest and dipped her head as if gathering all the applause and stage lights, then sunk down on one knee in a tottering curtsy.

I had a fizz of jealousy at that. "Did you play her mother?"

That received a stink eye from Minnie and Pip and a honk from Candy Doll.

"You should have seen our act in Orinda," I said. "We even brought Big Henry..."

Minnie wove her arm round Pip's and commandeered her down the hall, leaving me the satchel and Pip's hat to collect.

Candy Doll stared at me, her jaw hung open like a cow's. "You ain't scary one bit."

"Yeah, well, looks can be deceiving. You should think upon that." I hooked the satchel on my shoulder and put on the hat. It hit the bridge of my nose and bent my ears. "Do not comment."

⁂

MINNIE'S BACK PARLOR BOASTED AS MUCH GLEE AS THE FRONT waiting area, and I was impelled to wonder what man in their right mind would choose this for their spurious desires. The parlor held a round table, a bar top, a few beer signs nailed to the wall behind it, and a carpet threadbare as the paint on the walls.

Minnie floated in and made a show, twirling her skirts and providing us a peek and glimmer of her velvet mules, silk embroidered hose, and fancy garters. She tipped her head to one side as she sat and gestured grandly for us to sit on down. A hair clip peeked out near her temple. It had wiggled loose from its assigned position and the hair piece curled enough I could make out a few strands of gray poking out beneath the wig. "Take off your jackets and get comfortable."

Pip did. I didn't.

Minnie took Pip's coat, leaving a hand to run along her shoulder before she wafted over to the coat rack to hang it up. She took the hat from where I held it in my lap and stuck that on the rack, too.

A telephone rang somewhere in the house, stopped for a bit then rang again.

"Doesn't anyone get that?" I asked.

Pip watched Minnie the whole time, frowning out from under her eyebrows and with her face set like stone.

The phone rang again, two times then a thunk of the receiver.

The door squeaked behind me. Candy Doll came in with a bottle and three fluted glasses, scurrying around to Minnie's side.

Footsteps thumped down a set of stairs. A man coughed and he might as well have been standing right next to me instead of on the other side of the thin wall. A door opened and shut, again on the other side.

"He pay the full?" Minnie poured out the glasses and glanced at Candy Doll.

The girl tucked in her chin, taking on the look of a wet chicken, and nodded. She spun around to the bar, picked up a red bowl and held it out. "Sugar candies?"

I eyed them, but they were as shabby as the entirety of the room. "No, thank you."

Pip, with her sweet tooth, picked out an orange and white striped one and stuck it in her mouth. I watched her move it around her cheek, then she bit down and chewed it up.

Candy Doll pushed the bowl at her. "Try the cinnamon."

"She doesn't like cinnamon," Minnie and I said at the same time. She smiled at me and I fully expected a split tongue to come out in a hiss and her ass to rattle.

I didn't like her and that was that. It wasn't fair, I know. Sometimes people rub you the wrong way just by their existence. Minnie DuBois, who had once danced with Pip, did it to me.

When she flipped open a glass box and offered a choice of cigarette or cigar I lifted my hand and said, "No, thank you."

And when she lifted her glass to toast old times, I did not lift mine.

She raised an eyebrow, but other than that ignored me and took to pawing Pip's hand. Her gaze fluttered to Pip's face and I could see the revulsion curl on her lips. "Cullen do that to you?"

Pip shrugged and picked out another candy.

"Awful. But he always was such."

I scooted my chair back. "You mind if I head on to my room?"

"What's gotten into you?" Pip asked.

"Nothing."

Minnie leaned an elbow on the table. "I didn't do whatever she told you." Her voice couldn't decide if it was meant to growl or squeak, which puzzled me but mostly added to my dislike.

"I'm sure you've got a lot of catching up to do. Years and years of it." I downed the champagne—a shabby taste to it, too—and stood up. "I'll take the bag."

The telephone jangled again.

"You sure got a lot of activity for one in the morning."

Candy Doll shuffled to the door with me. "I'll show you down."

I took the hat and Pip's coat from the stand on my way. "Early start, Pip."

Pip accepted another glass from Minnie and settled back in her chair. "How'd you get from Spokane to here?"

"*Very* early, Pip." I raised my eyebrow to transmit my seriousness to her.

"All right."

"Before the rooster."

Candy Doll swayed from foot to foot, holding the red bowl.

"You got a root beer?" I asked.

She pushed a finger into the candy and shuffled it around. "No."

"I guess it's time for bed."

THE ROOM WAS DOWN THE CELLAR STAIRS AND BACK AROUND THE corner from the canned goods and beer casks. It smelled of kerosene and mold. I dropped the satchel on the single mattress and attempted to fluff the pillow.

"Is this the queen suite?" I tossed the pillow back then sunk down on the bed.

Candy Doll snorted. "It's got all the fineries, don't it?"

I leaned against the wall, crossing my legs and threading my hands behind my head. "Well, I will not complain." I reached into the satchel and took out the newspaper. I had noticed the train timetables listed on the front page and thought to peruse them.

Candy Doll eyed the paper then lifted her gaze to me. Her cheeks glowed. "I ain't never met anyone of notoriety before."

"There's a first for everything."

"I know all about you. 'Pretty Terror of the Desert,' that's what they called you. My sister Eudaly cut out all the articles. You're a real live honest-to-goodness bandit."

"Well, I had my moment."

"Did you really say it? 'I shall not be tried under a law in which my sex had no voice in making.' Did you really say that?"

My chest shrunk in a bit. "That wasn't me."

"No? I'm sure..."

"That was Pearl Hart."

"Oh, well." Her smile touched her ears and her eyes cleared of their dullness and shimmered in that same way the suffragettes' did when they moved on from Pearl and came to cheer me at in my trial.

"How many people did you really shoot?" She mimed pulling out two pistols. "Hold 'em up."

"I didn't say that. That's just a penny paper rendition...I didn't shoot or hurt anybody. You shouldn't emulate me."

"You didn't say that?" Her smile dipped in disappointment. She picked at the label on an industrial can of tomato sauce and got that wet chicken look again. Her shoulders juddered up and down and she dragged her bottom lip on her teeth.

"How old are you?" I asked.

"Eighteen."

"No, you aren't."

"Sevent—"

"Nope, not that, either."

"Well, what age do you want me to be?" Her chin disappeared completely.

I sighed. "Is she good to you? Minnie?"

"I suppose."

"How many other girls are here?"

Her chin came back in view. She rounded her gaze to the stairs. "Two or three. Depends on the day."

It pained me to see the state of her and the decline in houses of delight. I think Candy Doll might die of ecstasy should she get a look at the Paradise's parlor with the umber lamps and fringed pillows. Instead, I feared she'd die here, on her back, in a sea of gray shabbiness listening to the ringing phone and the grate of Minnie's voice.

"Where're you from?"

"Gravette, Arkansas."

"What's your real name?"

"Martha Ruth."

"That's a pretty name."

She shrugged and pulled the label some more. "My sister's is Eudaly Grace. I always wish I had that name. I think I might have stayed in Gravette. Martha Ruths just get stepped on, don't they?"

"I wouldn't know about that." The beans and ham and multiple beers hit me at once. I yawned and all my limbs went heavy. "I need to go to sleep now, Martha Ruth."

"Minnie's going to get the reward."

My eyes, which had drooped, snapped open.

Martha Ruth put a knee on the bed and her mouth to my ear. "There's a coal shoot just that way, it's easy to crawl up, I done it before."

Her breath tickled my ear lobe. I swatted at her to move a little.

"That phone ringing? That's Artie. When I answer, he's coming in with the Chief of Police. That's Mr. McInerny."

"What're you supposed to answer?"

Her eyes wobbled and swam in their sockets. *"They're here."*

"So, after Pip has a jaw and catch up with her friend, you're going to lock her down here, too?"

"Uh-huh."

"Then you'll head upstairs and pick up the phone."

"It'll be Artie."

I bit the inside of my lip and slapped my thighs. "You should see the world, Candy Doll."

She raised her eyebrows in confusion. "Oh?"

"When I look at you, I see myself. Well, that's not the truth, I don't see myself in you at all. But I do recognize someone who desperately wants something else."

"Okay."

"My guess is old Minnie upstairs saved your ass when it was kicked to the ground, am I right?"

"She was awful nice. Got me all fixed up."

"Gave you board and lodging and that see-through outfit you got on. Helped you get on your feet or at least on your knees."

"Sure she did."

I narrowed my eyes. "But you know about the coal shoot."

She gave a start and her skin went palish. "She said I'd get a percentage."

"You trust her?"

"Well, no."

"Listen." I scrabbled around in the satchel for Pip's wallet. "How much is a ticket back to your town of Blink and Miss It?"

"Gravette."

"As I said." I put my thumb to a dollar bill. "So?"

She ran her hand down her hips then across her chest, all the while staring at the load of money as if she'd gobble it up and swallow. She fluttered her eyelids and peered at the ceiling. "At least four dollars. What as I'll need a sandwich and all."

"Well, that's a deal." I flicked the bills for her to take.

"Deal for what?"

"What's outside that coal shoot?"

"The privy and a couple horse stalls."

A shiver drove up my back. "You got horses?"

"Just one mule." She rolled the four dollars and stuffed them in her chemise. "He's a nice mule. You know how they ain't, in general."

I stood from the bed, stuffing the wallet into my trousers, and strode over to the coal shoot. It was wide enough to fit in and shallow enough to climb up. And someone—no doubt Martha Ruth—had been kind enough to add a rope in case the wood grew too slick.

I pulled at my lower lip and let a plan formulate itself in my head. Then I tramped back to Martha Ruth and handed over another five dollars.

"You take this money and tomorrow morning, after Pip and I and that mule —"

"Theodore."

"Theodore. After Pip and I and Theodore are long away, you get yourself a travel outfit and a one-way ticket to your sister and that sweet old town of your childhood."

"I'm supposed to turn you in."

"If you want to be a bandit, you follow the code. And that never never consists of turning someone in. Never."

"I don't want to be—"

"Give me a dollar back." I poked around the shelves until I found a wax pen.

To My Good Friend Martha Ruth (and her sister Eudaly).

Good luck.
Pals forever, Ruby Calhoun

"Now tell me how to get to Burdick."

❧

THE COAL SHOOT GAVE ME NO GRIEF AS I CRAWLED THROUGH IT AND out to the yard. The privy was where Martha said, and the two-bit stable sat beyond.

Pip, who came down to the cellar only for me to shove her up the coal chute, loped across the snaggle of grass and into the shadows.

Martha Ruth had drawn out directions on the back of a scrap of paper, which basically consisted of squiggly lines signifying creeks and a water tower with an arrow showing our turn north. At a certain point, we would need to pick up the road proper. She drew a house with smoke coming out of it.

"I like maps," she said.

"I like timetables," I answered.

I had given her simple directions back: Tell them we've headed south to Abilene.

I wiped my trouser fronts and crept close to the building. The back parlor windows were open, allowing the night air in through the screens and Minnie's conversation with Candy Doll to flow out unimpeded to my ears.

"Are they locked in?" Minnie's voice lost all the rough velvet she'd put on for Pip. It came out like saw teeth through wet oak.

"Yes'm, yes, they is. Locked up tight like a fiddle gets locked up tight."

The phone jangled in the hall.

"Well?" Minnie snapped her fingers. "Well?"

"You want me to get the phone?"

"It's ringing."

"But should I get it?"

"Yes, you should get the phone, you stupid bit of a nothing."

I caught a movement from the paddock, a swish of tail in the moonlight. Pip sat on the mule, patting its neck. I wished she would get back in the dark, for the moon was bright as midday, and the corral plain open for anyone, such as the betrayers Timbo and Artie—and the damn barman—to see.

The telephone stopped.

I thought it high time to sprint across the lawn. I scrambled under the fence and shot across to Pip. "No saddle?"

"I could only find the halter and rope."

A lantern weaved its light out by the street.

"Come on." Pip legged the mule to the fence. "Get on."

I climbed the fence, gripped on to her hand and jumped. I wiggled my leg over the mule's haunches and wrapped my arms around Pip's waist. "This is Theodore, by the way."

"Let's get on with it."

Theodore backed up and shoved his ass against a stable door. He wobbled his long ears forward and back, then laid them flat like a cur.

Pip tsked and patted his neck. It didn't do a thing but make him swing around in a circle, his front hooves digging a hole to China in the dirt.

The light flipped on in the basement. "You have got to get this animal on the run."

"Tickle his haunch," she whispered.

"What?"

"Tickle his haunch and hold tight."

Which did the trick. Theodore popped over the fence and I held on to Pip for my life.

She had a hand on the top of her hat and the other on the halter rope. "This better be the road."

"It's the road."

Theodore's gait, to be kind, was bone breaking. My ass bounced and slammed down the length of a hay field and half another length of fallow land.

"You need to turn right at the—" My teeth cracked against each other.

Theodore kicked out his hind legs, huffed a grunt and doubled his pace.

I grunted and kept hold.

CHAPTER 19

ORINDA
1898
THE BOULDER STARTS ROLLING

My mother always said bad things came in threes. She'd stared at me as she said it. I had been a decent sort of child. Not as priggish and perfect as Rose, who had been no issue at all to mother when being born.

"She slipped right down that canal, pretty as you please," Mama said. "You know what her first words were, Ruby Desiree?"

I looked from my tower of alphabet building blocks. Mama kneaded a large clump of dough, her fingers clawing in and bending it all around. She grimaced as she worked and looked much like the witch in the story Grandma Ottoline liked to read me at night. The book scared the living hell out of me, and I think grandma got a kick out of that.

Mama's eye flicked like saw blades as she considered me. I do not know if she wanted to push my face in the dough or was worried that I was a demon child and was considering a second attempt at burning her at the stake.

The stake burning was not an original idea of mine. It had, in fact, been generated by Rose who'd slipped from the birth canal on a river of perfumed oil and the songs of angels. She'd gone as far as creating a stick and moss effigy of dear mother and shoving a lit match into it out behind the chicken coop. Apparently, being the Chosen One came with a heavy load of responsibilities and resentments.

I got stuck with the damn thing when it caught my skirt on fire. Rose was lauded by the family for her savior qualities.

"What were Rose's first words, dear Ruby?"

I chewed at one of the blocks.

"*How can I help you, mother?*" Mama said it like she was quoting a Sunday psalm, then wiped her forehead, leaving a swath of flour. "Those were her first words."

I kept chewing because there wasn't much I could say, both due to my young age and my lack of helpfulness in general.

"You are bad thing Number Three," she said.

I suppose Number One was daddy leaving with his pretty cousin. Number Two was Fairfax the dog choking on a chicken bone.

In a way, being Number Three in the prophecy brought great relief to me. Until Grandma Ottoline said it was all an old wives' tale meant to lull one into sanity. "Ruby," she said, "once that boulder starts a-rolling, there's nothing it won't pick up on its way down the hill."

Then she dropped dead, and that cemented the truth of her words.

❧

"I LIED TO CULLEN." PIP TIGHTENED THE RED SILK RIBBON ON HER dance boots and fiddled with the beadwork along the hem of her skirt.

I let go the strings of my corset. "You what?"

She gave a sly smile and admired herself in the mirror. "You heard."

"That is..." I wished I had an alphabet block to chew on. I could chew it and think of something to say besides words like *suicidal* and *insane*.

"You could say something." Her cheeks, already rouged, grew redder.

"Have you told him?" I squeezed my eyes shut. "If it's..."

"It's his. Jesus, Ruby, you look like you've just seen a funeral cortege."

"With an open coffin."

"That's not funny."

"It wasn't meant to be."

She grabbed a brush and dragged it through her hair. She glued on a smile and hummed a tune as if she'd not told me this tragic news.

Out on the stage, Verna rolled the bars of *Silver Threads Among the Gold*.

"You'd best get yourself cinched up and costumed," she murmured, her lips tight.

I nodded and returned to the business with the corset, then held up my arms for her to drop the dress over me. I smoothed it in place and tugged the neckline lower, then twisted up her hair and handed her a fan. It was a tight space, and our habits in dressing were another choreographed dance.

We stared at each other in the mirror. Pip had a strange look to her eyes, far away, desperate, and defiant all at once.

"Was this your plan?" I asked.

She shrugged.

"China Mary—"

"I don't care."

"Cullen—"

"He'll come around." She pinched her cheeks to pink them. "*Two* turns at the chorus of—"

"I know."

"You missed last night, so I'm—"

"I said I know."

"It's a girl." She feathered her palm across her belly. "I can feel it." With a rap of knuckles to the little wooden makeup table, she flounced around me and took a teasing step to the stage.

My darkish feeling followed me right up to the chorus. I missed the turn again and Pip gave me a murderous look as we took our bows and curtsies. She stomped off stage and out the back stairs to the alley, leaving me to unhook my own corset and put everything away.

I had heard tales of women in the sporting life who'd got themselves with child. None of them ended well. Miscarriages and madams not just tossing a girl to the wilds but beating them to near death before throwing them out. Frank told me half the women that followed the line or lived hand to mouth in cribs no bigger than sheds were there because of such untoward accidents. He'd known a woman who kept her baby swaddled in a basket, giving it opium to keep it quiet.

I pictured Pip wandering the desert and plains in a state of desolation, the wind whipping her hair around and the sun parching both her and the child she held tight until they were nothing but bones. Not a soul to call friend as she lay dying.

My throat clogged up.

I picked up a powder puff and threw it against the mirror. "It's your own fault you'll die there, Pip Quinn. Your own damn fault."

I shoved through the back door and out through the alley to the street. A couple of men whistled as I passed by. "How about a tickle or two with those feathers, Ruby?"

I waved a hand and kept going. Pip was a block ahead and nearly at Pascoe's.

"Hey," I called. "Hey, you wait up a second, Pip."

She didn't wait; she increased her pace.

"I need to talk to you." I lifted my skirts and jogged forward, causing the tiny bells I'd sewn on the hem to ring.

"That's a ridiculous costume, you know." She waited at the livery, one pink satin arm slung over the gate.

"It's an excellent skirt. You said so yourself. Don't pretend you aren't a bit jealous of it."

"What do you want?"

"If you're bound and determined to ruin your life, you aren't going to do it here."

"Is that so?"

"That is just so."

She narrowed her eyes but did not huff off as I expected.

"You're going to have a baby—"

"A girl."

"All right, then, a girl. When is this bundle of girldom going to join the world?"

"As far as I can figure, five or so months."

"All right, then."

"All right?"

"Yes, all right." I paced the fence line, stopped at the end to peer down Broad Street. I caught sight of Tommy Gee weaving between men who lounged outside the saloons and The Paradise then sidling into the shadows. My guess was he had four to five wallets stuffed in his pockets. I did admire the boy for his gumption and imaginative sideline businesses. I spun back to Pip. But she'd gone on in to spend time with her horse.

"Thank you for listening," I called out. "As per normal."

"IT'S LIKE DOMINOS," I SAID. "WE NEED TO BE VERY WATCHFUL."

"Dominos." Verna sat on my bed, one leg crossed over the other, swinging the whiskey bottle Joe had given me between two fingers. She sighed and watched me make another turn of my room. "You're going to wear a hole in that floor. Then you'll drop through and break both legs."

I paused and thought how Maggie might like such a thing to happen so she could replace me and add in her Anaconda Stroll.

I returned to the subject at hand. "She cannot have this child, Verna. She cannot."

"No, she cannot. However—"

"I have a very bad feeling about it." I swiped the bottle and took a swig.

"Pip will do what Pip will do."

"Maybe this once she shouldn't. Maybe this once she might think upon her actions and—"

"Oh Jesus, you going into your preacher mode?"

"I don't have a preacher mode."

"As you say."

"China Mary's going to drop her in the middle of the street, you told me so yourself. Then what happens? Then what?"

"Eventually she'll have the baby."

I smacked my thigh. "Before that tragedy, Verna."

"There's a few nice cribs down past Broad Street. She could work those until...they've had an outbreak of tuberculosis, though, so we might warn her off that."

"We need to save her."

"And how do we do that?"

I took another sip of the rye, set the bottle on the dresser, and crossed to sit beside her. My stomach hurt from the anxiety of the problem, much as it had when I needed away from Frank. I had let my nerves and sadness get the best of me and twist my thinking around until all I could see was getting out. Out before he stole another coin from me and tossed it on a table. Out from under his fist. It mattered not at all what train I took that morning. It only mattered that I took one.

If I had done it over, I'd have gotten him good and drunk, stolen his wallet with a prayer he had a few dollars, then refreshed myself at a hotel. Got my head clear and actually sat and waited until a Missouri bound train came. But no, I had no plan and got on the first to depart the station. Maybe Grandma Ottoline's boulder had started its roll then. Or maybe it'd always been rolling and I'd just gotten used to its shadow.

"Are we certain she's keeping the mongrel?" I asked.

"Adamant."

"We need a plan."

"You got one?"

"It'll come to me."

"Hopefully before the birth." Verna poured the last of the rye into a small flask. "There was only a little left..." She twisted on the metal cap and licked her fingers. Her eyes narrowed as she studied me. "You've got a strange glow to your visage."

"We could go on tour. You and me and Pip. There's plenty of other towns around. We can do two shows a town, and just keep moving."

"Until what?"

"Until she has that baby."

"And then?"

"Then we'll be in Missouri and rich and maybe we can buy our very own theatre and add acrobatics and trapeze and—"

"Cullen's not going to let her leave."

"You can't tell me he wants the child."

"It's not about the child. Those two go back a long time. On and off and on and off." She sniffed. "You know he owns most of the town. And God knows how many others."

"How's that?"

"They pay him each month or he burns the place down. Or he requests the deed."

"What's that have to do with Pip?"

"He owns her, too. She's tried to leave before and came back. He gave her Big Henry."

"Well, that was then. This is an entirely different situation. Why, he barely visits her as it is, I don't think he'd even notice. You've seen him carry on with Darby."

"He'll kill her." Verna stood, put her hands on her back and stretched. "That's what he'll do."

"Why?"

"Because he can."

I took Verna's comments with the grain of salted doom they had earned. Yet I could not shake Grandma Ottoline's words and a cold shiver slipped along my cheek. But it was the window cocked open for the cigar smoke and the frigid November air wanting in.

"We'll save her."

"Some people don't want saving."

"Even for their own good?"

"Even so."

"Hm." I tapped my foot and stared at her. "That is a conundrum and thank you for bringing up the barriers to our success so soon. It's a wonderful gift you have."

"You're very welcome."

THE NEXT MORNING DID NOT BRING ANY CLARITY TO THE SITUATION at hand. I cupped my chin in my palm and stared out the window of the 638. The sky was a sharp blue, which could fool you into thinking it a welcoming day, save the splinters of ice that caught the thin sunlight. Not many people were out yet. A few men trudged by, bent against the cold and their chins and noses tucked into scarves. One threw a yearning glance as he passed, for the saloon had a good fire in the pot belly stove, and my coffee steamed on the table in front of me.

I wondered if he felt like I did; trapped by circumstances, disconsolate, and partially under the weather from whiskey of a secondary grade.

Maybe I was meant to stay here until I fell over dead on a slag heap. Maybe Rose was the best mother for my children. She was no doubt turning them into miniature versions of herself. Which irked and frightened me to no end.

"Hey." Tommy Gee stood next to the table. His coat was a size or two too small which made his arms stick out funny. He pointed at my coffee, which took some effort and a twist of his torso. "You drinking that or you going to let it go cold?"

"How do you do that?"

"Do what?"

"Appear like that."

He stuck out his lower lip then smacked it. "I been standing here twenty minutes."

"No, you haven't."

"Have so." He shivered.

"That the only coat you own?"

"I'm saving for another."

"Well, sit on down."

I passed the mug across to him. He held it close to his mouth so the steam warmed his face before slurping on it and setting it down with a smile and sigh.

"Where're your mother and father?"

His eyes snapped up at me. "That's a stupid question." He took another slurp. "I got Wu Lin. When you got Wu Lin, you don't need anything else."

I refrained from saying the boy needed a larger coat. "Is he going to train you up in the laundry business?"

"How come you're asking so many questions?"

"I'm curious, is all. Seems to me like everyone around here is flotsam and jetsam."

"Which are you?"

"Neither. Maybe both."

"You don't make any sense."

"I make more sense when I've had my coffee, but you've got it."

He leaned over to spy the back of the saloon "Here comes your order."

"I didn't..." But there was a plate of sausages and another plate heaped with scrambled eggs. Two forks were set down and a slip of paper with what I owed for the meal. The bar man waited for me to hand over the money, then ambled back to his domain. "You just go on and eat it."

"Are you sure? There's plenty for both."

"I'm sure," I said.

He shoved a third of the eggs in his mouth and swallowed.

He bit down on a sausage. "I got news."

"Do you?"

"It'll cost a dollar."

"I already gave you plenty."

"Fifty cents," he said.

"No."

"Twenty-five with ten cents interest."

"I spent the last of my money on your breakfast." I pushed the chair back and wound my scarf around my neck. "If you find a shrunken cadaver in one of those washes, it'll be me. And you'll have to live with the guilt of being part and parcel to my starvation."

His chewing slowed then his jaw hung open, a hunk of sausage balanced on his lip. He flipped it back into his mouth and finished it off. "You having a delicate day?"

"A what?"

"Wu Lin says to be careful of them. If a man wants to survive and all."

"No, I am not having a 'delicate day.' You have offended me."

"Lady, that's a sorry attitude."

I lowered my voice. "You'd have this attitude, too, you little flea-bitten rat's ass, if you were stranded here and every week you hear the train whistle its merry way out of here and you're not on it."

He tipped his head one way then the other. "How about some smokes?"

I pulled on my wool shawl and lifted my chin. I would walk right by him. Like buying a horse. My daddy said you have to be prepared to walk away.

So, I did. I took the steps to the door and walked out into the bitter cold. I forced myself forward, the icy air burning the tips of my ears.

Tommy Gee, being himself and somehow able to run at the speed of the wind, rushed by me and then blocked my path forward. "Hey."

"That's a demon thing you just did."

"How 'bout a single smoke?"

"Well, all right, but just because I am impressed with your speed." I dug out my cigar case and shook one into his grubby hands. "Now, tell."

"You hear about China Mary's prize fighting cock?"

"I don't follow the sport and I did not know she owned one."

"You don't know about Aristides? Everybody knows about him. His spurs are the size of a long sword. Why one swipe'll cut open your stomach and set your innards to drip out. Two swipes'll—"

"I get the picture."

"Well..." He cut a glance one way, then the other, then gave a nod that seemed to mean he was satisfied we were not being watched. "There was a new cock last night. Name of Thor. He's a little spotty thing, but fast. Runs a circle around Aristides and wham and *pfft*."

Tommy made the universal gesture for getting one's head cut off.

"One swipe?"

"One swipe."

"Guess you can't mess around with Aristides," I said.

"Nah, lady, you got it all wrong. Thor took him out. *Pfft*. Aristides is in your stewpot right now."

"And?"

"And what?"

"There is a point to this, isn't there?"

"If you give me fifty cents, I'll lay it on Thor tonight for you."

"I don't gamble."

"Suit yourself."

I let out a breath. "I'm going across to my room. Thank you for the cock fighting news of the day."

He didn't let me go more than a step before tugging at my elbow. "You got a new boss, lady."

"What are you talking about?"

"China Mary bet the whole shebang." He did his hip swinging dance and honked a laugh. "The whole damn shebang."

CHAPTER 20

KANSAS
1905
WE ARE BURDICK BOUND—A NEW COMPADRE—SUSPICION ARISES

I grew truly sick and tired of the squiggly creeks. Martha Ruth assured me we'd have to cross Diamond Creek five or six times, which would have been fine and dandy had Theodore not intervened. The mule loved his water. It did not matter how we tried to get him to ford the creek. We pushed, pulled, coerced, and yelled. But each time, he'd amble on down to the bank and take his sweet time drinking. This was followed by a few nibbles of grass, which he followed with a long steaming piss.

The sixth time stretched and snapped my patience. "I am tired of creeks," I said. "I'm tired of crossing creeks, and wading creeks, and drinking and washing in creeks. I'm tired of throwing cars in creeks. I do not wish to see another creek."

But, of course, we did. There was no point to yell about it again.

In between the mule's breaks, we kept along the road. It being night, we passed the time trying to recall lyrics to songs. When those eluded us, we listened to Theodore's breathing and the thump of his hooves on the earth. Mostly, he remained a steadfast beast but went wall-eyed and skittered around every so often. I could not determine what caused the minor panics, but it made me keep my arms tight around Pip's waist.

I rested my head to her back and closed my eyes.

"Don't you fall asleep."

"I'm not falling asleep. I just can't keep my eyes open."

She jabbed her elbow into my ribs.

"What the hell, Pip."

"Stay awake and tell me a story."

"I can't think of any." I sighed and dropped my head to her shoulder blade. "When'd you get so skinny?"

"Tell me about your infamous robbery." She shifted the halter rope from one hand to the other and slapped my thigh. "Come on."

My throat felt thick with words. So thick I thought I'd choke on them. I burrowed my nose into her spine. "You know what happened."

"I know what I read."

"My mother said you shouldn't ever trust a newsman's words. Particularly if they're true." I lifted my head. "Tell me about Minnie DuBois."

Pip let out a long breath and rolled the halter rope around her hand, then unrolled it and let it drop on Theodore's withers. "We were an act."

"So, I gathered."

"And then we weren't."

Theodore slowed and ambled into the trees. Pip and I leaned over so as not to get whipped in the face by branches.

I swung my leg over his haunches and slid to the ground. My muscles felt gelatinous and prickly all at once, so I stomped around to gather back some feeling. "That's it? That's the story? You had an act and it ended. Hoorah. Let's clap for that thrilling dramatization of a dark period in Pip Quinn's speckled past."

"What does it matter?"

"I did not like her and I wish to know if my instincts are correct."

Pip stared down at me. "They're correct."

"How?"

"How what?"

I waved my hands then smacked them to my thighs. "What makes my uncanny sense of character correct? Did she rob you? Steal your limelight? Break your heart? Drag you into some form of indentured servitude?"

"All of that." She jumped down as if she'd popped out of bed and gave a deep swanning bow.

"How old were you?"

"Thirteen. Seventeen when she disappeared and left me to fend."

"That's when Cullen found you?"

"He found me before." She stretched her arms and swung them around. "Dawn's coming."

It surprised me to see the stippled light. "We're nearly to Burdick, then."

She tipped her head. The sun came like cream. She blinked as she looked at it, her mouth pursed in some thought.

"You sure know how to pick 'em, Pip."

"That I do." She gave a nod and turned to look at the mule. I saw the sadness before she hid it. She picked up the rope and headed for the road. "I think I'm going to walk some."

"A stretch of the legs seems just about right." We took to the road. I felt she needed me to hold her hand, so I did. "Look." I lifted our hands and pointed a finger. "A hill."

"That's just a mound."

"My guess is it's got a grand name, like Devil's Rise or Satan's Heights. It might even be on the map."

She kept her eyes on the hillock. "How're the blisters?"

"I don't feel them much. Other things on my mind."

"That's all right, then."

I swayed against her, bumping her arm with mine. "There's a windmill."

She sighed and took a look. "There's a windmill, all right."

"They make me sad."

"Windmills?"

"I don't know why. They have a solitary lonely air to them." The sky stretched from one infinity to another, peaches and pinks with a flush of blue in spots. "It's going to be a pretty day."

"That it is." She didn't let go of my hand. Gave a little shake to it. My guess was she was thinking of past things; Minnie and maybe Cullen and the Paradise fiasco. There was too much to think back on and I did not want Pip sad or the pretty morning ruined.

"Did you get the letters I wrote you?" I asked. "From prison?"

"Where would you have sent them?"

"Why, General Post."

"In Orinda?"

I lifted a shoulder. "It's the only address I had."

"I wasn't there."

"I determined that." With a squint in her direction, I asked, "Did you send that raccoon?"

"Did you like him?"

"He was a good little mouser. Until he grew up. I woke from a dead sleep once to find him mid-air and claws stretched out, coming right for my neck and eyeballs. If it weren't for my cellmate and her blanket, I'd have been a pile of shreds. I guess that was your way of telling me off."

"I thought it appropriate at the time."

Theodore ground his teeth and plodded along, content for now and in love with Pip. He stopped the teeth grinding to tickle her ear with his white muzzle. She rubbed his nose.

Horses and mules were like that with her. One shared look and ooh-la-la.

"You should have been a cowboy, Pip Quinn."

"I should have been a lot of—" She threw off my hand and gripped the pistol in her holster. "Don't turn around."

"Why not?" The question mattered not in the least, because I turned around. Someone followed us. It was hard to see with the sun in our face and the figure a silhouette. But as the stalker neared, I made out a squealy bicycle with handlebars that shook around and a wheel bent out of shape. The rider stuck up a hand and waved.

"Yoohoo!" The wave grew robust and somewhat panicked, on

account of the bike wobbling and the rider needing to maintain ballast. "Yoodeehoo!"

Pip squinted. "What in the hell?"

I shaded my eyes. "It's Martha Ruth."

"Who?"

"Candy Doll. The girl from that devilish hellhound's." I stomped my foot. "I gave her nine dollars to head on home to Watchamacallit."

Martha Ruth stuck her bony elbows out and peddled hard, wheezing as she went by us digging a heel to the dirt to stop. Dust flew up. Theodore sneezed. Pip dropped her hand from her holster. Martha wore that diaphanous nonsense of a gown, but at least she'd covered it with a good yarn sweater and put some sensible shoes on her feet.

She pressed her hands to her thighs and took a few big breaths. Her eyes bobbed back and forth between us. "You two are slow as molasses."

"You neglected to inform us of Theodore's obsession with water." I rubbed the new churned dirt from under my nose.

"You should see him down by the fishpond behind First Baptist Church. That's a sight."

"Be that as it may—"

"You get on out of here." Pip took a threatening step forward, which did not phase Martha Ruth in the least.

Instead, her grin grew, covering half her face. "Is that you being bandit dangerous?"

"What?"

Martha Ruth slung her leg over the bike and hopped about. She shook out one foot then the other. "Fiddly widdles," she said with a nod.

"Is that like pins and needles?" I asked.

She didn't answer. She rested the bike on the side of the road, untied a burlap bag from the handlebars and slung it over her shoulder. "We need to get a move on."

She ground her heel down and marched forward. Theodore abandoned us completely and trotted up to her side. The mule gave Pip a long look of goodbye, then nipped Martha Ruth's shoulder as if the two were at the start of a merry adventurous jaunt.

"Wait a damn minute." Pip set her hands to her hips.

"You need to come along."

"No, I am not coming along with you."

"Suit yourself." Martha Ruth gave a small skip. "It's your funeral."

Pip bit down on her lip and frowned. "Go grab that bike." She took off at a lope, leaving me, per usual, with the detritus.

I had tried many daring things in my life, but a bicycle had not been one of them. I pushed it forward by the handlebars, coming close to tripping when the bent front rim twisted around. I did, finally, manhandle it into submission and soon gained ground.

Pip was swearing a blue streak when I came abreast of them.

Martha Ruth nodded her head and every few curses mumbled how much she agreed.

"Can someone tell me what is going on?" I asked.

"Well, it's like this." Martha Ruth turned her palm to us and pointed at the fat of her palm. "This is where you just come from."

"Yeah?"

She pointed to one of the lines. "And this is our getaway route. As you can see, Burdick proper is up at the tip of my pinky."

"So."

"But along this ridge—" Pip and I leaned in close. "That's a straight road—well, not right there, that's just a callous so ignore that. That goes straight through and right here at my second knuckle is Tuckers Farm. The sheriff's going to ambush you. You don't want to meet that sheriff, but he's going to be there, all right."

"Was that the sheriff Timbo talked about?" I asked Pip. "Did something to the bartender?"

"We don't talk about that incident," Martha whispered.

Pip narrowed her eyes. "How do you know all this?"

"It's my job to answer the phone. Which I did. I explained to Minnie that it was Timbo looking for you, and I told her to tell him and Artie you had escaped and were heading south to Abilene. He asked why and I said Ruby Calhoun told me to tell him that and so I did."

"I see." Pip's scar stood out white as chalk.

"Then Minnie said he said *I'd* get a cut in the reward were I to share the direction you were truly going."

"So, you did."

Martha Ruth threw Pip a look. "No, ma'am I certainly did not. No. I said, 'I got nine dollars given to me by my friend Ruby Calhoun herself to escape this life and my mouth is buttoned in loyalty to her.'"

My heart warmed at the sentiment. "Thank you, Martha."

Pip smacked my arm and glared at Martha Ruth. "Then you tell me how a sheriff is going to ambush us halfway to Burdick?"

"I didn't say one word. That's the bandit's creed. But you two are on the front page of the *Emporia Tribune*." She squinted at me. "Do you really have a fiancé named Olaf? Because he's desperate to find you."

A sharp pang caught me out. "Oh. Olaf. Him." The pang turned to a mash of guilt, for I had not thought of him at all these past days.

"Mostly, though, you're wanted for attempted murder. In multiple counties. For multiple people."

Pip grimaced and walked a big circle. I kept my eye on her hand, wary she might tug out the gun and use her single bullet. She kicked at the bike. "So, you chose to come warn us. On a busted bike."

Martha Ruth lifted her shoulders to her ears. "I did. It's much faster travel when you keep to the roads."

"Well." I didn't have much else to say. Here we were nearly to Burdick and all such plans to find out if Verna was dead or alive had been kiboshed. "I suppose we need to hang up our plans, Pip. We could have a fake funeral here, in case Verna's dead. You still got that one Bible, don't you?"

Pip patted her chest pocket before yanking it out and slamming it to the ground.

Martha Ruth rushed over and picked it up. "You should never do that with the Good Book. Especially one like this. This is a fine red leather—"

"That's an Italian Morocco Levantine."

She looked at me. "That so?"

"It is so." I took it from her, wiped the cover and handed it to Pip.

Pip stared at it. "This will not help us."

"There's always something in it that can help," Martha Ruth said.

"You're going to get us to Burdick," Pip said. "Or I will kill you. Do you understand?"

Martha Ruth let out a high laugh.

"It's not funny," I said.

Her eyes fluttered in doubt. "Burdick." She held her meager pack of goods to her chest and swiveled around to take in the stretch of road and the fields. "That hill back there's got a name," she said. "I don't remember what it is, though." With a heavy shrug, she stomped through the sedge along the roadside and headed for the trees. "Come on."

Theodore gave a side eye; there may have been trees, but there sure as hell wasn't a river to lure him.

Martha Ruth let out a sharp whistle and Theodore took off at a trot.

"Huh," Pip said. "I could never get Big Henry to—"

"Whistle was meant for you, too." The girl and the mule disappeared in the brush.

"I guess we have to trust her, Pip."

"You gave her nine dollars of our money?"

"Well, yeah. I couldn't leave her—"

"All right then."

"She reminded me of Darby."

The next whistle was louder.

Pip shoved the Bible back and gave out a sigh. "Here goes nothing."

I tried to wrestle the bike through the high grass, but soon gave up. It wasn't as though we could all ride it, and, in its state, it wasn't much of a get-away vehicle. So, I ripped out some long grasses and covered it.

Another whistle came. This one from Pip. She waited for me and held back a few branches, polite as if she were holding a door. "You got a good heart," she said.

We were through into a dry wash. I took a little tumbling step as I realized we had put our lives in the hands of Martha Ruth, and I wondered if we should have taken a chance on the road instead.

Martha Ruth scrambled forward, as if she knew this place, and so I scrambled forward, too.

As we followed Martha Ruth, a weight cloaked me, such as a wet wool blanket would. It grew heavy and cold, and I shivered. Pip frowned and touched my forehead, but I batted her away.

"What's wrong with you?" she asked.

"Besides we're following a half-dressed painted lady and a mule with gas?"

"Yeah. Beyond that."

"What happens when we get there? To Burdick. To Verna."

"I'd like a long bath, personally. Well, after we find out if she's still breathing." Pip sniffed and we continued walking and watching Martha Ruth coo in Theodore's ear.

"And after that?"

"We go on to Hutchinson. We do what we planned."

"But what if this is the plan?" Various sprigs of thoughts grew quickly in my mind and I didn't like them one bit. "What if it was a plant? Verna's address. That Bible man. What if the cards we got were only meant to lure us to Burdick because we're kind people and it's the Christian thing to determine if one's friend is in good health or otherwise. Then we're right smack where he wants us. All together."

Pip gave a nod and hopped from one river rock to another.

I grabbed the sleeve of her coat to hold her back and lowered my voice. "What if Martha Ruth is part of the plan?"

"What are the odds he would know that girl? They got to be a million to one."

"Did he know Minnie?"

Pip froze, one foot on a rock and the other midair. "I don't want to talk about that."

"If you two don't mind," Martha Ruth called back, "I'd appreciate not being discussed without being a part of the conversation."

"Martha Ruth," I called back, "are you part of the plan to kill us all?"

"No, ma'am, I am not. Though I am very good with a gun should you need help at some point. When my brother Georgie blinded himself with a fishhook, it became my responsibility to shovel up supper. There ain't a squirrel going to beat my aim."

"Is that so?"

"You should all think on that as you consider inviting me into your bandit gang."

Pip squinted hard at her, like she was considering something, and not sharing it as was her absolutely annoying way. She trotted beside Martha Ruth and we continued along.

My back tingled, my guard being on alert. I checked over my shoulder every third step, in fear Cullen was stalking us beyond the tree line. I spied only a couple of frogs sitting on a flat rock, and a woodpecker who stopped to watch us pass before hammering away.

Theodore squirmed and shuffled around when a strong wind gusted itself down the creek bed and whipped up the dry silt. He curled his lips back, laid his ears flat and stared through the leaves.

"Storm's coming." Pip laid her arm on the mule's withers and bumped her hip to his ribs. That seemed to calm him.

I took off my jacket and tied it around my waist. The next gust came hot and damp. I rolled my sleeves.

A crack sounded behind me. I dropped to my knees and wrapped my hands to the back of my head. "It's him, isn't it?"

I stared forward. Not back. I didn't want to see that was there.

"Who's out there?" Pip had her Colt drawn.

Martha Ruth quivered in a tiny ball with her hands over her head.

Another crack. A small rock ricocheted off a trunk and tumbled down the bank.

Pip's eyes raked both banks of trees. A huge bird burst from the limbs and arced low, grazing the top of Pip's head before giving one huge flap and swooping high in the sky.

She shoved the gun in the holster. "You two get your quaking asses up and get moving."

Martha Ruth wiped off the knees of her dress and stood. "You are a bossy thing. I thought Minnie was, but you—"

"I have one bullet in this gun. And if I find out you set us up in any way, it's going to be aimed at you."

Martha Ruth flushed and hopped from foot to foot. "All right, then."

"Okay."

"You're very fierce when you're angry. I can see why Minnie—"

"I am not talking about Minnie. We are not talking about Minnie. Ever ever again. Jesus and Mary." Pip took Theodore's lead and stomped forward.

Martha Ruth gave a long yearning sigh. She glanced at me and dropped her shoulders. "Guess we need to follow."

"I suppose we should." It took all my control to not roll my eyes heavenwards.

"I heard she was a trick rider, too. So many talents."

"Ah, just go on."

I supposed the only good in the situation was that Martha Ruth would do anything Pip asked her, which made her accompaniment marginally safer.

But there was something that kept my spine ticklish. Perhaps it was the prospect of seeing Verna again after all these years or seeing her in such a precarious situation. Perhaps it was what happened after we saw Verna; when the rest of the road led to Cullen. I worried we would not beat him to the draw. I worried we would.

Not to mention the new wrinkly nightmare of the law bearing down.

A big part of me wanted to turn around, grab the bicycle and ride as fast as I could away from the whole of it.

But that would leave Pip to face Cullen alone. Or maybe not. She had a little lovesick puppy following her tracks.

"Hey." I loped up to Martha Ruth. "Did you know that I was nearly in Buffalo Bill's Wild West Show?"

She gave shrug. "Nearly ain't the same as in it."

"And there's an article written all about my stage robbery. I need to tell you about my stage robbery."

"I read about it."

Pip looked over her shoulder. "I was always the top bill, wasn't I, Ruby? Guess that hasn't changed."

"If it makes you feel good to think so, Pip Quinn, you go on with that delusion."

"Jealousy doesn't become you, Ruby."

Theodore swished his tail in a circle and gave a look that agreed. I did not as I am not the jealous type. I was, however, of the opinion that my escapades with the law exceeded Pip's and that Martha Ruth had chosen the wrong bandit upon which to have a crush.

CHAPTER 21

ORINDA
1898
WE HAVE A NEW OWNER

If there's one thing that runs around a house of ill-repute faster than the clap, it's a good bit of gossip—especially as it's gossip that affected each woman personally. No sooner had my foot touched the upstairs landing, but Verna peered out from her room and waved me over.

"You hear?" she asked.

"Sure, I heard. How'd you hear?"

"Tommy. You give him a nickel, he'll tell you anything."

"That boy's a born con artist."

"Never mind that. Get on in."

I sidled through the space she made, pushing aside the giant fronds she kept as ambiance, and found Maggie and Darby sitting on the edge of the mattress.

"Cullen Wilder won the business," Maggie said.

"Cullen?" My throat closed up.

Darby mewled.

Maggie patted her back.

"With that rooster of his." Verna held out a bottle. "From Tommy Gee's description of Aristides, I'd be curious to see the size of Thor."

Maggie took the bottle, poured it, and handed us each a thimble of whiskey.

"What about China Mary?" I asked.

Verna set the bottle on the window ledge. "Going to Sacramento."

"California?"

"She has family there."

"China Mary has family?" I hadn't thought of her as having kin; or if she did, I figured she ate them one by one.

"We need to be calm," Verna said. But she picked and pulled apart the knots on a curtain tassel and, when that was complete, moved on to the next one.

"Are we losing our jobs?" Maggie bolted from the bed and paced to the door and back. "I don't have anything else but this."

"Maybe he'll pay better," Darby said. She dragged her upper lip on her teeth. "He's always giving extra to Pip, isn't he?"

"He doesn't give her stink," Verna said. "Just a couple extra dollars to board her horse and a bruise or two for good measure. And I've seen how he looks at you."

Maggie stopped mid step. "I make sure—"

"I'm telling it how I see it."

"I know how he looks at me." Darby's skin was grey as old dishwater.

"How's he going to be a madam?" I asked.

Verna took the bottle and refilled the glasses. "Ashes to ashes." We drank again.

"We'd best get Pip." I strode from the room and knocked my fist to Pip's door. It swung partway open.

Cullen Wilder stared down at me, arms crossed, eyes at half-mast, stubble already darkening his jaw. His cheeks crinkled as he smiled. "Looks like I'm in charge." He made a quick move like he was going to backhand me.

"I'm not scared of you." I swallowed and thought how I damn well was.

"Maybe you should be. All of you running around doing whatever you want."

"Leave her alone, Cullen."

I stood on tiptoes to look for Pip, but he kept his shoulders to the space so all I could see was his satin vest and the gold pin in his lapel. "Meeting in ten minutes in the dining room."

⚜

THE DINING TABLE WAS TOO SMALL FOR OUR ASSORTED GROUP. Cullen took two seats: one for his boots and the other for his bum. He kept his eyes on the task of cutting his cigar tip to the exact right place.

Pip sat next to him, though not by her own volition. He'd pointed and she'd sat. As the conversation progressed, her arms crossed tighter and tighter to her chest and her glare at Cullen would boil iron.

China Mary sat at the head, as she always did. She eked out a miserable smile and tapped her very large emerald-colored ring to the wood. Three taps and then a single.

It was one of the codes. *Bastard.*

Darby and Maggie and Verna and I were left to squeeze along a bench.

Cullen lit his cigar and worked at puffing a couple smoke circles. They weren't much of anything, so he gave up and took to staring at each one of us in turn. You could see clear on his face what he thought of each of us, even though he tried to mask it in a smile. Maggie meant nothing to him. Verna annoyed him. Darby would need to watch her back. Pip was a second thought. China Mary was the vanquished. And I was nothing much but the size of an ant upon a sidewalk.

"No more shows," he said.

"No more shows?" Verna waved her arms up. "As in, not even one song and dance?"

"No more dance floor?" Maggie asked.

The liquor in my stomach took a flop and turn. No more job for Ruby.

I cut a glance to Pip, but she turned her head away to stare at the whitewashed walls and fiddled with her cheap cut glass ring.

"I don't believe in charity, ladies. And, respectfully to the madam here, you've been running one." He dropped his boots to the floor and leaned his elbows on the table. "We're going to take out the stage. Expand the tables throughout. Blackjack. Faro, of course. Wheels of fortune. That's where the money's won."

"What about us?" Maggie asked.

"Do your job. Butter up the men, give them a tip or two on how to play their hand. Then take them upstairs when they lose. Which they all will, in the end."

Verna leaned back. "Half our income comes from that dance hall."

"You're just going to have to work harder on your back, aren't you?" He stood up. "Friday's the final show. Let's make it China Mary's farewell. Ruby's, too, unless—" He raised his eyebrow.

"I got plenty of places I can find work."

"Pip's the new manager. You answer to her. She answers to me. Simple."

We sat around in silence, except for China Mary tapping that ring. Her face grew all manner of reds and purples.

I stared at Pip. "What the hell—"

"You have something to say, Ruby?" Cullen asked.

Verna hit my thigh with her fist.

"No."

"Then we're all agreed. Miss Mary, shall we go look over the books?" He stuck out his elbow for her, but she didn't take it. Instead, she huffed past him and out to the hall. "Some people are such bad losers."

He strolled out as if he'd been enjoying a light repast with friends rather than upending everyone's lives.

Once the door closed, our attention snapped to Pip. I thought she might be uncomfortable with her sudden improvement in station, maybe look downcast or show some humility. But she didn't.

"I didn't know any sooner than you did," she said.

"Well," Verna drawled, "It wasn't like this was unexpected. Aristides was what—ten or twelve. He's going to make a stringy meal."

"This is what you think about, Verna? Our supper's going to be a disappointment?" I asked. "How about the fact I am about to be a street urchin?"

"You're the one won't expand your job responsibilities."

"Pfft."

Verna's eyebrow rose. "I'm just saying."

"Whose side are you going to be on, Pip?" Maggie's question shut us up.

Pip gave her a blank stare. Smiled without showing her teeth. "You know I'm on your side."

"I don't understand." Darby stared at Pip, big eyes like a lost fawn.

Verna blew out a breath and shrunk down a bit in her seat. And me? Well, hell, who cared what I thought at that point? I would, within a space of days, find my ass in the yard with Wu Lin's chicken.

The thought came that I should find Joe and rescind my rejection of his proposal. But I knew if I did, his trust in my affection would forever be tarnished. I may not have loved him, but I did think well enough of him not to be so cruel.

I felt quite virtuous and self-sacrificing after thinking those thoughts, so I dipped my head and whispered, "No matter the pain and loss, I will live, so please don't worry about me or my future."

Verna rolled her eyes and made a noise.

I reached for Darby's hand, stroking the top of it. "You may have my room. It's got a good breeze. And Pip—" I threw out a silent prayer. "—she'll watch over you. And not steal most your wages such as China Mary did. She'll let me join you all for supper every so often, at least until I can get on my feet and move them towards—"

"Towards what," Verna interrupted. "The Jordan river?"

"Towards Missouri. Towards my home and kids."

"You have kids?" Darby asked.

"Why, I surely do."

"Oh. I'd like to have a kid."

"You're just a kid yourself."

"I'm fourteen. My mama had me at the same age, and Wyatt the year after. He died, though. Maggie's sure my dad done something to him and mama. But Maggie's always thinking wrong of people, isn't she?"

I had never heard Darby string so many words together. I thought her to have the personality of the wallpaper, but she had a tragic life and retained some sweetness. It gave me a rush of sentiment that I might miss her when I was booted out.

"The funny thing is, I still want to go home." Darby looked around at us. "Isn't that a funny thing?"

A horrific shriek came from the hallway, followed by a string of expletives mixed with Chinese and a smattering of Spanish and ending in China Mary slamming back into the dining room and then slamming out the back door.

"What was that for?" I asked.

"Maybe," Verna said, "she just found out the contents of the stew."

CHAPTER 22

KANSAS
1905
WE ARE NEARLY CAUGHT—WE REACH BURDICK AND MEET AN OLD MAN AND A DOG

O ur creek bed petered out, forcing us to lay low and determine what our next option was in continuing to Burdick. The clouds had turned a funny greenish gray, leaving us to look as if we'd just got off our deathbeds. Martha Ruth looked and said "Uh-oh" but didn't follow up with why.

Not that explaining was necessary: the whole of the sky opened at once, dropping hail the size of baseballs. Theodore tore off back down the way we'd come while the three of us clambered under the cotton-woods and hugged ourselves round the trunks. Limbs groaned and cracked. One swung so close the leaves brushed my back. I pulled it over us in the hope it might soften the blows of the hail.

"Ow!" Martha Ruth clutched the back of her head.

I cringed but did not admit to having knocked her with the branch as I maneuvered it.

Pip tucked herself under her coat like a turtle. "I swear if my cigar is ruined..." but I didn't hear the rest as she pulled herself tighter.

The hail diminished and after a dash of sunshine, the wind whipped up and another load of hail, this the size of bullets, came at a ninety-degree angle. I felt like one of the Egyptians forced to endure the wrath of the Lord.

"You thinking of Moses, too?" Martha Ruth yelled.

It was over as abruptly as it had begun. No wind, no hail. Just the leftovers slipping from the trees and the dry creek filled with ice.

I pushed aside the branch and stood. Pip rose, her jacket soaked through. Martha Ruth's gown clung to her legs and the arms of her sweater hung over her hands. She gave a whistle for the mule.

Pip strode by us, dropping the holster and shedding her clothes as she went, until she was her in all her grandeur. She crouched on the ice, scooped it in her arms and rubbed her face and chest with it. Steam rose from her skin, making her look like a river fairy released from a spell. Then, she flopped on her back and made a snow angel.

"You going to stand over there and steam yourselves dead like an oyster?"

❦

COOLED OFF AND CLEAN, WE AGREED A NAP WAS ESSENTIAL. WE TIED Theodore down under the trees, hung our clothes on some limbs and laid out in the shade in our altogethers. I took the crowbar from the satchel, set it to my side, then plumped the leather bag into a pillow. Pip stretched out, crossing her legs and resting her head on an arm. She chewed on the bit of cigar she had left and absent-mindedly rubbed her scar.

Martha Ruth's shift had dried quick as a snap and she spread it out like a blanket. She lay on her belly between us, cheek resting on her hand. "How'd you get that?"

Pip opened one eye—the green one—and closed it. She moved the cigar from one side of her mouth to the other. "I lost something."

"It wasn't your fault," I said.

Martha Ruth swiveled her head to consider me. "What was it?"

"Money. A big pile of money." Pip took the stub of cigar from her mouth and chucked it into the bushes. "Now be quiet because I want to sleep. We'll start again at dusk."

Martha toed Pip's leg. "How much money?"

"Enough." Pip closed her eyes and blew out a long breath. "Enough."

The girl turned to me. "Where is it now? All the loot?"

"How many penny westerns have you read?" I asked.

"*Deadwood Dick*, of course. Kit Carson's adventures weren't as thrilling, but they were authentic."

"So, the book cover said."

"It most certainly did." She sat up. "So, where's the loot?"

"That," I said, "is the age-old question." I grabbed the satchel and got up. "Never mind all of it. Just never mind."

"Where you going?" Pip asked.

"Over that way."

Pip grabbed my ankle. "Don't you leave me again."

"I'm not leaving. I want a bit of alone time, is that too much to ask? Gather my thoughts and such. Let go of my ankle you jack daw, horse rump, son-of-a—"

She freed me. I kicked at the dirt and stomped and stumbled over the slick river rocks to the other bank. A small sip of Doctor Kate's medicinal called to me, so I dug around in the satchel looking for it. I came up empty-handed. I kicked at the side of the bank.

Down under the shade, Martha Ruth fanned herself with Pip's hat and obsequiously did the same for Pip. Who stretched out with her hands to her chest and a Pharoah's smile on her lips.

"You don't even need me," I muttered. I pulled on my togs, then, with a small wincing squeak at the state of my blisters, tied up my boots. "Drag me all the way across the flats of Kansas on some death mission, and—you can have her!" I called out as I scrambled up the slope. "You two go on with your little love nest, but Martha Ruth? You should know Pip snores. You'll lose half your young life trying to get to sleep with the saw of it."

I stepped out to a field of tall grass that went on to a horizon dotted with barn and water tank and a couple wagons moving along and men milling about. They carried long implements, which had a fifty percent chance of being rake or hoe, and another sixty percent chance they all held shotguns.

🐚🐚

"HOLY HELL." PIP PEERED OVER THE GRASS THEN FLATTENED TO HER belly. I lay beside her, and Martha Ruth next to me.

"How many?" I asked.

"Four or five," she said.

Martha Ruth scooted in closer. "Can I have that Bible? This seems a time for prayer."

"Really?" Pip sneered.

"Well, if you're not offering, I can recite the Book of Job from my memory. My aunt Dora Lee taught Sunday school. She was a stickler for memorization. Do you know what my favorite quote is?"

A dog yipped in the distance. Another followed with a long howl.

I popped my head up in the direction I feared the sound had come from. "Dogs, Pip."

"Yeah. I heard."

Pip worried her lip against her teeth. "Martha Ruth—"

"Yes, ma'am."

"Show me that map again."

Martha flipped over her hand. "We're right here." She pinched the skin at the base of her pinky.

"And they're at the next joint."

Every part of me shook. "I don't want to go back to prison, Pip. I can't stand the food, I am telling you, there's maggots and fruit flies and—"

"Shh." She shaded her eyes, peered out another second and hunched back down. She studied Martha Ruth. "Can I trust you?"

"Of course, you can."

"Then here's the plan. You're going to get on Theodore. Make a big old stink and head due east as fast as that mule will go. You get the dogs on your tail."

Martha crouched, ready to sprint to the tree line. "When do I stop?"

"When you've lost them," Pip said. "Now go on before they let go of the dogs."

"Can I have a nickname? For my entry into your gang?"

Pip made a motion for her to move on.

"I mean, I may never see you again. A name would be a re-memory."

"Arkansas Spitfire," I offered.

"That's a very good name, though I wonder if something like Stone-heart Ruth—"

"Yes. That is a perfect name." I shooed her. "You are herewith a member of the Calhoun Gang."

"All right then." She flew off like a shot.

Pip and I stared at the trees. I crossed my fingers Martha Ruth's sense of direction was as accurate in real life as it was tracing the callouses and lines on her palm. I grabbed at Pip's hand and found her fingers crossed, too.

We waited an interminably long time. I swatted a fly that pestered around my nose. "Maybe Theodore got loose."

"Maybe you're right and she did set us up."

"You think they'll let us share a cell?"

Pip glared at me.

"Just thinking ahead, should your best laid plans—"

A terrible screech stopped my heart. Theodore bounded through the brush and straight out to the middle of the field. "Come and get me, you low life coppers." She gave another screech, and clung tight to Theodore as he galloped flat out.

Due east.

The men turned the wagons around. One of the men climbed on his horse and took chase. The dogs' barking grew wild. We remained prone, listening until all the hubbub faded away.

"What do you know?" I stood and shook out the foot that had fallen asleep.

"The Calhoun Gang?"

"Does it matter?" I asked.

Pip picked up her hat and slung it on. "Since I made a fairly brilliant plan."

"I wouldn't go that far."

"They're following her, aren't they?"

"What'll become of her?"

She shrugged.

"That's it? They all whispered about that sheriff, Pip. I'm feared for her."

"She's not like Darby. Not one bit. She'll be all right."

Martha Ruth had sacrificed herself for us. She wasn't as stone hearted as she wished to be named. She was brave hearted in my book, and I gave a salute to her valor.

Pip walked on, skirting the edge of the field to keep from leaving a long track of broken stalks.

"I believe she will be." I scurried to catch up.

We had Verna to find.

WITH THEODORE'S WATER OBSESSION NO LONGER SLOWING US down, Pip and I made good tracks into Burdick. We stayed along the edge of the main road, ready to lay down flat in the ditch should we spy anyone coming in either direction. Pip strode along in front of me, her shoulders forward and her attention on the scuff of her boots against the road.

Or maybe she wanted to be alone with the same thoughts that pummeled around my own skull. Each step closer to Verna brought us closer to our old lives. This made my stomach churn up a storm. For Verna was not the end of the road, but merely a waylay in the journey.

If we were lucky, she'd be alive and kicking. If we were luckier, she'd say she sent the death cards for a laugh, knowing it'd spur us to visit. Maybe she'd have rhubarb pie and a good bottle or two of whiskey so we could get a full belly and drunk enough to forget to talk about Orinda at all.

My optimism lasted until we hit the boundary of Burdick proper. A few rough and tumble wood buildings sagged along the packed dirt road, a couple of them shaded with gnarled old sycamores and the others stripped of most their paint from the relentless weather. Three chickens scrabbled about behind a picket fence. A house was half hidden behind rusted farm equipment. A buggy top sat in the shadow along the side, with two butter churns and a step ladder piled in its middle.

Pip put her hands on her hips and peered at the porch. A muffled thump-thump echoed, then an old coon dog ambled to the steps, stuck its nose to the air, and let out a wheezy bay.

The screen door opened. Pip clamped my shoulder and shoved us down along the fence.

"Who's out there?" A man's voice rasped. A strange wood clicking came. "I see you all. I got a gun and I see you."

I took a chance and glanced between the pickets. An old man in brown coveralls stared in the other direction from us. He held the railing post with one hand and kept the other on his dog's rope collar. The man worked his jaw and the clicking started again. Dentures.

The dog let out another wheezer and gave up midway, dropping down on all fours with his head and front paws hanging over the step.

"You stay off my property. It's my property proper and I'll shoot without remiss if you trespass it." He spit and clacked once more before disappearing inside.

Pip motioned me up and pointed to the ancient barn in the back-yard. We tread as light as possible among the junk and slipped inside. A couple barn birds flapped near a roof that was more beams and sky than boards. A buckboard wagon sat on bricks in the far corner, blocking empty stalls. Another corner was piled high with dusty bottles.

Pip spotted an overturned bench, set it upright and plopped down, stretching her legs out before her.

I peered out at the yard, making sure the dog didn't decide of a sudden it could see, hear, and smell. But all was quiet, so I turned back to Pip. "Well, we're here."

"Close, anyway."

"We'll go once it's dark."

"Yeah." She took in a breath and let it out on a long sigh. "Maybe Verna's got a map so we can get to Hutchinson a little quicker."

"About that..."

She cocked an eyebrow. "About what?"

"What happens after?"

"Why do you keep harping about this? You're like a cur with a bone." She ground her teeth and seemed to contemplate it. "We find him. That'll be enough."

"That day it'll be enough, but what about the next? And the week after that. The month after? Think about that. You won't have to worry you'll be dead before dawn, that's true, but now there's the law—"

"That's a wrinkle, all right." She pulled in a breath, let it out.

"I'd consider it more than a wrinkle."

"You talk too much, you know that?" The sun had dipped enough she was nothing but a shadow, arms crossed tight to her chest, one boot heel tapping the floorboard. "Too damn much."

"Okay, then, I won't say another word."

"That would be nice."

"My lips are sealed."

"Good."

We sat in our individual huffs. She bit at her nail and I listened to her do it. It took the fullness of my strength to keep my mouth shut, rather than warn her that constant chewing led to permanently marred cuticles.

A strange odor came from the direction of the hovel.

"What's he cooking?" I could not help myself. The curiosity was too much.

The smoke carried an amalgam of smells, none of which brought steak or pork chops to mind.

"Possum?"

"Hm." I sniffed. "Gamey enough."

"Pronghorn?"

"Is that what they smell like?"

"Never had one to know."

"Squirrel."

"Nope."

"Prairie dog?"

"Could be," she said. "Wouldn't put it past..."

A wraithlike figure snuck into the gloom. I bolted up and crashed into the wall.

A light bobbed about in the yard, illuminating the coon dog, who stood wide-stanced and panting at the entrance. The lamp came closer. It was bright. Bright enough to catch the glint of the shotgun the man aimed right at us.

"I don't want any trouble." He swung the barrel this way and that. "But I made up some extra vittles if you're in need. I'll set it on the back porch."

The dog snuffled the floor, turned tail, and followed him back through the yard.

My stomach did a flop, as I was both hungry and entirely unsure as to the ingredients in the proffered vittles.

"What do you think?" Pip asked.

"It's possible he poisoned it. We may be two in a line of travelers. There could be skeletons right underneath these boards."

"Or it's just stew."

"For someone so distrustful, that answer surprises me."

A SMALL OIL LAMP ILLUMINATED THE BACK PORCH. TWO TIN PLATES sat on the bottom step, both topped with a mound of hash and a slice of bread. I stared at the closed kitchen door. The light was on in there, and I heard him shuffling around, opening drawers and such. The light went off, and there wasn't any sound coming from this part of the cottage.

Pip stuck a finger in the goo and licked it. "I've got no idea."

That didn't stop her from rounding up a scoop on the bread and taking a big bite.

I tore off a corner and dipped in, finding the mixture to be pleasurably tangy. I couldn't determine the foundational meat, but I realized that when you're on the road and in hiding, you can't be picky about ingredients.

It hit the spot just right and gave me a jolt of energy. "Let's at it, then."

Pip reached to the screen and gave two raps. "Mister, we're looking for the Rolfe place."

"What the hell, Pip?"

The door creaked open an inch. "You one of them two girls?"

"Yes, I am."

He clicked and clacked, then said, "Sheriff's going to hang you if he catches you. He don't wait for courtrooms and judges."

"We didn't do anything," I said.

"That don't matter at all. Not to John Ward. He's not got the devil, he is the devil."

"Please don't turn us in." I wiped the sweat that had come of a sudden on my brow and neck. "We're bone tired and thankful for the meal and—"

He waved a hand to get me to stop talking. "Take a turn at Wilner's granary. Rolfe's is out a mile past."

Pip stepped back. "Thank you. I—"

"I hate Ward. Took my girl, took my land, took my health." He pushed open the screen and picked up the plates. Smiled his wooden whites. "Possum hash. Can't beat it."

CHAPTER 23

ORINDA
1898
CHINA MARY DEPARTS—A GRACIOUS GIFT—AN INGLORIOUS
SURPRISE

China Mary refused to stay one more night in the house. She barked out orders to Tommy Gee who had been tasked with moving her things from her room. She didn't like how he stacked the crates of clothes and fineries in the hall and chucked a candlestick at him. He ducked, because he's a fast fella, and the brass stick thumped against the wall. If I'd been one step lower on the stairs it would have taken off my leg and I said so, scooping up the offending weapon and continuing down.

"Sorry about that," Tommy said.

"You're not the one who should apologize."

The front door was propped open. Outside, two men I did not recognize lugged a large wooden crate from a wagon and carted it next door to the barroom proper. They came back for another, heavy enough they rolled it in on a dolly.

I scraped my teeth together and turned away from that dismal impending doom of a reality. "What time is it?"

China Mary yanked her velvet dressing gown tight around her middle, pushed past Tommy, and yanked the candlestick from my grip. "Don't take my things."

I did not answer; I could not answer. There was no answer. Not with the wonder of China Mary's bald head sans her intricate wig. I assumed she had hair under the thing—it was a madam's wont to change her wig styles and colors every other night, but in general, the wiggery was for effect, not subterfuge.

Tommy plucked the candlestick from her and wiggled it into the corner of a travel trunk stuffed with frills and what-nots. He slammed the lid and buckled it up. "All ready."

He ducked again, but she ignored him and shuffled on back to her empty room.

"It's a new world coming, Tommy," I said.

"You don't know nothing." He swiped at his eye then kicked the trunk.

"I know you're going to miss her. I don't know why, though." I raised my voice enough it'd travel through the door. "She's a mean old skin flint and she better be paying you ten dollars for all the times she stiffed you on the water delivery."

"I second that," he said.

Once her belongings were loaded, we stood outside and waved her off with "Good lucks" and "Good riddances." She did not respond, but stuffed her hat low on her head, took a sip from a small bottle of paregoric, and kept her determined gaze forward. The wagon stopped two blocks down, allowing China Mary to alight in front of the Eagle Hotel, at which she had a reservation for two nights, and would then take her official leave on the weekly morning train.

"That's that." Pip clapped her hands. She blinked and stared at us then strode back inside. By habit she started up the stairs but made a quick U-turn and sashayed back down. "I guess this is my room, now. And—" She reached in her skirt pocket, unfolded a piece of paper, and squinted at it. "I will need an accounting of each of your belongings.

This includes items such as soaps, perfumes, and ladies' essentials, so as we start on the right track for wages and such."

"China Mary should have left the ledger," Verna said.

"No, I..." Pip made a half-hearted point at China Mary's door.

"Why are you pointing at the door?" Verna asked.

"Because."

"We'll go with you and help you find it."

"No, you won't. Go do what I said. Or you won't get paid, how's that?" She screwed up her mouth like a small-time potentate.

Verna pushed past Darby. "Ladies, shall we find the ledger so we can get paid today?"

"You're not allowed in there. That's my place now."

⚭

THE INVENTORY RECKONING BECAME A HARANGUE BY CULLEN IN the misuse of products and the subsequent increase in our debt to the Paradise. A closet soon sported a lock, and that lock could only be turned by Pip and only after we'd sent a note in writing (slipped under her grand pasha door) as to the items we required.

Working hours increased, the parlor opened from nine a.m. sharp to whenever the last damn man wanted to leave.

Wu Lin's laundry services were curtailed to every other week. A plain oil cloth was given to each girl to save the ends of their beds from the scrapes of boots.

All the while, I watched from the stage as the dancehall transformed, with no room left for an audience to sit let alone take a turn or two around the room with a girl. Instead, men hunched over poker and faro tables, yelled at the craps tables, and drank far too many two-for-one drinks that Cullen so generously offered so as to loosen wallets.

⚭

IT WAS MY LAST MEAL AND THE LAST ACT. THE HOORAH TO END hoorahs. We sat and toasted the demise of Wu Lin's chicken. Wu Lin joined us for the early luncheon and didn't seem upset about the matter. He gnawed the last bit of meat from one of the wings and gave a nod of approval at the taste. Tommy Gee stuck five small potatoes in his pockets and no one called him out about it.

I sat between Maggie and Darby, though I think that irked them no end. Pip, being too good for us now, had taken Cullen's arm and pranced across to McQueen's for a fancier feast of steak and potatoes.

My stomach churned. I had no appetite at all, what with counting the hours until my welcome at the Paradise had run its course.

"You could rob the train," Tommy said.

"That's a helpful, though illegal, suggestion." I pushed a wad of boiled kale around my plate.

Verna popped a piece of chicken in her mouth and watched me. "Maybe you should have told Joe yes."

"That would be bigamy."

"Who would know? What judge here is ever going to find out about what a judge in...where'd you marry the Damn Bastard?"

"Independence. On a steamboat. I think the man was a judge." I shook my head. "Frank said he was."

"There you go, then. I would consider that marriage license null and void."

"But that makes Emma and John bastards."

"So?"

"Verna. Be serious. That sort of thing is a brand on the forehead. They won't be recognized by any polite society and how will John make his way in the world with that albatross tied to his ankle?"

"How much money do you need?" Darby set her fork and knife down. "To get home."

"A lot. I've got to get all the way back to Missouri. That's multiple trains at minimum. It'll take months to get the funds."

She reached into a small pocket on her skirt and took out a fifty-cent piece. "You start with this."

"Where'd you get that?" Maggie's voice was low.

"Never mind."

Tommy pointed with a chicken wing. "Mr. Wilder gives those out."

"Doesn't matter where it comes from." She pressed it into my hand. "If you go, it gives me hopes that I can go, too."

Maggie glowered and remained a lump of indignation, then out of the blue stood up. She dug a coin from the top of her bodice and slapped it down. "Goodbye and good luck."

Tommy added a quarter dollar and Wu Lin pushed three nickels across the table.

Verna plopped a two-dollar bill on top.

I pressed my hand over my mouth in surprise and to keep back a flood of gratitude and tears. It was enough to get truly away from Orinda, maybe even out of the Arizona Territory. "Are you sure?"

Verna stood, held up a glass of cider, and cleared her throat. "Heave ho with the drink." Which we all did.

The sun cut through the window in the way sharp suns do, making me squint. Even with my eyes half-mast and awash with tears, the light shone on everything—the mismatched cups, the dust motes hanging in the air like floating bed bugs, the curtains torn and oil splattered. Wu Lin sneaking half his meal to Tommy's plate while the boy waxed on about the silver he was sure had been hidden in the town well. Maggie cutting worried glances Darby's way and Darby humming in her improbably awful way. Verna rolling her eyes and sighing at it all. I loved them. It had snuck up like a tick on an ankle, burrowing into the skin while I blithely went on with life.

"I am overwhelmed. Your kindness and generosity—"

"Let's not get blubbery," Verna said. "It grays the joie de vivre."

I shut my mouth and scooped up the money.

"Better."

We gathered up the plates and slung the extra bits over the fence for the javelinas to enjoy.

❦

"WELL." PIP FIDDLED WITH HER BUSTLE THEN FLUFFED THE WIDE ribbons that cascaded down the back of her dress. "This is it, then." She refused to look at me; instead, she turned to the mirror and patted her cheeks to rouge them up.

I watched how particular she was, turning her head this way and that. Smiling with that one eyebrow creeping up that sent men's hearts to flutter. A weight pressed against my chest and my skin chilled though the room was warm as hell. And a thought came: This is the last time she'll be this carefree and beautiful.

I shook my head to dislodge the thought, but it stuck in place. "You should come with me, Pip."

"You got your life and I got mine."

"Well, I'm glad they crossed."

She slid a small silver filigree box across the makeup table and wagged a finger at it. Then pulled in her chin and mumbled something I took to be "I have been overly rude and am now groveling for your forgiveness."

"It's from Verna and me."

The box was an old piece with a bent corner, one I'd seen in her room that she kept her earrings in. I lifted the top. A roll of bills sat inside, wrapped up with a bit of silk cord. A rush of panic filled me. "Pip, where'd you get all this?"

"Never mind that," she said. "We've been saving aside, is all."

"This is more than that, this is—"

"Just say thank you, Ruby Calhoun. And don't say I didn't help out with your plan."

Out in the saloon, Verna rolled the chords for our entrance. Pip took the money out and pushed it down the front of my corset. "That's seventy-four dollars. That should get you home and get presents for your kids, too. Now close your mouth and put on a smile. We've got one last act to do."

Neither of us missed a trick. It didn't matter the house was half-empty and the majority of miners crowded around the Wheel of Fortune Cullen had put smack dab in the center of the room. He ignored us completely, intent on spinning the wheel and fisting up the money that flowed from the poor men's pockets. Pip did an extra few wiggles and flirty turns on the *Dandy* song to try for some attention, which should have annoyed me, but instead made me sad. We closed with a simple rendition of *Sweet Marie* and I saw a few hankies and a couple blown noses.

I slung my arm around her shoulder. She stuck her arm around my waist. Which made things all right. We threw up our hands and shouted, "Happy Blessings and Goodbye to All!"

IT ALL FIZZLED THEN, AS IF NONE OF IT HAD HAPPENED, AND THE Paradise and its denizens had been a dream.

The dressing area was empty; Pip asked if I'd like a drink or two with her, but her voice had the ring of someone asking because it was expected. I declined and we changed to our regular clothes without another word. She stood and brushed a kiss to my cheek before scuttling down the stairs and disappearing into the crowd of gamblers. I looked out at the empty stage and the piano with the top closed up for the night, perhaps for good. The chairs and tables sat empty; the men had moved to the saloon proper or drifted into the parlor to wait their turn with the girls.

Pip had cleared the shelf of makeup jars and brushes. The only thing left was the silver box. I tapped it. They'd done a stupid thing. That much money didn't come from saving tips. That came from skimming profits.

But come tomorrow, that was none of my affair.

I swiped the box and trudged out the back door into the yard. Out past the fence, the desert was pitch black and silent. I closed my eyes against the loneliness and did not stop for it to drag its claws along me. I stomped around to the kitchen door, yanked it open, and took the back stairs to my room. Tomorrow I would take the train away from this damn little town and back to my family. Why, if I kept good track of this money, I might be able to set myself up in a little shop and then what could Rose say when I asked for my kids back? Nothing. She would be able to say not one word.

My steps grew lighter. I made a small shuffle-ball-change to the rhythm of the piano tinkling in the parlor below. At the landing, I leaned over and blew a kiss of thanks. Then I pushed open my door.

"There you are, darling." A man stepped away from the window and into the light of a lantern sat on the dresser. A man as familiar as my own bones.

"Frank."

"Ruby Desiree. My love. I found you."

I gripped the box tight to my chest so as not to immediately sling it at his head. "What do you want?"

"Couldn't we..." He moved forward.

"Don't you take one more step. You take one more step, Frank Calhoun, and I will scream like a banshee."

He tilted his head and looked at me with those gemstone eyes and didn't stop. His arms were around me, holding me gentle as a lamb.

I did wish to remove myself and my dignity. But some things are like opium. So damn hateful and so damn hard to resist. So, I let him hold me. He peppered my head with soft kisses.

"Do not think you are forgiven."

"No, ma'am."

I breathed in the good smell of him. Let his kisses travel down my ear and neck.

"You need a shave."

"You're the only one knows how to do it right." He leaned back. "Everyone else gets the mustache wrong. Cut it too short or leave it too long. You know how long it took to grow out that disaster in Baker? I couldn't look in the mirror for months."

My shoulders dropped. I shifted away and set the box on the dresser.

"Where are you going?" he asked.

I shook his hand off my arm. "I've got things to do, Frank. Listening to your self-regard is not one of them."

"I don't understand. I traveled miles to find you."

"How did you find me?"

"That's a question that'll take hours to answer."

"Or did you come here for the new casino's easy odds?"

"I don't have that life anymore. It's poison. Makes a man crazy." He dropped to the edge of the bed. Ran his hands through his hair and set them to his knees. "I've changed, Ruby. You leaving...it made me think. Made me think on all I'd thrown out. I want us to go home, Ruby. I want to see the kids."

"I don't think they even remember you."

"You don't tell them about me?"

I shrugged. "No. I do not." I winced at the lie. "A little."

He nodded and sighed. "Would you come sit by me?"

I did. He took my hand in his, turning it over and running a finger along my palm.

"That tickles."

"Your hands are so soft." He kissed the tips of my fingers then cradled my hand in his. "What time's the train tomorrow?"

"Why?"

"Let's get on it. You and me. We can take a trip, go see Colorado Springs and Denver, maybe go on up to the Tetons—"

"I thought you wanted to see the kids?"

"I do. But I want to see you first. Get to know each other properly. We can settle down after. If Rose'll let us—"

He hadn't changed. I slipped my hand from his and stood. "That train leaves at eight twenty-three tomorrow. I plan on being on it. I'm heading back home. And not with you."

"But—"

"No. Do not talk."

"Ruby—"

"No. I know what'll happen. Somewhere between here and Denver or Wyoming you'll get antsy. You'll blame me for your troubles. That I'm holding you back from your life. And I'll believe you. And you'll leave me to fend for myself. Well, now I can fend for myself. I couldn't before, and that's why I crawled on back. But now I can stand on my own. I don't have to worry that something I say or do will land me in a heap with a busted nose."

"My God, I am sorry for all I've done." He dropped his head to his hands and swayed forward. "I am so sorry, Ruby."

I tapped my foot and put a hand to the door. "It's been nice seeing you, Frank."

He looked up, his eyes filled with tears. "I can make it up to you. Please, I don't know how to be without you."

"Well, you'd best learn."

"Give me one night then. Just one. Just to sleep, nothing else."

"You don't have money for a room, do you?"

"I spent it coming here. I've spent all I had looking all over the damn place for you."

"I suppose you're hungry, too."

"No need to go out of the way. I wouldn't pass on a bit of rye. Just a small glass, as I have given up the majority of snake juice. Just a tickle."

"You take the floor, I take the bed."

"As you wish."

One glass led to another as it does. One laugh led to even more.

He fell to sleep wrapped around me, his leg heavy across mine, arm tucked around and holding me close.

"Good night, you damn bastard," I whispered.

CHAPTER 24

KANSAS

1905

WE REACH VERNA ROLFE'S—TROUBLE

W e took the gravel road past the granary, as instructed. And there it was: a four-square farmhouse bone white under the moon. A single old tree grew next to it, throwing the top floor in shadow. A screened-in porch spanned the front of the house. It was all so neat and tidy, the siding newly painted, the lawn freshly cut, the line of daisies in copper troughs along the fence line.

Not a single light was on. No guard dog barked. The paddocks were empty, though I assumed we'd find horses or mules in the barn at this hour.

"Something doesn't feel right." Pip gave a gesture to move to the barn, so we did. She moved to slide the door open, pulling the handle a little bit at a time, then stopped to peer at the house.

"You can't even hear that bolt," I whispered. "It's oiled to an inch of its life."

We sidled in and she pulled the door shut. Unlike our last accommodations, this barn was water- and wind-tight. Which meant it was dark as Hades. I listened for livestock, and heard the scuff of hoof to floor, then slid my feet forward in increments until I came to a stall. "Over here."

"I'm already here."

My heart jumped into my throat. "Don't do things like that."

"Sorry."

I reached out to find her and patted her arm when I did. "Apology accepted. Now what?"

"We wait until morning. Then we knock on the door."

"Yeah?"

"We wait for her to answer."

"Okay."

"Then we know."

"Couldn't we do that now?" I asked. "I'd prefer to sleep in a bed and not the floor of this barn."

"It's too late."

"No, it's not, I think this is an acceptable time for visitors to call. Would you turn me away if I showed up this late? I think you wouldn't."

"I might. If I were a heavy sleeper, I certainly would. Besides, there may be a Mister Rolfe."

"He wouldn't be called Mr. Rolfe. He'd be Mr. Harrington, or Ludlow, or some such. And he'd be averse to two innocent women out in the dark by themselves. He might even give us a hot rum."

"Well, I am not ready. So, we're staying in the barn and getting well rested and prepared."

She sat, so I did, too, both with our back against the wood. The only noise was the crunch and grind of the horses chewing salt blocks or the end bits of grain.

"Verna thinks you were in cahoots with Frank."

I let out a laugh. "That's an upright wrong lie. Does she really think I'd do that?"

"You did take off."

"Not after him. That's just rude of her."

"You do have that nice cigar shop. That takes—"

"You're on her side? What the hell, then. Maybe you should have run right to her and left me to my shop that I apparently purchased with all that stolen money."

"Now, Ruby—"

"Don't 'Now Ruby' me." I jumped up and chewed my lip and thought how I wanted this all over. I drilled my fingers to my thighs, squeezed my eye closed, and flipped through my mind looking for the timetable of the Burdick train. But I had never heard of Burdick before The Black Witch of Imminent Chaos walked in my cigar shop. I blew out some short breaths, allowing my mind to wander over the schedule for the Missouri, Kansas & Texas line. "Fairdale, Muncie, Edwards, Forest Lake."

"What are you doing?"

"Shh. LaTrape...no. Bonner Springs. No. I think that's an Atchison Topeka, but maybe they both run through. Wait—*Frisbie*. Yes." I made a small circle so as not to run face first into the wall. "I can't stay here, Pip. She needs a talking to."

A muffled yelp gave me pause.

"Pip?"

Heavy thumps and a low grunt did not bode well. There was a scuffle of feet, then the barn door yanked open, illuminating the noise and confusion. A heavyset man hurried out into the moonlight. He had Pip slung over his shoulder. Her arms swung around as he spun back to pull the door.

"Boudreaux." The word caught like a fiery stone on my tongue.

"You're next." He slammed the door. There came an unmistakable thunk of a padlock.

I STOOD AS STILL AS A FUNERARY URN, NOT ABLE TO MOVE A FOOT, IN full shock as to this latest disaster. I blinked furiously, as if that would allow me to see in front of my face, but it didn't help in the least. I wanted to call for Pip, because she was fast-witted in situations, and a kidnapping would throw her into high gear. Except she had been the one absconded with.

By Barnabé Boudreaux. Who I had mostly forgotten about once we were out of Osawatomie, save for his gift of the Bibles and the address list that led us here to Verna.

My chest constricted and my breathing became a high wheeze. I bent over, put my hands to my bare knees, and sucked in air. I coughed it and the hay dust right out.

Boudreaux had kidnapped my friend. I needed to do something.

"Oh hell," I said. I swallowed a scream of panic and dropped to a crawl. The barn had more than the main door; every stall let out to a paddock. This I had seen when we approached it. I crawled along, reaching out to find a wall with my hand and not my head. One of the horses snuffled, so I zigged my way in its direction.

"Good horse," I whispered.

My shoulder slammed the corner of something. I winced and bit my lip to keep in the curse. I clasped the object's edge, determined it was a trunk, and ran my fingers along it as I neared the sniffly horse. The hay and grit on the floorboards transitioned to sawdust. I spread my hand to the wall and caught the corner of the stall door frame, then the door itself. Stood and slid the bar open. I slipped in, keeping my back to the stall and facing the horse.

"You stay on your side, and I'll stay on mine."

It snorted and swung its head, the hot breath like ants crawling along my arms.

I sidestepped, dragging my back along the wall, my hip setting the empty hay bag swaying. A loud kick reverberated in the space. I shuddered and scrambled for the back half door, my fingers reaching and clutching the bar, giving a tug.

It held fast. Boudreaux had locked it from the outside.

He knew we were coming.

"Not good," I muttered. "Not not good."

The horse pawed the floor, hoof scraping on the wood.

I made a dash for the inner door, scrambled over the top, and landed in a heap. I shook all over, as if my blood was poisoned and leeching its way out, taking my courage with it. I envisioned Pip outside somewhere and maybe already dead.

I could not help. Just like before. If I stayed, I would be next. Boudreaux said it and I believed it.

A feather fluttered against my cheek, spinning to my lips. I spit it away and sat up. I twisted around and crawled to the stall across. Stood and opened the bar. "I hope you're a good old horse." I waited until it walked over, its knees cracking as it moved close and nestled its muzzle against my collar bone.

Boudreaux would be back. I had one opportunity to escape.

I let go a long breath and ran a hand down its neck, tugging a bit on the mane and then rubbing the whorl of hair on its forehead.

"I knew a horse once named Big Henry. Now I don't need you to have the talents he did, as I surely do not have the talents of Pip Quinn, but if you could do me one small favor, horse, I will be ever grateful."

It pushed its head in for more attention and shifted a foot. I twisted a hank of mane near its ears and turned us both out of the stall, as if it were another day with the plow or saddle. I searched around for the trough, climbed on the edge then slung a leg over the horse. Its withers gave a little shiver, then it stood there awaiting my word.

I grabbed hold of the mane with both hands. "I thank you now in case there isn't another opportunity."

My ears rang, my attention fully on the big barn door. I walked the horse, who I named Fred for his equanimity, in a circle or two. The other horse kicked its stall again and whinnied. Fred ignored it, giving a small huff of annoyance.

Fred slowed. Raised his head.

The barn door slid open and with it came a sliver of moonlight. "Now, Fred." I lay myself low and gave a kick.

The horse barreled forward, aiming straight for Boudreaux, whose arms did cartwheels as he tried to stay upright. He grabbed my ankle as we sped past but couldn't hold on. I looked back as he fell face first in the dirt.

Fred was off. I gripped tight, slipping sideways when he took a sharp turn at the house and headed for the drive. The wind whipped my hair, stinging my eye. It was familiar: my heels in the horse's ribs, his breath rough, neck stretched out for the run, my panic tindering his own.

His hooves dug into gravel, sending it flying out around us. I squinted into the night. The white rails flew by, then we tore around the granary and onto the main thoroughfare.

A train whistled. I sat up, pulling at Fred's mane to slow him to a trot. A long plume of smoke lay on the horizon. The train headed into Burdick.

Pip and I had passed the one room depot on our way to the farm. I did not know how long the train would layover. Perhaps long enough for Fred and me to hurry behind it and I could hop in a boxcar as it pulled away. Leaving one place, going to another. Staying would be suicide.

That train was my way out.

CHAPTER 25

ORINDA

1898

Damn the Bastard—A Horrible Event—I Show My True Colors

Three clangs to the pipe woke me and stopped my heart cold. Three clangs meant trouble.

Doors opened and closed in the hall, and running feet went in both directions. I bolted awake, then grabbed my head to keep it from spinning. I looked down at my bare legs and my half-buttoned chemise.

"Where is it?" Cullen's voice rumbled. Darby whimpered.

"Frank." I pushed at the lump of blankets next to me. "Frank."

But there wasn't any Frank. Just the pillows and sheets. On the floor, my clothes strewn about. On the dresser, the empty bottle and tumblers. No silver box. I rolled out of bed and pulled on my skirt, then dug my hands in the pockets. I was certain I'd put the bills and coins there after I'd changed from my costume. I caught up my leather wallet and dragged it out, flipping it open to find nothing at all but the photograph of Emma.

"Oh no..." I stumbled back. "You no good son of a—"

The door slammed against the wall. Verna barreled in. She grabbed both my arms. "It's gone." She was white as a sheet.

"What?"

"The money. The safe was broken into."

My stomach twisted. "How?"

I knew. I knew Frank had pulled a trick same as he'd done other times when he'd drag me out of whatever hole or grand room we stayed in and set us both on the first train to leave a town.

A loud thump came from the hall, the crash of the spittoon. Cullen wrestled Pip to the floor. "Where's the money?"

"Stop." Her mouth was cherry red with blood, hair pink from the spittle. "Stop." He swung the toe of his boot hard into her ribs. Maggie and Darby pulled at his shoulders, digging their hands into his undershirt and tugging the fabric.

"Please." Pip grabbed his suspender and tried to yank herself up. He backhanded her, his fist curled around the handle of his knife.

"Is this what you want?" His voice quavered with rage. "I trusted you."

"I didn't do it. Please..."

Maggie tried to land a barefoot kick. She clenched her teeth and pulled back to kick again. Cullen grabbed her around the middle and threw her down. Darby beat her fists against his back. He staggered and shoved her hard against a doorframe. She made a noise, half grunt and half keen, and let go.

Cullen dragged in a breath and lurched forward, gripping Pip's jaw tight and holding her to the floor. He raised his knife like you see in a penny dreadful, then it arced down at Pip.

It was too fast, that blade. She didn't have a chance of raising her hands. Could only stare at him in surprise. She shook so hard her teeth chattered. She reached a hand to her cheek, fingers slipping in a pool of blood.

"Ruby! Help." Verna sprinted forward. Cullen let Pip go and twisted around, a look of surprise on his face. I do not know if it was due to Verna rushing straight for him or what he'd done.

He hit the floor with a wheeze. His hand clamped on Verna's wrist, and he clambered up, dragging her with him and twisting her arm until she cried out.

Maggie pointed at me. "She took it."

"No—that's—"

"You're playing us all like fools, aren't you, Ruby? I saw you. I saw that roll of money you took last night. She had it after the show."

"No. It was..." I stared at Verna, wishing for someone to help. No one had seen Frank.

"Don't you lie." Maggie's voice rose high.

"It wasn't her." Pip rolled on her side.

Cullen lurched towards her, yanking the collar of her nightgown. "So, you admit it."

"No." Blood poured from her cheek. Her eyes rolled back, and then she squeezed her lids tight and grimaced, awaiting the next blow.

The spittoon lay by my feet; I could have lifted it then and brought it down on his head.

But I could not move. I could not speak.

A loud bang broke my inertia.

Darby held a pistol at arm's length. The barrel shook. She kept it aimed at Cullen who lay face down, arms and legs spread eagled. "I'll shoot again, I will, I'll shoot you."

Verna darted over to Pip. "I need towels. Ruby—"

"Is he dead?" Darby asked. "Should I shoot again?"

Maggie took the gun from her. "It's all right."

"Ruby—" Verna pressed the edge of her nightdress to Pip's face. "Ruby, damn it."

"We need to go." Maggie waved the gun. "We can't be here. If he's dead, we get the noose. If he's alive, we get worse."

"Ruby." Verna barked. "Are you going to let her die or are you going to get yourself together enough to be of use?"

I pulled towels from the peg by the washstand and knelt next to Verna. Pip reached up. She kept her head bowed, hidden in the wild mess of her hair. She wore a white sleeveless shift—or what was left of one. Both arms bore red marks—fingers that had dug deep. Blood stained the front of the cotton, blood that pulsed and slid from the gaping gash in her face. She cut a sharp laugh and took a shallow breath. "I think he ruined my face."

"It'll be fine," Verna soothed. "We'll get it sewn up right."

"You all need to go." Pip's eyes fluttered shut.

"Go get water," Verna ordered.

"It wasn't my fault," I blurted. "I had nothing to do with it."

I stood and backed away. Then I ran.

❦

WU LIN CALLED OUT FROM THE YARD, BUT I KEPT GOING. STONES cut into my feet. I ran anyway. I had no rhyme or reason, just zigzagged between cacti and crawled over old slag, sliding down the other side and ending in a culvert on the back side of town. The train whistled. Frank would take it to the next town, maybe the one after. Buy a random ticket. Not care he'd put a death sentence on us. I gulped air, the panic bubbling and strangling at once.

The sun blazed above, the sky a hard blue. I turned my head to look up the hill, at the saguaro climbing the red rocks. Tommy Gee's voice echoed. *"Then there's the javelina. Eat your eyes out while you're sleeping. But it's your grave, lady."*

I crept low along the paddock fence and crawled under a broken wagon to wait as Matteo passed by, taking a horse to the hot walker. Big Henry's stall was three doors down. I stood and brushed my skirts, then walked with my head up like I had every right to take a halter and lead from a hook and every right to put it on Big Henry. I led him out the back, down again to the gulch, then scrambled up a pile of rocks and threw a leg over his back.

"I'm sorry, Pip."

One squeeze of my knees and we were off. I dug my heels to his sides and kept low to his neck as he plunged through the arroyo. My hands, clutched to his mane, were sticky with blood and smelled of metal. His hooves slid under the loose rock as I legged him up. His shoulder twitched when he scraped against a saguaro. He swung his haunches and swerved his head around to nip at the sting. I gave another kick, gathering more mane in my fists.

"Come on." My teeth cracked against each other. We shot up to a narrow ledge, enough room for Henry, but not for my knee or shoulder, both of which banged and slammed against the red rock outcrops. The path opened, and Henry skidded to a stop in front of a small fire pit.

Joe Harper scrambled up from where he sat, clawing out his revolver and holding it dead to rights at my head. He took a step closer and squinted. "Ruby?"

"I want to go home." I nearly collapsed with sobs and exhaustion.

Joe holstered his gun and loped over to help me down from Big Henry. "Don't cry." He pulled me against his chest, his hand cupped around my head, kissing my hair like my mother used to do when she liked me. "There there, Ruby, what's all this about?"

Pip's bloodied face swam in front of me. How she shuddered and swallowed moans.

I bit my lip and pushed my head harder to his chest. "I want to go home."

A rock tumbled from a ledge behind the claim. I hit the ground and clambered behind Joe's tent.

He scratched the back of his neck and stared up the cañon. He came over and sank to his haunches, his face a muddle.

"I need to borrow some cash, Joe. You have some, don't you?"

"Well, I—"

"Joe, please. I have got to get home. All I need is a ride to Superior and a ticket for the train, even if it's up to Flagstaff or somewhere. He'll..."

"What'd you do?"

"What'd I do?" I smacked his arm. "I didn't do anything. If you'd been there, you—Why would you think I..." But there wasn't time for acrimonies. "I need money."

"I don't have any, Ruby."

"I need to go home. Please, Joe."

"I don't have a penny."

"Nothing?" I felt the blood drain away, leaving me cold and shivering. I got to my feet and trudged over to him. "Then we rob a stage."

THIS REQUIRED PLANNING. JOE SAID HE KNEW A SPOT THE PAYROLL stage for one of the mines had to slow. The cañon narrowed and took on a steep decline, thus the driver had to pay great heed to watching the speed.

"We jump from behind the boulders, you see?" He held up his hands, fingers pointed towards the roof of the tent, as if he held firearms. "We need to be bold, Ruby. The payroll box would be impossible to lift but there'll be a few travelers I guarantee you that. '*We want all your money. Give it over and no one will get hurt.*' We say it bold, like that. You take the money, I scare them one more time by shooting off the guns, we get our horses and we're gone. You get to your train in Superior and I get..."

"You get half the loot."

"Yeah." He scooted closer to me, so we were shoulder to shoulder. "I have been wanting to try out Mexico. Maybe set up a bar there. We can travel together, you know."

"We need to split up."

"Why?"

"Because we do." I crawled over him and paced around outside. I stared at the other side of the cañon, at the ragged white strips that marked other useless claims and the march of saguaro and hedgehog cacti down the spines and gullies. The wind whistled and I thought how lonesome its tune was. And how alone I was. And Joe was. And Pip, who I thought was surely dead.

The West had once so enamored me. I blamed Buffalo Bill for providing such a romantic view. I had a burning anger over Annie Oakley and her vivacious costumes and confident shooting, for they alone made me long for a West that never really was.

The reality came down to this: desert, brutal men, searing sun, and not one place to land that was soft.

A hawk girdled the cañon, wings tipping as he caught the air pockets. Waiting below for some quarry to lose its caution and grow tired of hiding. So, it circled and watched and waited.

I spun on my heel and grabbed back the tent flap. "You take Big Henry down and get us some horses and get me a pistol."

Joe had laid back for a midmorning siesta. He pushed up on his elbow. "Right now?"

"Now."

THE HORSES WEREN'T ANYTHING MORE THAN A POKE AND A SLOW-poke, little chestnuts Joe traded for all his mining equipment. He snuck Big Henry around back of Pascoe's and I hoped Matteo would see fit to take care of him. Joe gave me a little .38 revolver and showed me how to load it.

"You know I love you, Ruby."

"I know."

"I don't want to see you shoot your eye out, so make sure you're pointing it away from yourself."

"I'm not going to shoot myself." I stuffed the gun in the wide belt I had borrowed from Joe. "All right. The stage comes. You jump out, then give me a signal. I'll hold up the passengers and you cut the traces on those horses, so they can't follow us."

"When do I talk to the driver?" he asked. "Before I cut the reins and such or after?"

"Well, I...I'll leave that up to you. You figured out the way to Superior?"

"We'll head up and spit back the other way. Then we just go down-hill." He put his hands on my shoulders and studied me, as if he was deciding exactly how to say what was next.

"Why are you looking at me like that?"

"It's all been wrecked, Ruby. The Paradise. It's all burned."

"You see Pip? Any of the girls?"

"No one. I'm afraid..."

"Well, at least she'll have her horse, now. If she's..." My throat closed up tight with a ball of grief. "Cullen?"

"No one's seen him. They're talking about him. But they ain't seen him."

I cleared my throat. "Let's get on with this business."

WE TIED THE HORSES IN A STAND OF CREOSOTE BUSHES, UPHILL FROM the bend in the road where the train slowed. It had grown stifling, with the sun straight above and the sky a flat blue. The bushes and a few palo verdes gave good coverage to the mounts, and Joe and I were able to shimmy down to hunker behind some rocks to wait. My foot itched. But I had on four sets of socks to fill out Joe's old boots and worried the stage would come by as I'd removed the set of them. I chewed on my thumbnail instead.

"What's your bar going to be like, Joe?"

"I've been thinking it might look good with a mahogany counter. Running from the front door to the back end. All the stools could have tufted seats, so people can settle in some. Maybe an outdoor patio, with a guitarist or some such thing. I could save money by living upstairs. All down pillows and a dog. I would like a dog."

"That's nice."

A black beetle crawled in front of our feet and we watched it until it found some shade.

"I shouldn't have left Pip." My chest burned and tensed.

"No."

"I shouldn't have left her. Them." I unknotted and re-tied my bandanna so it fit tight over my nose. I pulled it down, then wiggled it back up. "Pip was my friend."

We heard the stage at the same time. My back tensed up. The beetle wandered back the way he'd come and I followed its path while Joe twisted around to look out through the brush. "You ready?"

"Let's at it."

CHAPTER 26

KANSAS
1905
SAVING PIP—THE SNEAK

I wiped a hand to my eyes, but it did little to remove the grit of memories past. I had tried to leave Orinda behind. Worked hard to get a new life, go get my kids back, though Rose made that finish line an ever-moving target. If only I had not let myself be seduced by Frank that night. If only I had not frozen that terrible morning. I could have stayed Cullen's hand when he swung that knife.

"Stop." I pulled on Fred's mane which didn't do much of anything. He kept up a jarring trot that took us farther away from the farm and Pip. "No, damn it. No."

With a great pull to the right and my knee digging in, Fred turned around.

"We're going to get her, Fred. You and me. I do not know how, but it'll come to me. I'm Ruby Calhoun, horse, and you can count on that."

THE FARM STUCK UP IN THE MIDDLE OF THE FLATLANDS LIKE A SORE thumb, which meant Fred and I stuck out like two molars and could be spied from many directions. My only chance of sneaking up on and into that house was to crouch and crawl, which I had become adept at during these past few days.

I slid down to the dirt. Then slapped Fred's haunch. He took off like a racehorse, charging across the field towards the barn. I kept against the shadowy side of the granary, squinting to see if I could make out Boudreaux. Fred slowed enough to hop his way through the yawing barn door. I took a few steps forward, leaning out to view the farmhouse. A small light moved from one first floor window to another, before going out. I swung my gaze back to the barn. It remained silent and dark.

I stooped and hurried along the edge of the field to the fence line. The moon had dipped and ran long shadows along the drive, so I kept myself hunched down and skittered forward. The porch light came on. I dove behind a daisy trough and kept going.

My heart thudded in my chest and throat and ears. I had not one iota of an idea of what to do. So, I stayed tucked behind a trough, watching a ladybug crawl across a petal.

There was approximately twenty feet between my position and the front corner of the house. I needed to get close enough to see who was in the house, and where, and if Pip was all right and Verna.

But the window casings were too high up. My heart squeezed with regret that I had let Fred go, as I could have ridden right around the perimeter and seen directly through each glass to my heart's content. If Pip was here, I could have got a leg up and a quick look. That made my heart squeeze harder.

I measured the length and breadth of the tree that hung over the second story. If I could somehow shimmy up and onto that porch—

A gun went off in the house. I bolted forward, a single prayer on my lips: Don't damn die. My toe caught on something, sending me hard to the ground. I scrambled up to run, taking a quick look to see what had tripped me. Something silver. Something shaped much like Pip's pearl-handled $33.50 Colt. Past that lay her hat, turned on its crown.

I whipped the pistol up and shoved it in the waist of my trousers, then grabbed the first branch of the old tree and hauled myself up, one branch to the other until I was able to reach the porch roof on my tiptoes. I grimaced as I dropped to the tin roof, softening the landing by bending my knees. I thanked Pip for the lessons on Big Henry that allowed such an elegant fall.

My palms stung from my grip on the bark. I rubbed them to my thighs. Took in a deep breath and prayed the window was unlocked and as well greased as the barn door bolt. It was both. I pushed aside the lace curtain and straddled the frame, sticking my foot out to see if there was anything in my way. The path seemed clear, so over I went, twisting around on my belly and sliding as quiet as possible to the floor. The gun slipped. I grabbed it and held it against my thigh, then pulled it out before it could discharge and lose me my leg. Which would do no one any good at all.

A voice came from somewhere deep in the back of the house. I shoved the gun back in the waistband and crawled across the rag rug and around the foot of the bedstand until I was at the door. The voice tossed about and snaked through the keyhole. I put my ear to it but could not make out words, only the low register of a man talking to himself.

Not to Pip. Not to Verna.

Just rumbling and mumbling to himself and punctuating it with a kick against a wall.

I grabbed the knob and turned it, yanked the door open and leapt up to sprint to the landing. But Boudreaux's words stopped me dead.

"I'll shoot it again, there's good odds I will." Boudreaux made a long whistle after this pronouncement. He shot again. "Told you they were good odds."

I wrapped my hands to the top of my head and gritted my teeth. My breath came out in raggedy wheezes. The distance from my position to the landing wasn't more than a few feet. I could make it and the stairs in a matter of seconds.

We need to be bold, Ruby. Jump on out.

I thought of Joe waving around his pistol, bold as pie. Scaring the passengers half to death. If it had been me in their position, I would have peed my pants at such a surprise as bandits appearing from the ether.

Surprise is what it would take. I sat down, unlaced my shoes, and pulled them off. Keeping on my toes, I sneaked my way down the stairs. A yellow light shown in a strip along the bottom of a door. The kitchen. Foursquares, thank the Lord and the architect, had few surprises. I crept along the hall, peeking in the dining room on one side, and stopping directly across from the kitchen door. It was ajar, enough to see Boudreaux lumber into view. His vest was unbuttoned and hanging. He scratched his neck and stared at something under his nail. He smacked his hand to the counter and waddled away.

Boldness.

I did not have it before. I had left Pip once, and now I needed boldness drastically. For all I knew, Pip and Verna both sat at the table with their legs sprawled and a bullet to each forehead. He had shot twice.

But it was possible they were still alive.

I had a gun, too.

Surprise, boldness, and a single bullet.

I took in a long breath, reached for the gun, ready to kick the door wide. But the damn Colt had decided at the worst moment to drop again down my leg and settle in crook of my left knee. I crept back, slow as a possum, and slunk into the dining room. I pulled up my trouser and tugged the damn gun out and stuffed it to my pocket.

The light from the kitchen grew bright. I squeezed between a hutch and the wall. Boudreaux trudged down the hall and out onto the porch. The screen door snapped shut. The stench of smoke rolled its way into the house. Either he was being polite and puffing outside or he was waiting for someone.

I scrambled over, peeked out, then jumped across to the kitchen. A shotgun lay on the counter, an empty bullet box nearby. Boudreaux's jacket hung off a chair's spindle. A couple clean water glasses sat upside-down near the sink. But no Pip. No Verna.

I saw it. A hole in the floor, wood splintered around it. One then another then another. He was shooting at them in the cellar like they were fish in a bowl.

After a quick glance to the hall and a sniff of the lit cigar, I dove down, putting my eye to one of the holes. But it was pitch black. "Hey," I whispered. I pressed my ear down.

"Hey."

"Oh, Pip—"

"Don't 'Oh, Pip' me," she hissed. "You have any idea what a stupid, nonsensical thing you've done by coming back here?"

"It *is* Ruby," another voice muttered.

"Verna?" Relief came over me like cool water. "You're not dead."

"It would seem today is not the day."

"I'm going to get you both out of there. You just sit tight." I sat back on my haunches and looked around. I leaned over the blast hole again. "You got a telephone around here?"

"You think I'm Midas?"

"Well, it is possible Frank did not take that money. I been thinking on that, and this is nicer than my cigar—"

"Ruby?"

"Yes, Pip?"

"You got my gun?"

"Yes, I do."

"Then how about you stop talking and get it to me?"

"How?"

The screen door squealed. I crab-walked to the back door and reached for the handle. Boudreaux's steps grew louder as he neared. The handle clicked open and I tumbled through.

"What in the holy—" A chair thudded inside, and the door slammed wide.

I froze, as is my wont in the worst situations.

The steps groaned as he came towards me. His face and that large mustache grew bigger as he leered. "Why, it's little bitty."

I jumped up and whipped out the Colt. "You take one more step and I'm going to shoot you. As you can see, this isn't a toy, like the last time."

He faltered, and half-raised his hands. "I don't believe you can do it."

I took a step back in the spongy grass.

He tsked and shook his head. "You're just a little bitty coward."

"Don't you call me that."

"Teeny tiny ant-like good for nothing."

The cocking of my gun stopped him. He looked at the barrel, at me, then back at the barrel.

My body shook, as I filled with a strange brave energy. "I don't know how much Cullen paid you to catch us, but I sure hope it's worth me shooting you dead."

He jerked an arm to one side, which made me aim that direction. I wasn't fast enough. He clamped a hand to my shoulder and raised the other punch me.

Well, I thought, that's that.

I screwed my eyes shut and waited for the blow. A sickening thud came right before I was in free fall, landing hard to the ground.

Fast sharp slaps stung my cheek. I opened an eye. Martha Ruth peered down at me.

"Hi-dee-ho." She held a crowbar, pumping it up and down in victory. She pulled a halter rope from her shoulder and dropped in on my stomach. "We best hurry."

We made short shrift of tying both his wrists and ankles. The possibility of moving him was nil.

Martha Ruth stuffed a cloth in his mouth. "He's going to wake up. No need to hear him holler."

It took both of us working the crowbar to twist the padlock off the cellar door. I put a foot to the wall and yanked at the iron rod with all my strength.

"I been thinking about a bandit name." Martha huffed and pushed from her direction. "I been thinking 'The Sneak.'"

The metal clasp squealed as it came loose from the boards.

"Is that so?"

"You didn't hear me coming, and that man certainly didn't."

We changed positions and yanked and pushed again.

"We'll ask Pip," she said. "I think she will approve."

Pip and Verna were no worse the wear, save sore skin from their rope bindings. We stood over Boudreaux. The sun was tipping awake and elongating the shadow of the lump on his head.

"This is not good." Verna poked the shotgun into his side. "He used up all the shotgun shells, which leaves that out." She set the weapon against the house and stared towards the barn. "We can harness up—what's the mule's name?"

Martha Ruth stopped her fluttering and prancing around Pip. "Theodore Horatio Hobnob Clark. I did not name him. If I did, I would have called him Mule."

"Let's bury him," Pip said.

I gave a start. "You're kidding. Pip—we did not come all this way for that. He's not even dead. Look." I pointed to the hanky in his mouth. "It's fluttering around. That's a sign of breathing."

She looked at me with eyes hard as stone then turned her attention to Verna. "You got a wheelbarrow and shovel?"

Martha Ruth's eyes went wide. "I don't mind hitting someone in the head to save a life, but I agree with Ruby."

Pip gave her a long look. "This has nothing to do with you. So, get your mule and go."

"Well, that is rude, after all I've—"

"Go away."

Martha Ruth jumped, then slapped her legs and stomped to the barn. "If you need something else, I ain't answering."

"That was ungrateful," I said.

"Give me the gun," Pip said.

"I refuse that request. I should have refused when you sashayed your sorry ass into my shop."

"I told you I was going to kill Cullen."

"I understand that. But that is not Cullen. That is a Bible salesman."

"Did you count the holes in that floor?" Pip asked.

"He's moving," Verna called.

"Give it to me, Ruby."

"Pip—" I pushed her, but she wouldn't budge. "You listen to me. If you shoot him that is cold-blooded murder. You will hang for that. You have things to live for."

Verna strode past us. "This bickering is giving me a headache. You do whatever you want. I am making coffee."

The screen door swung open before she was near it. Cullen Wilder stood in the doorway, a revolver in his grip. "Hello, ladies. Nice to see you all together."

CHAPTER 27

SOMEWHERE OUTSIDE ORINDA
1898
I AM A TRUE-BLUE BANDIT

"Stop and elevate." Joe stood wide-legged and straight-backed in front of the horses. He cocked his Colt and held it facing skywards. "This is a robbery." He sauntered on up to the stage and peered at the driver. "Drop your rifle, sir."

I crouched low along the bush line, waiting for his signal. It was now or never. My hands sweat profusely, and I thought my heart might bang right through my chest. I darted forward. Three faces squished together and peered from behind the window. I dropped back on my heels and pressed my hands to my hips. "I think we might try another—"

"Get over there and get the money," Joe barked. He put a leg up on the carriage and yanked the driver to the ground, where he pressed a boot to the man's chest.

"He can't breathe like that."

Joe pointed his revolver at me. His eyes had gone wild, not staying in any one place, and when he pulled in air, he bared his teeth. "Dammit, woman."

"All right already." I pulled at the pistol stuck in my belt, but my hand slipped off the handle. "Dammit right back." I wiped my palm on my chest, then took the gun and waved it at the cringers. "Get out and line up."

The door creaked as it swung open. The first out was a fat man who kept his hands straight above his head. The man behind him wore his hair oiled back and parted in the middle, his scalp so white I had to blink against the glare. He clung to the fat fella, and both leaned forward and tumbled down in a mess of arms and legs that took a good kick or two from me to straighten up.

Joe was no help; he had knocked the driver out and was tying his legs up, which I felt was a bit overboard.

"Stand against the carriage," I said.

The last of the three to exit gave me heartburn and a load of boiling guilt.

He took his time, careful not to catch his long gray garment under his feet. I noticed his black boots shone to a high heaven, with not one single scuff.

"Good afternoon, Mr. Wu Lin." I couldn't look at him. Just waved my gun to where I needed him to stand.

He nodded.

"You have to put your hands up."

"As you request." He held them up.

His didn't tremble, such as the other two's did.

I sucked in a breath. "Now, shell out."

Mr. Pudge rolled his lip. "You're nothing but a little thing."

I stuck the gun in his stomach. "This is a little thing, too. I can make it go off, if you wish."

"I do not wish that."

"Then take out your wallet and toss it on the ground."

His skin went a motley red and gray and his eyes squinted to slits. He was trying to communicate something to the younger man next to him.

I sighed and strolled back and forth, realizing that they were terrified of me. Or the six-shooter. Or Joe with his boot on the tied-up driver's back and his own gun aimed at the poor man's head. I tipped my head and took a turn or two.

"I'm not going to wait all day for you to hand over your money." I spit over my shoulder to show I was serious about this entire affair and knocked the edge of the door for good measure.

Wu Lin held out a small black leather pouch.

I did not want to take it. Of all the people that could be on this stage, he was the one I least wished. I wanted instead to ask him all that had happened and if Cullen was alive and girls had gone to safety.

He dropped the pouch to the ground and pushed it to me with his shiny boot. His mouth quivered and then he gave a shake of his head before returning his features to a calm blank. He kept his focus on the mountain beyond.

I swiped the pouch and shoved it into my pocket.

"Now see how generous he is?"

My trigger finger, growing numb, twitched. Which made the other men jump, grab out their wallets and toss them my way to skid to a stop at my feet.

"Well, then." I bent down and flicked open the wallet that looked ready to burst. "How much is in here, Mr. Pudgeman?"

"That's fifty-three dollars right there." His voice took on a reedy thin timbre. "That is all I have to my name."

The other wallet was thin.

"There's only a couple dollars in there." The other man's forehead bristled with sweat.

I sank to my haunches and thumbed out the bills. I hooked my finger to it to count. "There's seven dollars. Which is five more than you said, which makes you a liar."

He started to hum a strange tune, and his eyes rolled back in his head before snapping to me. He swayed, his shoulders thumping the side of the coach.

I was concerned he was suffering from heat stroke, for we stood cooking in the full brunt of the afternoon sun. I surveyed the three of them, miserable and hot and penniless and scared.

I knew what that fear was like.

I peered back at Joe. "Let him up."

Joe pulled him upright and shoved him against a wheel. "Stay." He jogged over and stuffed the wallets into a pack he'd slung around his neck.

"Turn around and face the stage," I barked. "No one move for ten minutes."

I stuffed the gun into my belt. Joe and I scrambled up the hill and jogged over to spy. Wu Lin moved first, sprinting to the driver to untie him, then joining the other men as they fell over each other trying to get back on the stage. The driver shoveled up his rifle and climbed back up to his perch. He peered up the mountain and took a wide shot before grabbing the reins and snapping them down, setting the horses into full flight. The dust swirled under their hooves and spit out behind the coach wheels.

"Joe?"

"Yeah?"

"They're headed right on down to town."

"Yeah."

I smacked him on the arm. Then I punched him.

He held a hand to his mouth. "What the hell?"

"You are the sorriest, stupidest, dumbest, mud-brained, son of a damn vacant-headed horny toad."

"You just hit me."

I swung another punch. "The traces, Joe." I clamped my teeth and punched my own head. I pulled off my hat and smacked it to the ground, then shoved it back on again. "You were supposed to cut the traces."

৩৶৩

Joe's mistake gave the driver ample time to drop the passengers and sic the law on us. Twice I'd seen the tops of their hats and the sheen off their guns. There was not much opportunity to reflect on our lack of plan. After a desperate grapple up the mountain and crisscrossing the same damn path so many times I grew weary of seeing it, we found ourselves well and truly lost.

The sun dropped like a ball and not a slice of moonlight shone into the deep gulch we pulled up in. My horse's ribs heaved under me. She needed a breather, so I slung my leg over her neck and slid off.

Joe turned his horse in circles, the poor creature panting and reluctantly turning at the "Move about," Joe barked.

"We have to stop, Joe."

He gave a hard kick against the poor horse's ribcage, hard enough I felt it in my own. I jogged over and yanked at his reins. "Get down. Let her rest."

"I hear 'em down below. You hear 'em, Ruby?" He dug in his heels and spun away from me, pacing back and forth, the two of them bounding up one side of the gulch to slide down and do it all over on the other side.

My horse, who I named Poke, lowered her head in exhaustion and gave no fight when I hobbled her.

"Are you thirsty?" I unplugged my canteen and took out one of the tin bowls from the knapsack tied to the back of the saddle. Poke took a good long drink. I unsaddled her, running my hand along her withers same as Pip used to do to thank Big Henry for being a good damn horse.

Her skin rippled at my touch, ending in her shaking her shoulders and stomping a back hoof. She gave a long deep-chested sigh and didn't lift her head; just took a hobbled step towards the one bit of grass she could nibble on.

"They're going to find us, Ruby."

"It'll be your fault." I lugged up the saddle and moved it to a place with a fewer rocks than where I stood.

"This whole thing is your fault," he said. "And when they find us and we get hauled to prison I'm going to state that fact as such."

I thomped up a ways and unbuttoned my trousers to pee. "You're going to kill your horse. Then what'll you do?" I let go a breath of relief, then buttoned up and jumped down directly in front of his path. "We need to get to Superior then out to the train. And I'm not taking you on the back of my horse, so get the hell off yours so we can sleep some."

He sniffed. "All right, then."

"Don't put your saddle next to mine. You just go on over to the other side and take care of your own damn self."

"You're what's called a witch."

I had no need to continue the conversation, so returned to my encampment. I unbuckled and rolled out a wool blanket and wrapped it around me like a cocoon. I sank down and dropped my head to the saddle seat.

The temperature made a steep dive. I shivered and pulled the blanket up to my chin. Above, the sky was so deep it looked like infinity, and all the stars glowed like chipped ice. It reminded me of the first night I slept out in Orinda, after I'd left Frank and taken that train to wherever it went and got off where it ended up. That roiled my stomach and brought me to a few tears. "I'd like to mail Mr. Wu Lin back his money."

There were scruffing noises and a groan. "Two dollars and fifty cents of that is mine."

"You have no charity."

Some rocks tumbled on a ridge above us. Poke lifted her head and gave a snort.

I froze solid. My heart thudded hard as a stick against a drum. Anything could be above us: mountain lion, javelina, old trapper. The law. Cullen.

Joe clicked his gun. "I will shoot."

Poke swung her head around and sniffed the air. She stepped back, swayed forward, her hobbled front legs crippling an escape.

I lowered the blanket and crawled on my knees until I could reach her and remove the ties. "Please don't run," I whispered.

She didn't. Just shivered and pawed.

I sunk back and wished I hadn't put my gun in the saddlebag. Not that it would do any good.

I hadn't loaded it.

THE NEXT THING I KNEW, THE COLD WAS MORE DREADFUL THAN IT had been, and my eyes blinked open to lumpy low clouds and a spritz of rain on my cheek. I found myself bound in my blanket and Joe's plaid one, which he must have given me during the night.

The horses nibbled at some plant a few yards down the way.

Joe, stalwart guard, slept with his head thrown back and his mouth open wide enough to catch the Gila monsters that caught the flies. Drizzle beaded on his skin and along his mustache. He cradled his gun on his chest, his palms crossed over the cylinder and trigger and the barrel aimed dangerously at his manly parts.

It would not do well to startle him.

I got on my knees and crept to him, leaning over to his ear. "Good morning, Joe." I blew a breath.

His hand jerked to swipe at the tickle, which gave me enough time to pick up the gun.

He smacked his lips and ran his tongue over the white salt on them. He opened a red-rimmed eye. "It's drizzling."

"It'll be a cooler ride." I put the gun on the ground next to him and headed for the horses. "They're going to need some real hay. Maybe there's a ranch where we can steal some—"

Joe's gaze snapped to the right. He jumped up, tore by me, then skittered to a stop to grab my arm.

I stumbled forward. "What are you doing?"

He pulled a bridle and reins from my saddle horn and tossed them to me. "Come on."

"I need my saddle. Joe, stop."

"They're watching, Ruby. They're just up the hill." Joe picked me up around the waist and raced to the horses. He lugged me onto Poke's back, bridled her, and took one leap to his own horse, looping the reins around his neck and reaching to drag on the bridle.

"You got to hang on, Ruby."

I grabbed the mane and the reins with both hands and screwed my eyes shut.

Just relax and trust, Ruby.

I opened my eyes, thinking I could see Pip next to me, her sombrero tipped back, hands on her hips, boots dusty.

You should have stayed a trick rider, Pip.

Some things just don't go the way you want, do they?

My throat closed up because she wasn't there.

Five horses lunged up the incline, five riders spurring them on. One split off and charged in pursuit of Joe while the other four surrounded Poke and me. I do not know which of us gave up first. The poor horse dropped her head, and I lifted my hands above mine.

"Hold your breath. I am guilty of whatever you're about to say."

⚜

THEY CAUGHT JOE THE DAY AFTER MY TRIAL ENDED. HIS TRIAL began and ended in half a day. Joe refused to talk to me, though we were two cells apart while awaiting transport to our sundry prisons. The jail keeper peered in at me on my last night there, spitting a plug of tobacco on the floor by his feet and scruffing the neck of his mangy hound. "People don't learn, do they? You may want to be Pearl Hart," he drawled. "But she's a spitfire tiger cat. You're just a teeny, miniscule nothing."

"I have no idea who you're referring to." I crossed one leg over the other and turned a shoulder him.

"Meow." He ambled away, taking his snot-nosed dog with him.

"You know who he's on about, Joe?"

"I am not talking to you."

"Be that way then."

"I will."

"I wrote my sister," I said.

"Did you?"

"She's not happy."

"No, I don't suppose she is."

⚜

I HAD ALSO WRITTEN A LETTER TO PIP AND SENT IT GENERAL POST. *I'm sorry for being such a coward.* But there was no answer to it or any other I sent explaining my side of things.

Seven months later, I received a gift, but no card to identify the giver. It was an intricate bentwood cage and inside, curled up asleep and cute as the dickens, a tiny baby raccoon.

CHAPTER 28

KANSAS
1905
THE STAND-OFF—OUTLAWS

I had concluded, based upon experience and hearsay, that there are four types of men in the world: the good, the weak, the mean, and the dastardly bad.

Olaf represented the good men. I knew, as certain as anything, that were I to send him a telegram and that telegram were to say, "Oh hell, I am in trouble," he would lock the door to his haberdashery and make his way to my side to assist. If he knew where I was, which he didn't. Which was a good thing, as Olaf—being a good man—was not a very smart man. He would feel the need to save us and maybe confront Cullen directly. Discuss the issue. End the conversation with a handshake. Because that is Olaf and that is what a good man would do.

Thus, he would end up dead and have mucked things up, and Pip and I would be in the same boat we were in to start with.

Joe Harper was the weak of the male species. They tended to have charm, which Joe had in spades, but in serious situations that charm spoiled and turned into tantrums and fits. In between the two moods, men like Joe did what was asked of them, though. And if the directions were simple enough, the job could be done. Such as: "Get us horses to rob the stage, Joe." Which he did. It was everything else I left to his machinations that went to hell.

The other men in my life fell into the final categories of mean (Frank) and dastardly bad (Boudreaux, Cullen).

Frank was mean, but like Joe he had a charming side. Which got me in trouble too many times to count. I had no idea where he was; for the other side of his meanness was a propensity to take what he wanted and run.

Boudreaux, I think, was a mix of weak and mean and bad. He did not know us, had been keen on killing us, and did it for money. Maybe that made him eviler than Cullen. At least Cullen had a personal connection.

"I see you all got my calling card."

"You're quite the artist," Verna said. She put a hand on her hip like she wasn't afraid in the least, but she clawed at her skirt and that gave away her fright.

"Should I kill you first?"

She lifted her chin. "Go ahead. It's how it goes, round and round."

"I took the money." Pip's voice was low and steady.

"No, Pip—"

Cullen tilted his head and smiled. "You've become ugly, Pip. But I am happy for the truth."

"That's not the truth." I had hold of Pip's lapels. I started simpering and shaking and my knees got soft.

She twisted me around, ripped the Colt from my pocket and aimed straight at Cullen. It came to me that Pip would surely die, and, perhaps, that had been the plan all along.

"Wait," I blurted. "You both have things to live for. You have a little girl."

Pip cut a look at me. "Shut up, Ruby."

I spun to Cullen. "Are you going to kill the mother of your child?"

"It appears so."

The next happened as bad things do. Quick and brutal. Like a second of time had splintered off. Cullen took the advantage and shot.

The Colt dropped. Pip clutched her chest, staggered back, and collapsed.

Cullen wheeled towards Verna. "Who's next?"

"Oh, God." She covered her face with both hands.

"You killed my friend." I bolted forward, grabbed the Colt from the ground and squeezed the trigger. Nothing happened. Just a click. Then another. "Damn you to hell."

My vision blurred. I shook my head to clear it. Cullen stepped to the yard and shot, tearing up the grass by my foot.

"Damn you." I cocked the gun and prayed. It went off with a dreadful loud bang, the recoil jolting my arm.

His legs buckled and he dropped face first, his cheek scraping against the gravel.

Verna jumped from the stairs and put the shotgun to his back.

"Where did you—when—did I just kill him?"

A high whistle came from the barn. Martha Ruth jumped around and pointed down the front drive. "They're coming. They got their dogs."

The law.

"You got to go," Verna said.

"Not without Pip. I can't." I squeezed my hands into fists and pressed them against my eyes. How in the hell was I to move forward without her? We'd come all this way together. How was I going to bury her? A sob came up and I curled forward. "I don't know what to do."

"You can start by helping me up."

I spun around and stared. Pip lay with her knees bent and her arms splayed out to her side.

"First time you have no words. Wonders never cease." She groaned, rolled over, and pushed herself up.

The dogs bayed. Martha Ruth hopped around, pointing into the barn.

"You all right, Verna?" Pip asked.

"No one steps on my land without consequence. Go on."

Pip considered me. "You coming?"

My words stuck so I nodded.

"In for a nickel, in for a dollar." She dashed across the yard.

I took off after her. "How are you alive?"

She patted her chest pocket then pulled out the red Levantine leather Bible. Cullen's bullet struck dead center in the cover. "I believe I was saved by The Word."

She took off running to one of the horses Martha Ruth had at ready and leap-frogged to its back. "Let's at it."

❧

"It wouldn't have been fair, you know. Me having to go to prison again and you getting off scot free to cavort with St. Peter."

"Life is not fair, Ruby, we have determined that multiple times." Pip flipped the reins around in her hand and peered at the horizon. We had come to a part of Kansas that frankly stunned my senses, as the endless grasses turned to packed earth and towers of limestone. The sun dipped behind them, stretching blue shadows long across the valley we'd crossed that morning.

Martha Ruth rode ahead, shoulders back and eyes peeled forward. We had assigned her the role of scout. Though it was Theodore the mule we relied on to find water, which he did even in these badlands.

It had been a week since our fateful meeting with Cullen. I had shot a man. This did not sit well with me at all, and I did not believe Pip when she said I was a terrible shot and had taken out a second-floor window.

"I'm going to ask again—"

"And I'm going to tell you again. Verna knocked him out with that shotgun. He was out before you even pulled that trigger." Pip pushed back the brim of her brand-new sombrero. "You are a terrible shot."

"Well, I don't want to get better."

Fred snorted in agreement and I patted his neck.

"You like your new duds?" she asked.

I shifted around in the saddle we'd sneaked from a farm two days back and admired my shiny boots and leather chaps. My shirt was, as per usual, too long of sleeve, but one cannot complain when plucking items from a clothesline at full gallop.

Pip had found the reddest skirt and jacket possible and said it was her new favorite color being as it had saved her life.

Her horse sidestepped and swung its head. She murmured something that got the beast settled and then turned it into song. *"I ain't got no regular place that I can call my home.'* You know this one, Ruby?"

"Course I know it." I joined her.

"I ain't got no permanent address, as thro this world I roam,
Portland, Maine is just the same as sunny Tennessee,
Any old place I hang my hat,
Is home sweet home to me."

Our song echoed off the limestone and I caught a flash of us with our feathers and bells in the limelight of The Paradise. Then it slipped away, its place taken by the stone towers and cliffs turned umber and gold in the sunset.

"I do love your voice, Ruby Calhoun, that I do."

"We never made it to Hutchinson."

"No, we did not."

"I don't need to see it."

"Me, neither."

"Do you know *When the Morning Glories Twine Around the Door?*" I asked.

"I'm not familiar."

"Then I'll teach you. There're only a few verses, but some complicated harmonies."

Theodore took a sharp turn off the trail with a high step trot and ears pricked in glee.

"Water," Martha Ruth called.

Pip heeled her horse to a canter. She climbed up and did a one-foot stand, her hat glowing and skirts flicking and flapping.

"I thought we were learning a song." I sighed and urged Fred to hasten his pace. "Hey, Pip," I called, "we've got to make a plan. For getting your girl from those nuns. It'll take some trickery. But I'll figure out something. I'm Ruby Calhoun, you can trust me on that."

DON'T MISS THE NEXT
WILD-WILLED WOMEN OF THE WEST ADVENTURE

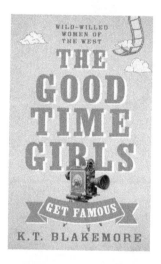

The law is still after Pip and Ruby, but so are the theater producers and then the moving pictures.

With the silent film industry booming, and Westerns are wildly popular, Ruby and Pip find themselves contracted to star in the story of their confrontation with a notorious outlaw.

But they are outlaws themselves, wanted in multiple counties across Kansas. They'll need all their wiles to take the film money to the bank and evade John Ward, the sheriff who has tracked them across the plains to the foot of the Rockies.

Will their new fame and Ward's single-minded obsession keep them from the Mexican border and freedom?

Visit https://www.ktblakemore.com
for the latest Good Time Girls news!

ACKNOWLEDGMENTS

Many thanks for the generosity and invaluable information provided by Vernon Perry at the Gila County Historical Society, Globe, Arizona; Chris Reid at the Pinal County Historical Society and Museum, Florence, Arizona; Alan Magary from the National Association of Timetable Collectors; Kansas Historical Society; Library of Congress for their collection of Sanborn Fire Maps; Katie Nelson of River City Historical; Bill Engbretson for his valuable contribution into the workings of a 1903 Model A and a lesson in early car manufacturers; and Threat Dynamics in Sherwood, Oregon for teaching me about historical firearms, their uses and drawbacks, and how to shoot from the hip.

My gratitude is boundless for the impeccable creativity and support of Jacqueline Vick for her incisive feedback on the initial draft; Kerry Cathers, copy editor extraordinaire; Kevin Moriarty, interior formatter, for his keen eye, patience, and humor; Valerie Biel of Lost Lake Press for her marketing prowess and never-ending positive vibes; and James at Goonwrite.com for a fabulous cover.

I want to give a huge thanks to the people who have cheered this novel on from its infancy and also so supportive of me stepping into the indie world:

Jackie Vick, again, but this time for our Friday morning accountability meetings, your sage advice, and most importantly, for our friendship.

Valerie Biel of Lost Lake Press, without whom I would be lost. Thank you for your sage advice and keeping the marketing gears tuned and running.

Katherine Genet, who has read and provided content notes on every book I've written and said, "I've been waiting for you to finally say you're going indie."

PDX Writers, Alida Thacher, Thea Constantine, and Gail Lehrman for cheering this novel from the first words written years ago about a 19th century saloon and the parasol dance performed on its makeshift stage.

My mom for reminding me that humor is sorely missing in the world and it might be a good idea to add some back in.

Dana, my cheerleader and love. I am always and ever grateful for your unwavering support.

BOOK CLUB QUESTIONS

1. In "The Good Time Girls," how does the author weave humor into the narrative? Which scenes or characters stood out to you as particularly comedic?

2. The friendship between the main characters is a central theme in the novel. How does Blakemore portray female friendship in the context of the Old West? Were there any specific moments that resonated with you?

3. "The Good Time Girls" offers a feminist take on westerns. In what ways does the author challenge traditional gender roles and expectations? Did this reshape your perception of the genre?

4. The setting of the Wild West plays a significant role in the story. How did Blakemore's descriptions of the landscape and atmosphere enhance your reading experience?

5. Several historical figures and events are referenced in the novel. Did you find these historical details enriching? How did they contribute to the authenticity of the story?

6. "The Good Time Girls" tackles themes of independence and self-discovery. How do the main characters evolve throughout the book? Were there any moments of personal growth that stood out to you?

7. Blakemore incorporates elements of romance into the narrative. What did you think of the romantic subplots? Did they enhance the overall story or distract from it?

8. The author blends humor and drama in the plot. How well do you think these two elements were balanced? Did one aspect overshadow the other?

9. The novel addresses social issues such as class, and justice. How effectively does Blakemore explore these themes within the historical context of the Old West?

10. The ending of "The Good Time Girls" leaves some room for interpretation. What were your thoughts on the conclusion? Did it satisfy you, or were there aspects that you wished had been explored further or resolved differently?

ABOUT THE AUTHOR

K.T. Blakemore grew up in the west and never left. Her novel THE GOOD TIME GIRLS is the first in the Wild-Willed Women of the West Series, featuring women who take no prisoners and succeed through sheer grit, determination, and a parcel of luck.

She also writes award-winning historical suspense and young adult historical fiction under the pen name Kim Taylor Blakemore. She has hung her hat in California, Colorado, and currently the Pacific Northwest. The rain does not deter her research whether it be train timetables from 1905 or the best way to catch a loose horse.

Visit her at https://www.ktblakemore.com/.
Subscribe to her newsletter and join the ride!